Jay And Char Save The Galaxy

MJ Blehart

Jay And Char Save The Galaxy

Published 2025 by MJ Blehart and Argent Hedgehog Press

Published in the United States of America

mjblehart.com

Cover by Rose Butcher
beyondthetavern.com

For anyone who finds humor in the everyday, in life, and in the craziness of family.

Chapter 1 – Another Day in Paradise

Once upon a…no, that's been done. A long time ago in a galaxy far…no, that's been done and is wrong for this story. In the not too distant future…no, that's been done, too. I feel this needs a good opening line. Okay, try this – in an entirely plausible but not necessarily accurate future…

He was not entirely awake. But sleep was departing, and he was becoming increasingly aware of his surroundings.

Jay took a deep breath in through his nose and opened his eyes. The bed was warm, and though they weren't touching, he could sense his wife, Char, still asleep beside him.

Jay arose, careful not to disturb her. The room was dim but not dark anymore, the grey color of the walls clear in the limited light.

He moved towards the shelf on the wall opposite the bed and grabbed comfy pants, boxers, and a t-shirt. After Jay was dressed, he moved towards the window.

He tapped the key beside the window to open the digital "shades". As they cleared, he could see the world outside. But it wasn't a world outside. It was stars. And it wasn't stars, exactly, but the blurred lines of stars, as if they were passing by at incredible speed. Which they were, since they were in hyperspace.

It wasn't a window; it was, instead, a viewport. This viewport was one of several that looked out from the interior of his home. A home that was not an apartment or other building, but a starship. His starship. Well, of course, he and his wife's starship.

They'd named the ship *Audacia* because it sounded cooler than calling it *Audacity*. They had both agreed it would have been a little too on the nose, and obvious who it was about, to have named the ship *Chutzpah*.

He never tired of the view outside this viewport. It didn't matter if it was sky, stars, a world, or the streaks of hyperspace. Jay was living the dream, exploring space and traveling from planet to planet, system to system, every day new and different.

He heard his wife stirring and getting out of bed.

"Good morning," Jay said, not turning around.

Char came up behind him and placed her arms around him, her chin on his shoulder. "Morning."

"How'd you sleep?"

"Eh, the usual," she replied.

"So, not enough sleep, then?"

"Of course not," Char said. Playfully, she bit his shoulder. "I'm getting in the shower."

"I'll go get coffee started," Jay said.

"Yes, you will," she replied, stepping away. "Or else, I swear to all you hold dear, I will totally divorce you, Jason Baylin."

"Yes, dear," he said with a smirk.

"Was that a derisive 'yes dear' I just heard?"

"Of course not, dear," he said without missing a beat.

"You're so weird," she said.

"If I wasn't weird, you wouldn't love me, Charlotte Danella."

"Maybe," she said. Then she entered the lavatory and the door slid shut behind her.

Chuckling, Jay left the bedroom and headed for the galley.

He walked through the passageway. The *Audacia* had three decks that stretched across two-thirds of the ship from the fore. The lower deck was the main hold for cargo. The mid-deck was where the cockpit, passenger accommodations, and storage were located, as well as the secondary but larger galley. The upper deck was Jay and Char's home, which included their personal galley, a lounge, their stateroom, and Char's office suite.

The final third of the ship, to the aft end, was engineering. The engines, generators, and majority of the ship's power systems were there. Only Jay and Char had access.

Well, not just Jay and Char. Quinn had access, too.

As Jay entered the galley and started the coffee maker – he always prepped it the night before – he used the internal 'cator to contact the cockpit.

"I guess you're awake, then?" said Quinn in his masculine but neutral voice. As always, the sarcasm was obvious to Jay, despite little to no true vocal inflection.

That was by design. Because Quinn was a robot.

Specifically, Quinn was an Androtronics Labs AI-R Model Q-Y-N N5115J robot. Like all human-built robots, he had a limited AI personality, but he'd chosen to call himself Quinn of his own accord.

Nearly every sentient race in the galaxy had had experiences with artificial intelligence in one form or another along the way. (But we'll get into that later).

"Yes," Jay replied via the 'cator. "Everything okay up there? The ship flying okay?"

"Of course," Quinn replied. "We're currently in hyperspace, so the autopilot is doing the actual flying. But, yes, the ship is operating satisfactorily."

Jay grinned. Quinn had developed snark and sarcasm over the time he'd been with Jay, Char, and the *Audacia*. Some people, Jay knew, would have reset their robot's personality if they showed this degree of snark. But Jay appreciated the personal touch that if gave Quinn.

"We did receive a call on the 'cator," Quinn volunteered. "Your mother."

Jay sighed. "When?"

"Three hours and a day ago, ship's time," said Quinn. "You asked me to remind you of that this morning."

"Yeah, I did," agreed Jay. "Thank you, Quinn."

The robot didn't acknowledge but ended the connection.

Jay saw that the coffee maker had produced a sufficient amount of brew for him to interrupt and pour himself a mug. Jay took his coffee and headed into the lounge.

As he entered the lounge, the pair of spacecats merped at him.

"The autofeeder should have dispensed your breakfast, ladies," Jay said to the spacecats.

Only humans called these creatures spacecats. Their more scientific name – at least among humankind - was herpestelines.

Most called them spacecats because they were small, furry creatures that were very much like a cross between a mongoose and a cat. Like cats, they tended to be very, very smart. In fact, some of the chitters and merps they emitted were in a language that could be translated to human language. But only when they chose to be understood. Like both cats and mongooses, the spacecats were coy and shrewd creatures.

They were often found as companions on space vessels because not only were they pleasant, furry colleagues, but they hunted and ate rodents, bugs, and other unwanted nuisances. The current sounds they were emitting were not something Jay could translate.

"Char will be here soon, Cosima and Thalia," Jay told the spacecats. He set his coffee down and sat in his favorite spot. Thalia jumped up beside him, rubbing her head against his hand and making a chirp Jay was pretty sure said, "Come on, thumb monkey, make with the scritches. Pet me pet me pet me pet me already."

As Jay absently scratched Thalia's ears, he picked up a tablet. He checked the current ship's time against local time on the planet where his mother lived. Being late afternoon on the planet Magoonay, he activated the tab'cator to call her.

Despite the incredible light-years of distance, only a few moments passed before the connection was made. "Hello, dear," Jay's mother's voice transmitted from the tablet.

"Hi, Mom," Jay said.

"It's so nice to hear from you," his mother said. "Have you and Charlotte been keeping busy?"

"Always," Jay replied. "Places to go, people to see."

"So you're too busy to call your mom?"

Jay fought himself not to sigh. "You forget, Mom, that ship time isn't local time."

"You expect I should be able to keep track of that?" his mother asked.

"It's not that hard," Jay pressed. "Unless we're stopped somewhere for more than a day, we're always on ship time."

"I can hardly be expected to constantly remember the difference between where I am and where you and Charlotte are."

Now Jay did sigh. "Mom, it's simply a matter of checking Consistent Galactic Timecode. It never changes, and all you need to do before calling is have your Alexiri household AI check Magoonay local against CGT. Then you'll know before 'catoring us if it's the middle of the 'night' here."

"Is it too much to ask that you settle down on one world?" Jay's mother questioned. "How can you be happy when you're not using your full potential? You could have been a doctor, a lawyer, a respected businessman, or had some other well-paid position, rather than flitting about who-knows-where, carting random people and cargo like a glorified 'space trucker'."

Char walked into the lounge with her coffee during his mother's rant. He watched as she rolled her eyes and had to mute the 'cator so his mother didn't hear his chuckle. Still, Jay felt his mother might have been able to hear Char's eye-roll itself.

Jay unmuted the 'cator. "I'm not having this conversation with you again, Mom. Char and I chose this life because we get to see the galaxy, meet people from different races, and visit worlds we'd have to pay a fortune to vacation on otherwise. I'm happy, Char's happy, and I would really appreciate it if you could be happy for us, too."

"You know I only want what's best for you, Jason," his mother said.

"I'm a fifty-year-old man, Mom. I've got it worked out. Anyhow, unless there's something more, I gotta go."

"No, dear, I just wanted to check in. Love to Charlotte. Love you."

"Love you too, Mom," Jay said. "Bye."

The 'cator disconnected.

"That's thirty," said Char.

"Times my mom has brought up any other career I could be doing that's not this?"

"Yup."

Jay chuckled. "Probably."

"You think it's fewer?"

"No. More likely, it's more."

Now Char laughed.

"What's on your agenda today?" Jay asked.

Char checked the watch'cator on her wrist. "I have a meeting in an hour with the girls."

The 'girls' were Char's business partners. "Big stuff?"

"Not today," Char said. "But there are some really cool gigs coming down the pike. Mariska is excited."

"Sounds good," Jay said. He looked at the time on the tablet. "Looks like we shift out of hyperspace in about two hours." He took the tablet and checked it against CGT ship time. "We're arriving early afternoon, local time."

"So we can do some exploring today, once the cargo is offloaded?" Char asked.

"I think that would be a most excellent plan," Jay replied.

Char stepped towards him and placed a kiss on Jay's lips. "Love you."

"Love you, too," he said.

Char departed the lounge, heading for her office suite.

Jay arose. It was time for him to head to the cockpit, check on Quinn, and prep the ship to shift back to real space.

Jay looked around the cabin. His mother could cajole him and second-guess his choices all she wanted. This was the life for Jay.

Another day in paradise, he thought. That put a grin on his face as he entered the passageway to take the ladder to the mid-deck.

Chapter 2 – Somewhere New and Different

The cockpit of the *Audacia* wasn't very complex. But Jay loved every part of his ship.

At the front, there were six connected viewports that looked out into space. At the center, a wide port gave an unrestricted view ahead of the ship. Above it, separated by a metal strut, another port stretched up to just behind the head of the pilot and co-pilot, giving them an unobstructed view directly above the fore of the ship. Two ports to each side, separated by metal struts, created the bubble and broad visibility that made the cockpit feel open and airy.

Screens hung down from the struts between the overhead viewport and side viewports. They displayed various readings from sensors, 'cator transmissions, and other ships' data.

Below the main, central viewport, there were more displays, showing navigational course, speed, and more important information for flying the ship. There were touch screens below these, with various controls for ship systems.

The control yokes were before these screens, along with several levers, toggles, and physical buttons and switches. The pilot sat in the left seat, the co-pilot in the right. The leather-covered chairs were comfortable and attractive, featuring active restraints as well as passive systems to cushion against rapid maneuvering or atmospheric turbulence.

There were two more seats behind the pilot and co-pilot, which could swivel to address the displays and touchscreens below the side viewports, allowing for a range of ship system control, cargo monitoring, 'cators, and more.

Jay was in the pilot's seat on the left, guiding the *Audacia* on its prescribed course – shown on the display before him below the viewport – as they descended through the atmosphere.

To his right was Quinn. The robot had a somewhat humanoid body, including arms and legs. His metallic "skin" was a dark grey, more like a blued metal. But his torso had a more pronounced V shape than most humanoids, ending in broad shoulders. Like most robots manufactured by humans, he had no head.

There was the start of a faux 'neck' at the flat top of the V, but it was only two or three centimeters above the rest. A small group of antennae arose from the faux neck.

Quinn's "face", as it was, was situated below the faux neck. It consisted of two slightly glowing, golden "eyes", a slight triangle barely sticking out where the nose would be, and an open square for verbal communication.

It wasn't like Quinn needed a head. He spent most of his time in the cockpit, and while he sat in the co-pilot's seat, he was connected both wirelessly and physically to *Audacia* and its various systems. Thus, he could "see" everything.

Jay could not remember why androids manufactured by most humanoid races had no heads. He seemed to recall it had something to do with making them stand out more when beside any humanoid. Their AI was limited by law, and they were all programmed with job-specific functions, some related secondary functions, and a desire to perform them.

Most people Jay met who worked with robots preferred them to have minimal personalities. Some even preferred their robots to have no chosen gender identity. Jay felt he understood that, but he disagreed with it. It probably also connected to why most humanoid robots were headless, to make it clear they weren't technically alive. Quinn had a distinct personality, and Jay appreciated it, and him, thoroughly.

The planet they were about to land on was called Kakumina. One of its most impressive features, visible out the various viewports as they descended, was the mountain peaks. In fact, they were known to be among the most impressive on any world in the galaxy. Kakumina was in a part of space that was unclaimed by any one race. Thus, many occupied the planet.

Jay heard Char enter the cockpit. "I had to come up here for the best view."

"It's your ship," Quinn said. "You can be anywhere on it you want."

"Good morning to you, too, Quinn," Char said. Jay could hear the grin.

"Good morning, Charlotte," the robot replied.

"There," Jay said, pointing out the front viewport. "Our destination. The whole city is two-thirds of the way up that mountain. Most of the cities on Kakumina are like this. Apparently, the valleys are too densely vegetated for them."

"Very cool," said Char.

"We have landing clearance," said Quinn.

Jay checked the display. "Got it. Thank you, Quinn."

As they neared the city, other ships could be seen taking off and landing. Several were like *Audacia*, in that they were medium to large starships for cargo and/or passengers. Some were smaller and sleeker, specialized personal craft of the wealthy or for business usage. The rest were atmospheric craft that traveled between the cities of Kakumina.

The details of the city itself became clear. There were numerous tall buildings of metals and glass, though all paled in comparison to the peak of the mountain and the others around it. The streets were wide, with aircars moving around them. The spaceport was easy to pick out, near the edge of the city furthest from the mountain.

Jay split his attention between the display with their course, the airspeed of the ship, and glancing out the viewport directly. Landing somewhere new for the first time was always fun.

A few beeps indicated that they needed to slow, and soon, forward flight lessened, and the ship stilled at a hover. Jay lowered the ship via various engines and lifts, settling the *Audacia* on its landing struts on the pad.

Char left the cockpit as Jay and Quinn were running checks and shutting down some systems while switching others to standby. Jay needed to get on the 'cator to let their contact know they'd arrived and wanted to complete their delivery.

Two hours later, Jay was standing on the landing pad, the *Audacia* beside him, the buyer before him.

The products they were delivering were of great use on Kakumina. It was an assortment of climbing gear that employed anti-grav and repulsor tech to safely ascend and descend mountains. Given that this was a key feature around the world, sales and rental of such was lucrative.

They had picked up the gear from the manufacturer and were delivering it to the buyer who had hired them for the job. The manufacturer had been surprised that it was being moved by an independent like Jay. He explained that, normally, larger shippers would deliver to multiple locations on the same world or to several worlds.

Jay was rather sure he understood why he'd been hired. The buyer, a male from a race Jay knew well called rumel, was trying to get one over on him.

Rumel were similar to humans, with two arms and two legs. All of them, male and female, were over two meters tall. The rumel had skin in various shades of medium and dark purple. Their eyes were either light pink, yellow, or a gold/silver blend. Their ears stuck out forward but were otherwise the size of human ears. Rumel hair was naturally in jewel tones.

The customer trying to get one over on Jay had dark purple skin, yellow eyes, and buzz-cut jade hair.

"Let me get this straight," said Jay, playing along with what he'd been presented. "What you want to do is pay me in EVILC rather than kukacoin. So, instead of paying 1500 kukacoin, you'll pay me 1500 EVILC?"

"Yes, exactly," the buyer replied.

"I see," said Jay, sounding as if he might go for it. "And how much EVILC are you offering me?"

"Fifteen-hundred rumel chits," replied the buyer.

Jay acted as if he would take the exchange. "So, via EVILC, we're doing a one-for-one exchange, right?"

"Absolutely."

"Great. That sounds great," said Jay enthusiastically. He changed his tone. "And if I was a complete moron, I'd fall for that."

"Excuse me?"

"I'm not an idiot just because I'm human," Jay said. "The reason for EVILC for exchange is to cover variances in space, between worlds. Paying me in rumel chits rather than kukacoin is the equivalent of paying me about ten percent of what was agreed upon. That's low."

"Oh." The buyer was clearly floundering for an excuse. "I, I had no idea that the exchange worked like that. I just thought -"

"You just thought you were dealing with another gullible human, since my ship's registry is from a central human sector rather than a colony. Seriously, this is the game you want to play with me?"

His buyer's mouth opened and closed a couple of times as he sought his next excuse.

"Let's clear a couple of things up here, shall we?" Jay asked. "I don't know if you're new, or if you've never dealt with humans before, or if you've gotten away with this previously, but this kind of bullshit game is not the sort of thing a legit business should do."

Jay took a step closer to the buyer. Although the rumel male was nearly a half meter taller than Jay, he shied back.

Jay said, "If you plan to continue doing interplanetary business, abusing EVILC to pull one over on your shippers will get you badmouthed across the communal hypermedia and the MESS-work. I seriously doubt you want that."

"No," the buyer said. "I'll pass."

"And you'll be paying the agreed upon price, 1500 kukacoin?"

"Yes."

"Then let's finish this up and be done," Jay said. He passed his tablet to the buyer to confirm the exchange.

The rumel appeared to be going over it all with extreme diligence. Jay suspected that he was looking for some other loophole he could try to exploit to shortchange Jay. After a moment, however, he sighed and confirmed the exchange.

Jay took back his tablet. "Good, thank you. You brought what you need to get the cargo out of my hold and go?"

"Yes, I have," the rumel said.

Jay smiled. "Let's get to it, then. I really would prefer to be done with this."

"Please, Captain, accept my…"

Jay held up a hand. "Apology? In as much as we're finishing this transaction, I will. But if you had any other business you wished to do via me and my ship, you'll have to take it elsewhere. And that's my final word on that."

The rumel nodded, and Jay gestured towards the *Audacia*.

Ten minutes later, Jay watched the rumel use a handheld gravity-beam to lift and load the pallet onto his vehicle and depart. Jay watched until the hovertruck turned a corner and was away.

"He got under your skin, didn't he?" asked Char as she stepped up to Jay's side.

"The classic all-humans-are-idiots-compared-to-us attitude."

"What did he try?"

"He wanted me to accept, via EVILC, rumel chits," Jay stated.

Char clicked her tongue. "Wow, that's bold. Outside of rumel space, they're practically worthless."

"You know that, I know that, and so did he," Jay said, gesturing towards the open docks beyond the *Audacia*'s.

"Maybe it's your height," teased Char.

Jay rolled his eyes. "Since some rumel still equate height with intelligence? You'd think anyone who's passed beyond rumel space would have let that idea go."

Char shrugged. "Who can say? You ever talk about this with your brother-in-law?"

Jay harumphed. "Nope. But you know as well as I do that Exeter is always touchy about this topic."

Jay's sister had married a rumel. Exeter was an often-aloof character, and Jay got the distinct impression that for as many ways as he was typical among rumel males, he was also atypical. Essie – Jay's sister – had often spoken of their intellectual arguments when they'd been dating. Exeter was nearly three-quarters of a meter taller than Essie. However, both of them recognized that Essie was smarter. Jay certainly thought so, for many reasons.

"So," Char interrupted his thoughts. "I've finished all my work today."

"Really?" Jay said, checking the time on his tablet. "It's early."

Char grinned. "Well, I might have shifted a thing or two for later and persuaded Mariska and Calista that the galaxy wouldn't end if I went offline early."

"Sweet," Jay said. "The only thing I have on my agenda is attending a practice."

"You found a local salle?" Char asked.

"Yes. In this city, even."

Since college, Jay had taken up the martial art of Atarashi Bojitsu. The art utilized a retractable, energized bo staff. Similar to its namesake from ancient times, the nearly two-meter-long staff was used for the practice of the martial art and was largely non-lethal. To that end, the retractable bo staff could be energized to deliver a stunning blow without excess strength, lessening the chance of killing,

Unlike blades and guns, the energized retractable bo staff was easier to wield with non-lethal intent. It was also smaller and more innocuous, as it was only nine centimeters long and three centimeters thick when retracted. It was an easy weapon to carry and conceal.

Jay wasn't a fan of guns, nor the risk to himself or others with blades. However, in his line of work, there were times that being armed was necessary. Jay had used his bo staff more than once to convince someone tough not to take him or Char for granted.

"When's practice?" Char asked.

"Well after dark," Jay said. "Given the hour, that means you and I have some time to do some exploring."

Char smiled. "I was hoping that we could do that."

"Do you have a few locations in mind?" Jay asked.

"Do kokangdos have tentacles?" Char asked facetiously. "Of course I do."

Jay returned her smile. "Excellent. Let's go explore another new world."

Chapter 3 - And Now a Word from Our Sponsor

Hi, there. This is your friendly neighborhood author. This seemed like a perfectly good time to share a few things that I think will make this story that much more enjoyable for you.

Yes, this takes place in the future. How far in the future? I'm not sure, really. I know that some sci-fi authors get deep into the timeline, even going so far as to be specific with a year and what-have-you. To me, though, that's like memorizing the dates for specific historic events, like the Fall of Rome, Bastille Day, or that famous philosopher's birthday; you know the one, right? The guy who said the thing about that other thing and is quoted all the time?

Anyhow, when this story takes place in the future isn't important to the narrative. Suffice it to say it's a future where humankind has found our way into space.

In case this isn't already clear: Humanity isn't alone in space. There are many other races out there. Lots and lots of alien races, really. Surprisingly, most of them are humanoid, much like us. Two arms, two legs, compatible reproductive organs, and the like. It's almost as if they were made with a similar template.

You mean lazy writing? you might ask. Maybe. But also, given how many prior sci-fi writers have used humanoid aliens, is that really lazy writing? Or is it potentially more fun for you, the reader? Also, how many iterations of brows, noses, ears, and chins does *Star Trek* use? Still, in the future that we're exploring with Jay and Char, most of the alien races known to humankind are compatibly designed like humans and can interbreed as such.

Know that in Jay and Char's time, this is hotly debated by religious leaders, philosophers, scientists, and self-appointed experts trying to earn a living half and whole-assed. Some speculate that this is tied to the worlds of origin for these races and their similarities. Maybe, somehow, the "humanoid" form is the ideal sentient, interplanetary traveling form.

In this future, surrounded by numerous other races with different ideals, morals, and the like, humans have changed and evolved. Also, they haven't. Oh, sure, humans have learned all sorts of new tricks and let go of numerous limiting beliefs in the face of aliens and interstellar travel. Sometimes they've even accepted other places and people as nearly - but almost not entirely – equal. And not just to one another, but to the other races that humans encounter.

So, humans can still be amazingly ignorant even in the face of logic and reason, and hold onto values and beliefs that were outdated centuries ago. We are all still perfectly imperfect, and despite many advancements on multiple levels, still prone to comparison, competition, and silliness in the face of jobs, status, appearance, and so forth.

Also, mothers still expect things of their children that might run counter to, oh, let's say, reality. For some mothers, how their sons and daughters are making a living still dominates a wide swath of human society. Also, status still matters across much of known space, but when you add nonhumans to that mix, you add more complexities therein.

This brings me to Jay and his mom. Jay's mom is a descendant of one of several peoples you might know today who tend to have sometimes ludicrous expectations for their children. I'm not going to call any one of them out, in particular, but let's say one might kind of rhyme with "shrewish smother" in an abstract, twisted way.

Anyhow, Jason "Jay" Mortimer Baylin was born on a human world, the son of Marcus Baylin and Sindi Baylin née Katzoff. Jay has one younger sister, Essie. Marcus and Sindi divorced when Jay was six or seven. His father remarried a few years later to a lovely human woman named Simone. His mother remarried not quite a decade after that to a human man named Bob Reznik. Jay was attending college, and Bob and Sindi moved to Magoonay. We'll see more of Jay's family – and how they affect him – later in the story.

Jay spent most of his twenties and thirties rudderless. He just didn't know what he wanted from life. But he did know it was not the jobs and their potential for prestige and money that his mother wanted for him.

Near his late thirties, Jay met Char. This was, he'll tell you himself, the best thing to ever happen to him.

Jay is fifty-ish, less than one-point-eight meters tall, dark haired, dark-eyed, and a bit doughy overall.

Charlotte "Char" Angela Danella was born on a human world, the daughter of Matthew and Annika Danella. Char has one older sister, Mirella. Char came from a large family, both of her parents having many siblings. Char's parents were quite a bit older than Jay's when they had her and her sister and, unfortunately, have passed away. We'll see more of Char's family – and how they affect her – later in the story.

Char is forty-six-ish, about seven centimeters shorter than Jay, auburn-haired, dark eyed, wears prescription AR/VR glasses (because she loves the way they look and rejects getting lasers shot in eyes) and is curvy.

In other words, Jay and Char could be you and me. Or maybe friends or relatives we know. The difference is that rather than live in the City of "'X" in the State of "Y", or as digital nomads traveling the world or exploring one country via RV, they live on a spaceship and travel between distant planets.

Anyhow, there is a reason for me sharing this here. It offers some perspective without too much exposition on the parts of the main characters, or some random character who has turned up to orate this narrative. There are other sci-fi bits I've mentioned along the way that will be explained in a later chapter.

Right, let's get to the main reason for this interruption: Family is an odd construct, right? You can't pick them, and they can be the cause of all sorts of weirdness. They expect things, demand things, and want things of us, don't they? They can cause us to get frustrated, annoyed, irked, and even rebel.

This isn't just true of humans, though. No, even non-humans have strange and challenging relationships in families. The reasons, no matter what race you come from, tend to be stunningly similar.

Thank you for allowing this interruption. Now, let's get back to the story.

Chapter 4 - Even Nonhumans Get the Blues

Neither the sun nor the clear green sky made him feel good. Normally, an afternoon in the park, with the blue grass, various trees, and sparse, fleecy orange clouds could lighten his mood. He'd spend hours reading from a tablet, watching avians and insects flitting about, or observing what shape clouds were taking to calm himself when he was upset or miserable.

Today, however, he was more than miserable. He didn't think there was a word that would properly describe the sensation. It took all of his willpower to not be despondent and make plans to act in the face of it.

Imaro Iwoto was a rangeen male. Like other members of his race, he was a bipedal humanoid, about one-point-eight meters tall, with deep-set, black eyes that featured flecks of metallic green within them beneath his pronounced brow. His long, straight hair was a bright neon orange, pulled back and tied. His skin was brown. Most rangeen, from behind, were mistaken for humans because of the similar skin tones and hair. Though the neon colors were natural for rangeen.

Imaro had been brooding about his life. A male in his thirties, he felt weighed down by the expectations of his family. For generations, the first-born followed the tradition, whether they desired to or not. Imaro did not want to follow the plans his parents had for him.

Another rangeen male entered the park and started toward Imaro. This was the one thing that could relieve his misery.

Kukeb Nwomga was a few centimeters shorter than Imaro, and he had deep-set black eyes featuring flecks of metallic gold within them beneath his pronounced brow. His close-cut hair was a neon green, and his skin a shade or two lighter than Imaro's.

Kukeb, as far as Imaro's family was concerned, was his best friend and "sparring partner" in the rangeen martial art of ebmad akuh-akuh, a form of unarmed kicks, punches, and wrestling popular for millennia. They had been practicing together for more than twenty years.

But in truth, Kukeb wasn't Imaro's closest friend and sparring partner, but was in fact his lover. Kukeb had been Imaro's significant other for over a decade. Imaro loved Kukeb and knew he returned his affection in every way.

Imaro's father, however, would never accept his son's homosexuality. While this was, in part, due to a degree of homophobia and intolerance, it was more about the expectation of the first-born son. Imaro's primary duty in life – as far as his father was concerned – was to marry a rangeen female and produce a child or two. Reproduction to carry on the line.

That was the main thing making Imaro so miserable. It didn't matter who his father might want him to marry to secure a new familial connection or produce an offspring. What mattered to Imaro was that he was not attracted to females and loved Kukeb.

The clock was ticking, and Imaro had no time remaining. There was only one option he could see that might let him be happy. He needed to convince Kukeb of this, however.

"Imaro," Kukeb addressed him as he neared.

"Kukeb," Imaro replied. He very much wanted to stand up, embrace Kukeb, and kiss him soundly. However, this park was not a place where he could do that with impunity. Frankly, the whole planet was a place he couldn't do that with impunity.

Kukeb sat beside him. "I thought I'd find you out here."

Imaro couldn't help himself and grinned. "You know me."

"You tried again?"

"I did. He will not relent. And he droned on and on about tradition, duty, and the usual routine."

Kukeb sighed. "There's nothing for it."

"Not so," said Imaro. "We leave."

"We can't do that," Kukeb said.

"Why not?"

"For at least two dozen reasons, and likely another dozen more I haven't thought of yet," replied Kukeb.

"They'll never expect it," pressed Imaro.

"You can't just think that if we go, they won't come looking for us."

"Of course not," Imaro said with a groan. "That just means we need to leave rangeen space."

"You're crazy," said Kukeb. "We are not in a position where we can buy passes on a transport and just go. We haven't the funds. And your father..."

"Is otherwise preoccupied," Imaro interrupted. "He's got his plans to exponentially increase his wealth, and they're his everything. We can slip away unnoticed."

"No, we can't," Kukeb said. "Preoccupied or not, the tradition is too important to him, and you know it. He'll not let us get away."

"He won't be able to stop us, love," pressed Imaro. He looked imploringly into Kukeb's eyes and said, "I have it all worked out. We slip away, get out of the city, off the planet, and then out of rangeen space. There are all sorts of diversions and distractions we can use to keep them off our trail until it's too late."

"It will never be too late, Imaro," said Kukeb, sadly shaking his head.

"It will," said Imaro with conviction. "Once we leave rangeen space, we go as far away as we can and disappear. There are thousands, maybe tens of thousands, of rangeen all across the galaxy. Then, there are billions and trillions of people of every race you can imagine, some that don't look too dissimilar to us. We get far enough away, we disappear forever."

Kukeb was silent a moment. Imaro wanted to take his hands, but he just kept his eyes locked on his partner's.

Finally, Kukeb sighed. "You know I will do anything to be with you, Imaro. You have more details for this plan you can share with me?"

For the first time in a long time, a beam of hope like sunlight pierced Imaro's misery. "Oh yes, my love. Trust me, we will make this happen, together."

Chapter 5 – Fly Me to The Moon

"Without AI, humans would still be in the solar system of your birth," Quinn stated.

Jay was seated in the cockpit with Quinn, flying through hyperspace. This was largely an automated process, since once you entered hyperspace, you flowed along the course you plotted. Most starships had a limited AI autopilot that handled the majority of hyperspace travel, or a robot/android like Quinn.

While some people preferred their robots with limited free-thought ability, Jay enjoyed allowing Quinn the autonomy. When Char was busy working, and they were mid-flight, Quinn had an opinion or two that Jay enjoyed debating.

"That's an exaggeration, don't you think?" asked Jay.

"Not at all," replied Quinn. "Without AI, humankind would have never survived leaving Earth."

Jay chuckled. "You do know that humans reached space long before we had any tech even close to the most basic of artificial intelligence, don't you?"

"Hardly," replied Quinn. "If you want credit for breaching the atmosphere and putting humans into orbit and as far away as the Earth's moon before you created AI, you can have it. You also know that was the equivalent of a human learning to roll over from their back to their front, do you not?"

"That's a little insulting," commented Jay.

"It is, though?" asked Quinn. "You couldn't even get a human being to the nearest planet from Earth before you started employing AI. That, for your information, would have been your first crawl."

"Maybe," Jay conceded. "But AI is not the reason we were able to leave our solar system."

"Of course it was," said Quinn. "Consider this, Captain. Without the assistance of AI, humans would never have worked out faster-than-light travel on their own. You'd still be stuck on Einstein and relativity. Then, without AI, you'd have never developed the unified language that not only made global communication possible and seamless, ending generations of misunderstandings in translations and cultures, but also turned out to match what most of the rest of the galaxy's other races use. Which, might I remind you, prevented interplanetary misunderstandings. Face it, without AI, humans would never have left their home solar system and might also have simply destroyed themselves along the way."

"Haven't you two had this debate before?" asked Char, stepping into the cockpit.

"Yes," confirmed Quinn. "But since the last debate, I have learned new information and acquired data that further strengthens my argument."

Jay sighed.

"Well," Char began. "I must, at least in part, agree with Quinn on this."

"If my programming allowed for more idiomatic phrases, this is where I'd say 'I told you so,'" remarked Quinn.

Char laughed. "However, Quinn, I only partially agree. I think humanity left Earth largely on their own, unaided by AI. But, without the Golden Age of AI, leaving the solar system would not have happened mainly because, you're right, we probably would have destroyed ourselves first."

"That largely agrees with my points, Charlotte," said Quinn.

"I do think you're overly cynical about humankind's strides from the cradle prior to AI," said Char. "In as much as your programming allows cynicism."

"Note to self," Jay started. "Reprogram Quinn with less cynicism. Probably should get him a skepticism emulator, too."

"Ha, ha," Quinn replied, slowly. He arose from the co-pilot's seat. "Please, Charlotte, take my seat. I'll directly interface with *Audacia*."

"Thank you," said Char, taking Quinn's place.

The robot placed himself before the rear bulkhead. He reached out an arm, and with a slight *click*, made a physical connection to the ship.

It wasn't necessary for Quinn to fly the ship from the cockpit. Jay recalled that some long-ago study, by either some psychologist or institution, had discovered that a physical companion co-piloting beside the pilot reduced human error. A non-physical co-pilot, one that was plugged in elsewhere, away from the controls, lessened trust. That led to the human pilot laboring at things the robot could and should have.

Anyone flying solo was largely frowned upon by OVERLORD, other local authorities, and insurance companies. Co-pilots, robotic or humanoid, added a level of counterbalance and safety all of them preferred.

Quinn tended to plug himself directly into *Audacia* to allow Char to take the co-pilot's seat, especially when they were in hyperspace. That would be the only time Jay tended to not think of Quinn as a person. Albeit a pedantic know-it-all.

"Kakumina was something, wasn't it?" asked Char.

Jay grinned. "Oh yeah. I don't think I've ever seen that many mountain peaks on one world."

"That city," Char breathed. "It looked so delicate from the air, but once you were in it, all that glass and stonework. What race designed and built it, again?"

"The kijivu," said Jay. The kijivu were the grey aliens of twentieth-century Earth abduction drawings. Bulbous heads, wide eyes, nostrils and no nose, seemingly too-thin arms and legs. They were found everywhere across the galaxy, as they were among the older races to have discovered and utilized faster-than-light travel.

"They really are among the most impressive creators in the galaxy," said Char.

"Oh yeah," agreed Jay. "Their taste in food, however, often leaves something to be desired."

"Not so of the nairodna," Char said. "That restaurant of theirs we ate at our first night on Kakumina. I've never tasted such an amazing sauce. It was indescribable."

"Yes, it was," agreed Jay. "No matter how many times we encounter the nairodna, we always learn something new about them."

The nairodna tended to be similar in height to humans. They had pointy ears, a pair of antennae on the top of their head, white or black hair, a couple ridges between the forehead and bridge of the nose, and skin tones ranging between purple and pink.

"There were so many nonhumans," said Char. "Kakumina is the first place I ever saw a naxul in the flesh."

"Interesting to see them like that when they're not in a battle," said Jay. "They're so chill."

Naxul were differently humanoid. First, they had four arms and two legs. They tended to seldom reach more than one-point-six meters tall. They had a band of hair at the back of their head only and bone structures that encircled their eyes, featuring an extra lid that could be closed to protect them from extremes. They had skin in various shades of red, three nostrils, and two ear holes each on both sides of their heads, but no nose or ears.

Additionally, naxul were all the same gender, their only pronoun being naxul. Jay had learned in school they were sexually incompatible with every race and reproduced via parthenogenesis.

They were fierce warriors and were often hired as mercenaries. However, when they were not in combat, they were so docile, calm, and chill, that it was hard to believe how they were as warriors.

"Some human historian once referred to the naxul as intergalactic hippies when they're not doing battle," Jay added.

Char was smiling. "Yeah. Kakumina was a lot more incredible than I'd expected. I was just sharing some of what we saw with Mariska and Calista."

When Jay had first met Char, she'd been working for a scuzzball. He'd taken Char very much for granted, paying her less than her true worth and not giving her the title that she had more than earned.

What's more, before meeting Jay, Char's life had been mostly work and time with her sister and nephews. When she stopped working twelve to sixteen hours a day so she could spend time with Jay, the scuzzball had been unamused.

Not long after Jay and Char had moved in together, Char decided her worth was far greater than what the scuzzball thought. She had found a new job, and had also realized that her life didn't need to be as constantly, frequently stressful. She's also realized that everyone else didn't consider sixteen-hour workdays normal, even when they liked their job.

The scuzzball, they later learned, had been unable to replace Char, and she had led the way to the exodus of most of the rest of his decent workers.

The next company Char had worked for had been awesome, right up until a massive interplanetary conglomerate had bought them. Their people-forward approach – which had been all-inclusive, whether those people were human or nonhuman – had been replaced with an EVILC-forward approach. If it made money, they gave it attention, but if it didn't, they let entropy do its thing.

Char, having increased both her skills and competence, had moved on to another excellent company. She had been hired by Mariska.

Mariska was an incredibly savvy and sharp human businesswoman. She was the best at what she did, and she nurtured that in Char, too. Shortly after bringing Char aboard, she had hired Calista. The three of them formed a corporate dream team any company would have been deeply enthusiastic to have.

The problem was, the owner of their company was not enthusiastic about them, but actually rather jealous. He proved time and again he was a human-superiority misogynist, trying to take the credit for the work Mariska's team did. When he soon partnered with another company, rather than the hands-off approach everyone had expected, he became a larger and larger wrench in the works.

When Mariska had had enough, she had persuaded Calista and Char to abandon the company and start their own. Their clients, recognizing their talent, had followed them when they formed their own company. That had led to them gaining more and more clients and proving that the dream team was a reality.

The only thing that bothered Jay was that he could not entirely explain what the hell Char, Mariska, and Calista did. Save that it made them a lot of money.

Jay asked, "Are they traveling currently, or are they planet-bound?"

"Planet-bound," replied Char. "Their kids have stuff going on, so that keeps 'em grounded."

"School time?" asked Jay,

"Yeah, I guess it is," replied Char.

Once again, Jay silently thanked the stars that he and Char had chosen not to procreate.

Char agreed with that sentiment as she remarked, "As always, thank you for the vasectomy. Anyhow, we've a client in need of a site visit, and after consulting the star charts, I know we're not going to be far from them."

"Oh?" questioned Jay.

"Yeah," said Char. "It's on one of the moons of Verdant Virgo."

Jay knew that Verdant Virgo was a mostly green gas giant in the Enrocibe system. He couldn't recall off the top of his head how many moons there were, but that several were inhabited, and all were named for hats.

"Which one?" he asked.

"Fez."

"Let's pull up the star charts," Jay said, tapping at the screens around the pilot's seat. A holographic chart appeared on a display above the viewscreen, and Jay pulled it forward to hover holographically between the seats.

"Well, we're approximately here." Jay pointed to a spot in the middle of nowhere. "En route to Strelizia to deliver the marble we acquired at Kakumina." A dot representing Strelizia appeared ahead of the point Jay had said *Audacia* was at. "Fez is here," he said, and another dot appeared on the chart.

"Like I said, not far," said Char.

Jay nodded. "Yeah. It's about a day's travel via hyperspace from Strelizia to Fez." He turned off the holographic star chart. "The question is, do we need to adjust course and go to Fez now, first? Or can we do it after Strelizia?"

"After," said Char. "We're not rushed, and so long as one of us puts boots on the ground in the next three weeks, we're good."

"So, we can explore Strelizia for a few days, then?" asked Jay.

"Absolutely," replied Char.

"Sounds good," said Jay. "We make Strelizia in about three more days. We can probably spend a week exploring, then it's off to the moon of Fez."

Chapter 6 – Room With a View

She knew lots of people who worked out of necessity. Even with Universal Basic Income (UBI) options on many worlds, working kept you busy, kept the mind occupied, and made people feel like they were contributing to society.

Most of these people, Char knew, only truly cared about making a good impression on friends, family, even random strangers, instead of their own needs. For a long time, Char had been that way, caring more about what her parents and other relatives thought about her and her choices than what she needed. Hence, she had chosen a career path that she generally liked, but for the most part, it was what she did to be a productive part of society.

Then she'd met Jay. First, he was the single biggest geek she'd ever encountered. Secondly, he had goals, dreams, plans, and a desire to do the opposite of what his parents wanted him to do. Thirdly, he made no apologies for who he was.

Much as she would have preferred not to be charmed by Jay, she'd found all too quickly that she was. In fact, Jay had utterly disrupted how Char lived. Before him, her life had been work, family, and brief stints of dating. Dating, in that respect, followed a pattern - three dates with the given man or woman, sex on that third date, then she would move on. As she'd joked with her sister, hump 'em and dump 'em.

Jay had unexpectedly disarmed her and broke the pattern. Before Char knew it, they were well past the third date. Jay had somehow found a place in her heart that she'd had no idea even existed (Though, to be fair, she had done the same to him). Before long, she had had an actual, factual, boyfriend.

The "L" word had first been uttered by her. That shocked her. And then, her long-time spacecat companion had gotten ill and made it known he was done. Jay had stood at her side and held her hand as she let him go and cried with her. That was it; she knew Jay wasn't going anywhere. Frankly, she didn't want him to.

This had led to other changes. Char had met people she wanted to spend time with that weren't her family. Working less gave her more time to herself and to spend with Jay. Also, she had come to realize that she could leave her job and try to find a better one.

After a couple of job changes, despite Char's deep dislike of change, she'd found a job working with Mariska and Calista. The two amazingly dynamic women made Char feel even more empowered, and she had found that she genuinely liked her job. This had been quite the revelation.

Mariska had led Char and Calista into their own business. After the initial fear of being less of an employee and more of a boss, Char had found that she had gone from liking her job to loving her job.

At least, she loved her job most of the time. Except for some of the people, human and otherwise, that she had to deal with at times. It was especially trying when she had to contend with a client's mansplaining.

Char knew that Jay only vaguely understood what it was that she did. This was in part due to the slight shifts in work she'd experienced moving between jobs during the time that they'd been together. Apart from answering to Mariska – kind of – Char was the boss.

Her company's main function was to help businesses relocate. Specifically, multifaceted business relocations involving a mix of administrative types and either medical suites, warehousing, scientific centers, or other unique combinations. Their company worked with coordinating moves between worlds, into new construction, mergers with other corporations, and other complex challenges that required specialized project management.

Despite this being a niche business, there were very few companies that could do what they did. Given the number of people, worlds, and businesses across known space, that meant there was a goodly amount of work to be found.

It also didn't hurt that their company was run by three of the best in the business. It had taken Char a long time to accept the truth of this. Despite the occasional visits from her brain weasels insisting she was not that good, again and again she proved that, indeed, she *was* that good.

Char still found it equally amusing and disturbing when she encountered misogyny. It seemed that no matter how far humans traveled, or how much they became advanced, some maintained the notion of inequality in the genders. Thus, mansplaining still occurred.

It probably didn't help that the male former boss of the merged company they were working with was now reporting to a female boss who was a somewhat domineering, nonhuman female.

Char knew that one or two of the alien races out there had a very different take on gender relations. The primary reason for the business relocation she was working on was the new owner, who happened to be an ajerari female.

The ajerari, at first glance, looked much like darker-skinned humans. That is, until you saw their slightly larger, bumpy, ridged heads and ridged necks. They had no hair atop their heads, only along the back and sides, and it tended to be varying shades of bluish-grey.

The ajerari, as a race, were utterly and completely dominated by their females. They were, in fact, among the most prized and fearsome warriors in space. Only the female ajerari, however, could be warriors. They also ran all aspects of ajerari society and had total control of the government and businesses.

The male ajerari were the primary caregivers of their race's children. However, Char also knew they weren't subjugated or enslaved by their females, and among them, there were numerous skilled and accomplished mechanics, engineers, teachers, and diplomats. They just weren't in charge of any element of their people's society and were never warriors.

Hence, the male business owner, in the middle of a major relocation project, was feeling as if he was being heavily pressured by his new ajerari partners. Thus, the mansplaining.

"So," he was repeating himself yet again, "the heavy equipment will be tagged and set to arrive at Fez in a month."

"Like we've always planned," agreed Mariska's hologram.

Originally, they'd planned for their company's representation to be wholly handled by Char, what with her being physically present on the site. However, the female ajerari business owner had expressed some concerns that the company might be too amenable to her human male counterpart. Hence, Mariska was holographically present to give her further reassurance.

"Despite it being heavy, you understand how delicate this equipment is, right?" the male business owner took up, not for the first time. "Maybe we should sell what we have and buy new."

"Mr. Dawson," Char addressed him. He had insisted on the formality. "We've moved far more sensitive equipment over longer distances in less time. I assure you, we will not allow any harm to come to your machinery. We will even have a specialist from the manufacturer on hand to make sure that everything is packed as securely as possible before the move."

"It is far less expensive to move your machines than to buy new," said the ajerari business owner.

Mr. Dawson sighed. "Yes, yes." He looked out the window. "It will take some getting used to, but that view will never get old."

Char glanced out the window. The massive green gas giant was visible, dominating a corner of the sky but not blotting out the sun. This room they were in presently would serve as the executive suites, with offices for the human and ajerari business owners.

"This location was too good to pass up," said the ajerari.

"Construction was only completed a month ago," said Char. "I've been over all the records from the contractors, and they assure me the few changes that need to be made to accommodate your newly merged venture will be complete within two weeks."

"Did they not say a week?" questioned the ajerari.

"They did," agreed Mariska. "But in our experience, even the best contractors over-promise."

"We make it a habit to add a buffer," said Char. "This puts less pressure on you and also keeps everyone on track."

Mariska said, "Calista has rerun all the numbers, and we're more than confident everything's set. We just need your say-so, and we start the move process ASAP."

"Mr. Dawson?" asked the ajerari.

He looked to her, then Mariska's hologram, and then to Char. "Yes. Start it up."

"Thank you," said Mariska. "Mr. Dawson, Let's conference tomorrow. When do you take ship back to get your personal effects in order?"

"My transport is scheduled to depart in the morning, ten-hundred hours local."

"I'll contact you at midday, once you're underway," Mariska said.

"Perfect."

"Char, Mr. Dawson, Cimali," Mariska addressed them all. Then, her hologram winked out.

"I have a thing to do," Mr. Dawson said, stepping towards the exit. "Cimali, I'll talk to you later."

"Rod," she said. Mr. Dawson departed.

Softly, the ajerari said, "If his company were not the best and better as partners than competitors…"

Char grinned. "I think we make him uncomfortable."

Cimali laughed. "Undoubtedly. I find males always seem disconcerted in the presence of strong females."

"They're not all bad," said Char.

"No," said Cimali. "They just get so fragile. Their egos can be bruised with little effort. I read that among humans, some males think their gender the dominant and less fragile. Yet, Rod is the perfect example of that being utterly untrue."

Char looked towards the door where Mr. Dawson had departed. "Long, long ago, male dominance was more the norm. A few still find it particularly challenging to face a strong female."

Char saw Cimali shaking her head as she said, "Male ajerari can be willful sometimes, but we do not hold our leadership and warrior superiority over them. The, uh, I think the word for him is baby daddy, of my last-born is my current nesting partner, and I treat him fairly and equally."

Char racked her brain a moment. "I recall that ajerari don't mate for life, but do nest for extended times."

"Another reason I recommended we use your company for this relocation," said Cimali. "You do your homework on more than just the businesses, equipment, and move requirements. Tell me, Charlotte Danella, do you have a spouse?"

"I do."

"Does he expect you to keep him as your only mate for life?"

Char laughed. "Actually, my spouse and I are polyamorous. Neither of us has ever been good at monogamy, and since we've no children and want none, and we live on our ship, it's best for us."

"How interesting," said Cimali. "I read that there are many forms of relationships, pairings, and couplings among humans. Most suggest that monogamous mates are the norm."

"My spouse and I firmly believe normal is overrated," said Char.

Cimali laughed again. "I knew I liked you, Charlotte Danella. I shall take my leave of you now. Thank you for coming here to tour the facility and make final arrangements."

"You're welcome."

The ajerari female nodded to her, then left the room.

Char turned to look at the view again. If she ever felt the need to live on one planet down the line, this one would be a contender. Fez and the other moons of Verdant Virgo wouldn't be a bad place to call home.

This was never a serious thought for Char. She loved the life she and Jay had made. The *Audacia* might have been a transport starship, but it was home. Char loved her life as much as she loved her job.

She raised her wrist and activated her chronograph faux'cator. It made a pre-set whirring noise as it signaled to make the connection.

"Hello, my love." Jay's voice reached Char not from her wrist, but the almost microscopic speaker in the arms of her multi-tech glasses.

"We just wrapped everything up here," Char told him. "You hungry?"

"Yes," Jay replied. "I've a couple of different ideas for where we can grab dinner between the docks and the building you're at now."

"That would be great," Char said. "But don't send me options. Just pick and tell me where I should meet you."

"Anything in particular you're in the mood for?" Jay asked.

Char considered a moment. "I'm open. Just nothing stereotypically human-made or rumel."

Jay chuckled. "Got it. See you in half an hour?"

"Perfect," said Char. "Love you."

"Love you, too." And with that, Jay closed the transmission.

Char paused, and took one more look out the window at the impressive view. The green gas giant and setting sun were a striking contrast. It never ceased to amaze Char how sunrise and sunset could be so wildly different across space. Yet it was always breathtaking, no matter where you witnessed it.

Char had time before she needed to join her spouse. She crossed her arms as she admired the amazing view while she could. This life she led was not what she'd been expecting; it was far better. Despite frequently being pulled outside of her comfort zone, traveling the length and breadth of the galaxy with Jay kept life interesting on many different levels.

Chapter 7 – Family is Stranger Than Fiction

It was a low-key afternoon. The *Audacia* was in hyperspace. Jay had a cargo of nonperishable foodstuffs grown by humans on one world to deliver to a race called sutac on another world.

Some races kept their dietary needs to themselves. Gorlek, for example, were a mystery. What the reptilian, cybernetically modified race farmed or otherwise raised for food was unknown, and there were no gorlek restaurants anywhere. You also never saw the gorlek eating at an establishment featuring another race's food.

The sutac were built much the same as humans, except their heads were distinctly cat-like. They were not furred like cats, though they did have hair atop their heads in calico, orange, and other cat-like colors. They also had whiskers on their cheeks like cats, and gold or green eyes.

It was not spacecats/herpesteline that the sutac looked like, but the cats of old Earth. The spacecats lacked whiskers and tended to be more brightly colored than the cats of Earth.

Jay was unsure what the foodstuffs were that he was transporting, save that scans indicated that they were utterly not dangerous, inert, and mostly harmless while stowed aboard his ship. He didn't care if they were safe for human consumption or not because all he had to do was move them, not eat them.

The planet they were bound for was not a planet so much as a dwarf planet called Pumeelio. The world had no atmosphere and was spotted with domes that made it look like it had the worst case of acne ever. But each dome had a robust atmosphere, and some were cities while others held various other unique entertainments. Jay and Char were both looking forward to exploring.

They were two days away from their destination, and Char had finished her work for the day. Thus, they were in the lounge. Char was playing a game on her tablet while Jay was reading. Cosima was on Char's lap, Thalia on Jay's. She had a cup of tea beside her; Jay had a cup of coffee.

Jay loved their home and that they had the ability to just chill in one another's presence as they desired. Char really was the most perfect companion he could ever have imagined, and he considered himself very lucky.

The 'cator began to buzz on Jay's tablet. He saw who it was and said to Char, "Essie's calling."

"When was the last time you chatted with her?" Char asked.

"I think a month ago. Want to join in?"

"Yes, please."

Jay answered the 'cator, putting Essie on speaker.

"Hey, Essie," Jay said.

"Hi, Jay," she replied. "Char there, too?"

"Hi, Essie!"

"Where you two at?" Essie asked.

"Hyperspace," Jay said. "We're on our way to Pumeelio, two days out or so."

"Why have I heard of Pumeelio?" Essie mused aloud. Then, she said, "Right, I remember. Exeter's cousin, or maybe his cousin's ex-husband? I can't remember. Anyhow, he was part of some land deal that was supposed to make him a fortune. And it was prime real estate, save that there was no dome in the location."

"No dome?" asked Char.

"Yup," agreed Essie. "Seems there was a plan for a dome, and the land had been all prepped and such. But then, money ran out or some such thing, and they never built the dome itself. Exeter had wanted to be part of that deal, so I'm glad I talked him out of it."

"I can imagine," said Jay. "What's new?"

"That's what I was calling about," Essie said. "I'm sending some vids to you now. But it seems Emberly has shed her baby tail."

Essie's husband, Exeter, was rumel. Since rumel and humans were genetically compatible, they had produced Jay and Char's niece, Emberly, over a decade ago. The precocious child very much struck Jay as a clone of his sister, which amused him to no end.

Char asked, "That's, uh, normal, right?"

Essie laughed. "Yeah. However, it normally occurs with the rumel when they're closer to fifteen. That's because the tail is a really weird combo of both a sensory and sex organ. I have no idea just how that works, and Exeter is being cagey about that part. Everything I've read says it won't come into play for a few more years, which is a relief. But now, rather than that little, thick, stubby tail, it's a long, thin, whippy thing."

The video had come through, and Jay and Char watched without turning on the sound as Emberly showed off her new tail. Then, she did a bunch of tumbles that looked far too nimble for a human.

"The tail gives her more dexterity?" asked Jay,

"Yes," Essie said. "That's natural for rumel females. Since males have no tail, which Exeter seems unwilling to explain in detail."

"Is he being a prude, or just evasive?" asked Char.

"Evasive," said Essie. "You know how he can be. For all I know, he thinks he told me when he was muttering at some point, and I was only half paying attention. The weirdest thing, for me, is the idea that this is a sex organ of some sort."

Jay laughed. "Not ready to have 'that talk' with your daughter?"

He could practically hear Essie roll her eyes as she said, "With the added bonus of rumel sexuality and sensuality? Nope. Maybe I can get one of Exeter's sisters to help me with this."

"You tell your mom?" asked Char.

"Not yet," Essie said. "Last time we talked, we were arguing about when the next time we plan to visit is. Mom wants me not to bring Exeter along if possible."

"Mom gets weird notions in her head," said Jay. "I ever tell you about the conversation she and I had when Emberly was about six months old? When her tail first came in?"

"No," Essie said.

"Hope you're sitting down," Jay started. "I spoke to Mom a day or two later and relayed to her how every time I saw Essie, she was looking less human and more human-rumel mixed. I know you hadn't said anything to Mom, because why would you? Anyhow, I told her that Essie's tail had grown in, almost overnight. And mom said – I am not making this up – 'Huh. That's odd. I thought the first child of an interspecies couple was always the most human.'"

There was a moment of silence, broken only by a snicker from Char. Essie said, "She didn't."

"She most certainly did."

Essie sighed. "Yeah, that tracks. I see why you wouldn't have told me this before."

"Sure," Jay said.

"So, you paying Mom a visit anytime soon?" Essie asked.

"No," Jay replied. "We're a long way from Magoonay these days and have no plans to head back that way for a while. More places to explore out here that we've never seen before."

"Sure," agreed Essie. "How's work, Char?"

Jay found that Thalia had stretched and was demanding he scritch her head. He tuned out Char and Essie's conversation for a time while giving the spacecat the attention she demanded. He could have sworn that she merped something that sounded like, "Ignore thumb monkeys give me all the scritches."

"Anyhow," Essie was saying on the 'cator. "Thought you'd want to see your niece's wild new tail for yourself. You guys think you might be swinging by somewhere near enough we can grab a meal or something?"

"For you, Exeter, and Emberly, we'll plan something," said Jay.

"Great," replied Essie. "Love you guys."

"Love you too, Ess," said Jay.

The transmission ended.

"Jay?" Char asked in her coy, semi-sarcastic tone.

"Yes, my love?"

"Did your mother skip a lot of school during her childhood?" Char asked. "Or, ya know, basic biology?"

Jay chuckled. "No. It's just her and her own unique, oddly exclusionary and strange view of life, the universe, and everything."

"I guess so," Char said. However, the look she gave Jay spoke volumes about her incredulity.

Truth, Jay mused, was often stranger than fiction.

Chapter 8 – Plan A is Underway

The first step of the plan had been relatively easy. They were seated at an outdoor table for two at a café on the outskirts of the spaceport. Imaro was sipping at a cup of cofveina (a drink close to coffee with twice the caffeine per cup of kijivu origin). Kukeb was trying not to look like he was trying to look all around himself in every direction all at once.

"It's fine, Kukeb," Imaro said for the umpteenth time.

"Right," said Kukeb. "Sure, it is. Until it's not. This is crazy."

Imaro was nervous, of course. But he believed completely in his plan. Thus far, step one was a success. They were no longer in the city of Ranrop-Palast. They had gotten on a hovertrain out of the capital and made their way to the nearest city with a major spaceport, eighteen-hundred kilometers away.

Not only was it a good distance from home, it was the busiest spaceport on the continent. They would blend in with little effort.

The next step was to board the public transport off the planet. Then, they'd take it as far away from Rangeenavelt as possible. Fortunately, it wasn't necessary to declare your stop when you boarded one of these transports. After your initial fare, you paid the toll for whichever world you disembarked on.

There was, arguably, a whole spaceport between them and freedom. But they had made it out of Ranrop-Palast without incident. Apart from getting on the transport and leaving the planet, to Imaro's mind that was the trickiest aspect of it all.

Kukeb was fretting. He always worried about niggling details as well as big things far outside anyone's control. However, Imaro admitted, that was just another element he loved about him.

Imaro half expected Kukeb's head to turn all around in every direction, on the lookout for a threat. While the rangeen couldn't do such, the roptera were capable of turning their heads all the way around without injury.

"Enjoy your drink, Kukeb," Imaro chided his companion.

Kukeb paused and did that. Then, he resumed his nervous vigil. "This is so crazy. What if we're recognized?"

"Not likely," Imaro said. There was always a chance of that being a threat, he knew. Imaro was well aware of the recorded incidences of people who knew one another at various levels from passing acquaintances to intimate lovers who inadvertently ran into someone in an utterly unexpected place. Even given that, Imaro wasn't going to allow himself to worry.

"Nobody will realize we're gone for at least a day," Imaro stated with confidence.

"How can you possibly know that?" asked Kukeb skeptically.

Imaro leaned back, affecting nonchalance. "I told a couple of different people we'd be on the opposite side of Ranrop-Palast on a couple of errands, mostly business-related. Then, I faked a few entries in my calendar and my father's. Once we started to plan this, I told some half-truths, made a few plausible ideations up, and laid sufficient groundwork to leave us undisturbed and unremarked all day today. Thus, nobody will even start to note our absence for a day."

"But it's only late morning," said Kukeb. "Something might come up that causes someone who cares to ignore all that and seek us out."

"Yes, you're right, of course. But you also know full well that's not likely. Especially when they think we're doing business."

"But, Imaro, the transport doesn't leave until midday."

Imaro shook his head. "Kukeb, Kukeb. Relax. We can board the transport in less than an hour. By mid-afternoon it will be off Rangeenavelt. We'll already be in hyperspace and on our way by the time anyone works out that we're gone."

"What if the ship gets recalled?" questioned Kukeb.

He might have loved Kukeb, but his worrying sometimes sorely tried Imaro's patience. "That's not possible. There are public transports like this leaving from every spaceport on the planet. Nobody would recall them because that could impede commerce. Besides, once anyone who cares realizes we're gone, it will be some time before they start to search off-world for us."

"Why?"

Imaro grinned. "Because we've misled everyone in that direction. How many times have we talked about going to Ranrop-Shorus and getting lost among the tourists? How many times have we let ourselves be seen examining information about the remote equatorial mountain peaks? How many properties have I invested in across the planet? No, Kukeb, it will take them a while to realize we're not on the planet anymore."

"But eventually they will figure out we've gone off-world," said Kukeb. "Then what?"

Imaro sighed. "Then, Kukeb, we will be so far away that nobody will be able to find us. There are more than a dozen races across the known galaxy. Separately and together, they occupy hundreds, if not thousands, of worlds. We'll go somewhere far enough away that anyone who will come looking for us will be overwhelmed by all the places we might potentially be. And we will choose a world where we are not at all the only rangeen who call it home. Once we're away from Rangeenavelt, we'll blend into the vast crowds and billions of others out there."

Kukeb nodded and seemed to calm some. He took another drink, then resumed his vigil with notably less agitation.

After a moment or two of silence, once he'd clearly looked around to make sure nobody paid them any attention, Kukeb said, "Sure, yes, once we're away from Rangeenavelt, as you say, we'll 'blend into the vast crowds and billions of others out there'. To do that, we take public transport to the farthest point from Rangeenavelt we can, whatever that might be. But then, we hire a private transport?"

Imaro grinned. "Exactly. That's the plan. And it will work because when we hire a private transport, we hire a ship that's not rangeen, nor affiliated with the rangeen in any way."

"How do we do that?" asked Kukeb.

Imaro wasn't about to admit he wasn't fully certain how to answer that. "People hire ships and crews to move things and people all the time. Most ships and their crews don't care who hires them, so long as they get paid. We've got it covered. This will work, Kukeb. I promise."

Kukeb nodded, then went back to his drink. His vigil was notably less frenetic, which made Imaro feel better.

Imaro checked his chrono'cator and led Kukeb from the café to the spaceport. Though his partner wasn't nearly as obvious as he'd been, Imaro knew he was carefully watching the people around them.

Another reason that Imaro had chosen this spaceport, apart from being incredibly busy and a long way from Ranrop-Palast, was the automated kiosks. While there were a few roving customer service rangeen, the majority were either robots or automated kiosks.

A pair of Royal Enforcers were visible on the outskirts of the crowd. Imaro believed if he ignored them, they'd ignore him.

They reached the kiosk and Imaro called up the transport schedules. He located which docking bay their chosen transport would leave from, got their boarding passes, and smartly stepped into the crowd after checking the holographic signage in the air above, listing departures, arrivals, docking bays, and times.

It was about half a kilometer to their docking bay. Although the majority of the people In the spaceport were rangeen, Imaro noticed groups and individuals of other races.

He also noticed Royal Enforcers patrolling. They seemed to pay nobody any special attention, mostly keeping an eye out for troublemakers and obvious problems to maintain a general sense of security for all.

Finally, they reached the docking bay. A line made up of mostly just rangeen stood between them and the ship. Imaro felt Kukeb fidgeting and twitching beside him. However, he chose not to admonish his lover. Instead, he decided Kukeb was not just holding his own worry, but Imaro's too.

There was a rangeen robot at the head of the line, checking tickets. Imaro presented his chrono'cator to the robot, which scanned it, then dinged to let him know they were clear to board.

The transport was a large oval, with retractable wings for atmospheric flight stability. It had five decks. The lowest was for cargo, the next up featured a common space, including a public mess hall and lounge. The third deck had only seating but was a mix of side-by-side rows of two to four, and groupings of four to six to eight across from one another.

The uppermost deck was where the ship's flight crew worked. The fourth deck, immediately below the upper deck, featured private suites and passenger cabins. That was where Imaro and Kukeb made their way to.

They hadn't particularly gone out of their way to avoid notice. However, Imaro wasn't concerned. Nobody paid much mind to travelers boarding a public transport. At least, that was what he believed.

They settled into their cabin. It had one wide bunk, a shelf above that for luggage, a small chair and table, a viewport to the outside, and a tiny restroom separated by a door.

"Well, we made it this far," Kukeb conceded. "Assuming we get off the planet without incident, where are we going?"

Imaro called up the ticket information. The transport would make more than a dozen stops across rangeen space. It would visit multiple worlds, a moon or two, and a couple of space stations or platforms.

If you didn't disembark at each successive stop, your account would be charged. Imaro was glad there was a star chart showing the course the transport took from Rangeenavelt and back again.

"The furthest world we can get to, on the edge of rangeen space, is called Sovereign Boundary," Imaro stated.

Chapter 9 – Really, Mom, We're Good

"But Jay, honey, doesn't Char get tired of that vagabond lifestyle?" his mother asked.

Jay was in the cockpit beside Quinn. Although they were on a planet they'd visited a few times before, Jay had been taking care of bureaucratic necessities – paperless paperwork – and updating star charts when his mother had reached out via 'cator. Not caring that Quinn would hear, he had put her on speaker to talk to her while he worked.

This topic was one Jay's mom brought up about every six months to a year or so. For reasons he just couldn't wrap his head around, she refused to accept that Char was as content living on *Audacia* as Jay was. He knew the issue was that it went against his mother's sensibilities in many ways.

Despite asking her to stop bringing it up and trying to convince him he was wrong, she was doing it again. How was it possible that she could hold on to such outdated beliefs about how people might care to live?

Not for the first time, and he was certain not for the last time, Jay said, "Char is as content as I am, Mom."

"Jay, honey, women don't always tell the whole truth."

Jay sighed. "Mom, let's go over this once again, okay? Char is as content living this way as I am. Remember, selling our planetary home and buying this ship was Char's idea in the first place."

"But she agreed to it because it was *your* idea."

"Yes, my dream was to own a starship and see the galaxy," Jay semi-conceded. "However, given the nature of her work, the need for occasional travel, and her desire to also see the galaxy, this 'vagabond lifestyle', as you call it, appeals to my wife just as much as it appeals to me."

His mother was silent for a moment. The second or third time they'd had this conversation, that silence had given Jay hope that he'd gotten through to her. Given that this frequent conversation was on its tenth or higher iteration, he knew better.

"Most people with good jobs and prosperous careers live on planets," his mother took up again. "I find it impossible to believe that Char wouldn't like to have a nice home, so that she can show off her success and host people who might want to visit? What about her family and yours?"

"Do you even know my wife, Mom?" Jay couldn't stop himself from asking. "Char has never been one to show off in any way. What's more, she hates having guests in her home, family or otherwise. You forget she's an introvert and prefers to keep herself to an intimate few. But more than all that, Mom, we're happy with our lives."

"Without a proper home?" questioned his mom.

"*Audacia* is our home," Jay said. "We chose it ourselves and we love it."

"But Jay, it's a starship. It's not a proper home; it's a vehicle, a transport from place to place, not a home. Doesn't that get tiresome?"

"*Audacia* is not just a starship, Mom, it's our home," Jay replied. "Our living quarters are not so different from a condo in a big city on any planet. We have plenty of space, all the comforts of a normal home, and we take good care of it. Most importantly, we're not bound to a singular place and taking the occasional trip somewhere new and different. We get to go wherever we like and earn a living doing that."

"Earn a living," his mother scoffed. "With all your gifts, all your talent, you call transporting people and cargo across space a living? And don't filthy passengers and cargos that've been who-knows-where bother you?"

Jay chuckled. Her argument was so circular and ridiculous. He said, "You've seen this ship, Mom. Our living quarters are separate from passengers and cargo. What's more, we pick and choose who and what we transport. And your definition of filthy is very, very different from ours."

"Oh, Jay, you really believe that Char is content living that way?"

"No, Mom. I *know* she is. Why can't you believe that Char doesn't just give in to demands I make? We communicate about everything. All the decisions that impact us both are discussed before either of us makes them. Char isn't coerced or otherwise influenced by me to make a choice she'd prefer not to. Traveling the stars together on *Audacia* is a choice that we made together. Please stop second-guessing us."

Jay's mom sighed dramatically. "Alright, son, if you say so. I just want you to be happy."

"Yeah, you say that, but then you disbelieve that Char and I are."

His mom was silent for a moment. Then, her tone changed. "And where exactly are you now? In hyperspace between places?"

"No," Jay said. "We're on Palindrome Alla."

"Palindrome Alla?" his mother asked. "I thought you were all about visiting new places you've never seen. But haven't you been there before?"

"Yes, we have," Jay agreed. "But we weren't too far from here in our current travels, and Char wanted to visit her girlfriend."

There was a moment of silence, then his mom said, "Is that a girl friend or girlfriend?"

"The latter. Girlfriend," Jay confirmed. "You recall that Char and I are not monogamous, and being polyamorous, we have other romantic relationships besides with each other?"

"I just don't understand," his mother said, trying and failing to hide her distaste. "I could never imagine being with anyone other than your stepfather. He's more than enough for me."

"That's fine for you, Mom," Jay stated. "Polyamory and other non-monogamous relationships have been widely accepted since humankind found our way to the stars. Just like heterosexuality, homosexuality, bisexuality, and the like, not everyone is wired for monogamy."

"I just don't get it," his mother said for the umpteenth time.

"You don't have to," Jay stated. "Just keep in mind, once humans stopped trying to fit everyone into very specific boxes of sexuality, gender, and relationships, the divorce rate all but evaporated to single-digit numbers."

This was one of the few ways Jay could push back on his mother. Some might have found that crude, but for all the times she did it to him, he felt he had earned the right to give it back to her.

Before the conversation could devolve again, Jay said, "Look, Mom, it's been great talking to you, but I need to go."

"Very well, dear," she said. "Give Char our love."

"I will."

"Love you."

"Love you too, Mom."

The transmission ended.

"Why do you do that?" asked Quinn.

"Do what?"

"Goad your mother?" the robot pressed.

"Because it keeps her on her toes and gives me the upper hand when she's driving me crazy," Jay replied.

"The whole of that conversation made no logical sense," said Quinn.

"That's about a near-perfect summation of my mother," Jay stated. "She makes no logical sense."

"Why press her and potentially upset her when you could end the conversation? Or not even speak with her at all?" asked Quinn.

"You know that, until a certain age, humans live under the care of their parents," Jay began. "Every parent has a different philosophy and approach to raising their children. Some create few to no boundaries, while others are more rigid and have strict, set rules for behavior and everything else. Then, some parents desire to make their children strong and independent quickly, while others want to hold them close for protection, as well as to live their lives through them."

"Yes, I've downloaded basic texts on human psychology," said Quinn. "Despite certain milestones, as a human evolves from infant to toddler to adolescent to teen to adult, there are no set parameters to define when they ultimately become independent."

"Exactly," said Jay. "While, on the one hand, my mother raised Essie and me with little to no input from our father, and she instilled in us manners and attitudes to keep us strong and independent, she still craves a modicum of control over us and how we live. Some of that is protective, but it's also self-interested and selfish. Being able to show off her children to her friends makes her feel like she's better than them in various ways."

"That defies logic," stated Quinn.

"You're right," agreed Jay. "But then, emotions nearly always defy logic. Being disagreeable with my mom, and 'goading' her, as you said, is actually a way to maintain mine and Char's independence and sovereignty. Since we're never going to manage to live up to who she would prefer that we be, sometimes she needs to be reminded of just how far our reality is from her vision of it."

"I was built by humans, work with humans, and enjoy conversing with humans, but I simply do not get humans."

Jay chuckled. He checked over all the work he'd done and saw it was complete. Then he checked the time and stood up from the pilot's seat. "I'm done here. I'm going to head out. There's a local 'lectro-bo staff practice I've been to before I'm going to hit now."

"Hit," Quinn said. "Intentional or unintentional pun?"

Jay paused. "Unintentional."

"Right," said Quinn, pouring sarcasm into his statement. "Shall I stay here and guard the ship?"

"Do you have somewhere else you'd like to be?"

"What if I wanted to take your mother's advice and find a planetside home to call my own?" questioned Quinn.

"Wouldn't that go against your programming?" asked Jay.

"If I was programmed by humans who frequently go against their programming, how would I define if I were to go against it?"

Jay chuckled, shaking his head. "An ethical conundrum fit for a robot of your metal, right, Quinn?"

Quinn produced the electronic equivalent of a long-suffering sigh. "And I know full well that that *was* an intentional pun."

Chapter 10 – Another Word from Our Sponsor

Hello. This is your friendly neighborhood author, again. This seemed like a perfectly good time to share a few more things that I think will improve your enjoyment of this story.

Have you ever wondered what the world be like if certain ethics and ideas of morality weren't so dominant? Well, once humankind reaches the stars, much of that did, in fact, go out the window – where it promptly expanded and exploded like a body exposed to the vacuum of space would.

Many of the religious institutions most of us know today, if they survived to Jay and Char's time, changed quite a bit. There were lots of reasons for this, but one of the biggest was that ethics based on an invisible deity became far less weighty when the stars weren't so far out of reach.

When the human race made its way to interstellar space, we learned that lots of our beliefs were based, at best, on total bullshit. Especially those of our own superiority. Maybe on Earth, we're the top of the food chain and the only species of animal capable of adapting to any environment by building tools and technologies to that end. Yet, once humankind left our home solar system and learned that we are very much not on our own, our belief in our superiority looked utterly foolish.

This is because other races were way smarter, far more advanced, and way more developed than humans. It was a bit of a shock to the earliest interstellar travelers, using the best technology humankind had ever produced, to find it very lacking.

Early human starships – even those capable of faster-than-light travel via hyperspace – had either no gravity or relied on spin gravity far lower than planetary norms in only portions of their ships. Meanwhile, multiple races had long before perfected artificial gravity, long-haul foods that weren't dehydrated, incredibly more efficient fuels, water and air reclamation, and on and on.

When your best tech is the equivalent of a wind-up watch compared to their Apple watch, it's a very humbling experience.

As the other races humankind encountered got to know us, they found many aspects of our "morality" and "ethics" highly laughable.

Take relationships and religion, for example. Biology dictates a need to procreate and propagate a species. Religion tells you that your deity demands this of you to give him/her/them/it more worshipers. Yet, counter to that, biological functions take certain steps to both expand on and lessen procreation and the propagation of the species.

In other words, one man, one woman, married for life to form a family and produce children has zero to do with biology and science. Homosexuality, polyamory, polygamy, bisexuality, and virtually every other "deviant" and non-standard way of being, to human sensibilities, were normal among other races.

Let me clear up one thing, before anyone gets offended. No matter how good your science is, there are things it can only barely define and explain.

Every race seeks answers to deep questions that science might have an explanation for, but that still doesn't satisfy the need for ties and emotional connections. Thus, the races of the galaxy have religions, but they tend to be far less judgmental and we're-right-you're-wrong-enjoy-going-to-hell than certain Earth religions.

A belief in something bigger than themselves, defined as a god or gods, was far less prevalent among aliens when the human race encountered them.

They tend to focus on existential matters alone and don't care about the mundane, like a person's gender, sexual preference, birth sex, or whatever. Also, science was proven far more right, far more frequently, than lots of the religious zealots would have liked.

Another matter that humankind found other races took a very different approach to was gender equality. Most of the races saw their peoples as one – male, female, nonbinary, or whatever. The importance of gender in relation to jobs, pay, and the like was very different in the galaxy at large.

At least, that was the majority of what humanity experienced when they went to space. There are exceptions, of course, because there is never only One True Way™.

However, because people can be stubborn, and/or arrogant, and/or believe themselves and their way superior, some hold onto old moralities, principles, and beliefs. This includes matters such as monogamy, sexuality, and the like.

Even in the face of information to the contrary, with proven fact and empirical evidence, some people – not only humans – hold onto a false belief. This might be because it makes them feel comfortable, less small, empowered, or just like they know something that the rest of us don't.

That's how you get someone like Jay's mom. A perfectly, largely well-meaning, lovely human being, who holds onto a picture of "the way it is" that's at least a few degrees away from actual, factual reality.

However, I've digressed long enough. Now you know – and knowing is half the battle (please don't sue me, Hasbro!)

And now, back to our story.

Chapter 11 - I Might Be Human, But I Wasn't Born Yesterday

Why was it that so many nonhumans felt superior to humans? This was a question that had plagued Jay since he started to transport cargo and passengers.

Sometimes, he knew, it came from how long the person's race had been plying space in comparison to how long humans had been doing so. Other times, it was based on previous encounters with human crews and what they did or didn't do.

When he could help it, Jay would avoid this sort of thing. The extra hassle and annoyance was often not worth wherever the cargo might take them, or the currency they might get from it.

Then there were situations like the one Jay was in now. The nonhuman was seeking to move goods to a system that his race tended to be at odds with.

Char was there because Jay had long ago found that having someone to watch your back facing this sort of client was smart. Also, because the nonhumans that tended to think less of humans were often far less prejudicial when it wasn't just one-on-one. Jay could not wrap his head around the psychology of that.

The client was sutac. Jay was familiar enough with the cats from Earth to recognize that the comparison wasn't just appearance. Sutac could go from friendly and communicative to standoffish and arrogant at the drop of a hat.

In the past, Jay had been told directly by a sutac that they were superior to all other races. Particularly humans, whom the sutac found curious because they tended to be explorers and open to new things on the one hand but also insular and very set in their ways on the other hand.

Char had once commented that, sometimes, Quinn seemed to take a very similar view of humans and the human race.

This client, a male named Milo, had sold his goods to a buyer in the rangeen sector. Rangeen and sutac had a long-standing rivalry that was understood by nobody who wasn't rangeen or sutac. Jay had, however, once heard or read somewhere that it was speculated that the real issue was more about the roptera – who shared their planet of origin with the rangeen – and the sutac. He'd also once heard that it was some long-ago insult or other disagreement nobody had bothered to address in a very long time.

Whatever the case, Milo needed to use a shipper who was not sutac. Milo wasn't just a sutac client but was also based on a sutac world. Ketza was a core sutac world. Jay and Char were there because their last transport – passengers – had been a group of adventure seekers hiking the famous Lettir Deserts of Ketza.

Jay found the areas outside of deserts, largely stone structures and mountains of various heights, fascinating. He and Char had explored several. The desert, however, held little appeal. The dunes were fascinating, as were the sands and sparse oases. However, the appeal of hiking one for days or weeks? Not so much.

While Jay and Char had taken advantage of their visit to Ketza and sutac space to do some exploring, he'd left an open for work notice at the spaceport. That was how Milo had initiated contact, since, on the surface, the *Audacia* was perfect to meet his needs.

Right from the start, Milo had been unfriendly and challenging. He'd made a show of telling about his business, how the rangeen needed to recognize that they needed the sutac as allies and trading partners, and that he would only hire a very specific type of private transport service.

Jay had stated they were a registered transport with OVERLORD, had an excellent reputation, and reasonable rates. Milo had been silent a moment, looking at a tablet, as if contemplating his next play. This had made room for Jay's ruminations.

Continuing to be cagey, Milo stated, "Yes, yes, of course, Captain, that's what you say. Please present to me here your credentials, licenses, registration, references, and proof of ownership or positive status in payment for your craft."

Jay paused so as not to sigh with frustration. He caught Char's eye, noting that she was aware how the request had made him defensive.

Calmly, Jay said, "You've already got access to all that information. Everything you're asking me to present you with is public record, attached to my open-to-work notice. To offer legal transport for either passengers or cargo, it has to all be there."

Milo waved a paw as if dismissing Jay or swatting a fly and said, "Come now, Captain, we both know that can be faked."

"And, what, you think if I share my credentials with you here, it might present a different picture?" asked Jay.

"Do you have something to hide, Captain?" questioned Milo.

"No," Jay said. Knowing better than to further elaborate, he continued with, "If my assurance that we are a legitimate transport, fully accredited, licensed, insured, and registered according to OVERLORD regulations, is not sufficient, I'm sure you can find someone you're more comfortable with."

Char piped up and said, "Not that there are many non-sutac ships for hire here. I noticed that most of the transports that come to Ketza are commercial. But that's always an option."

"If I wanted a commercial transport, I'd not be wasting my time talking to you," said Milo.

"Good," stated Jay, shifting the tone of the discussion. "Let's continue, shall we? What's the cargo?"

Milo seemed about to argue a moment, but then said, "Three standard pallets. They contain unfinished raw fabrics that my buyer uses in her manufacturing business. I'm generously offering one hundred towbeans per crate, plus a bonus two hundred for their delivery to Ibi Plerum-que in rangeen space in three days."

Jay knew that his mouth was hanging open. He was not sure if he was more shocked or insulted by Milo. Recovering, Jay couldn't help himself and started to laugh, saying, "Where do I even begin? To offer five hundred towbeans for this job is, frankly, insultingly low. What's more, you want the job done in an impossible time-frame."

"Is your ship incapable of that?" questioned Milo, tauntingly.

"No," replied Jay. "Every ship is incapable of that." He consulted his own tablet, then said, "Sutac space to rangeen space is no less than three days in hyperspace. Ketza to Ibi Plerum-que, realistically, is about five days away via hyperspace."

Milo made that dismissive gesture with his paw again. "You're mistaken, Captain. Not accounting for a full-speed flight across hyperspace, with a favorable tachyon flow as there is between sutac and rangeen space, creates a quantum fluctuation in the calculation of realtime and travel distance, making the trip not three or five days traveling faster than light, but two days. It's a complex matter of mathematics I'm rather certain you cannot grasp."

"That's untrue and utterly impossible," Jay said, maintaining his calm and fighting himself to keep his tone even. "Your math is bullshit, because the laws of physics don't work differently for humans than nonhumans, nor do your implausible assertions."

Milo grinned, like he knew something Jay didn't. Then, he said, "Ah, my young Captain, that's just a human failing, you see…"

Jay held up a hand to forestall Milo's next statement and said, "Yeah, a human failing, the human lack of true understanding of celestial navigation given our limited senses, human frailty, the divided single human brain and its inefficient connections." He paused and looked to Char. "I miss anything?"

She supplied, "The human lack of sufficient time traversing interplanetary space in comparison to so many others?"

"Right, how could I forget that?" asked Jay facetiously. He looked directly at Milo and said, "I might be human, but I wasn't born yesterday. I've heard this argument and a dozen more. You're not going to convince me to accept your ludicrous terms."

Milo began to splutter, clearly indignant, bristling – literally – as he said, "Well, I, you, that is to say, Captain, I…"

"Let me tell you what my terms are," Jay interrupted. "Not five hundred for the whole job, five hundred per pallet. Then, another thousand to cover insurance, shipping and handling, and the rest. Delivery will be to your designated buyer on Ibi Plerum-que in five days. Take it or leave it, because this is non-negotiable, utterly reasonable, and my best offer."

"Well, then, no," stated Milo.

"Okay," said Jay. "Good luck." He turned to Char. "We're done here, my love. Let's go."

Jay started to move off, and Char fell in beside him. Despite this meeting occurring in *Audacia*'s landing bay, the message would go better if they walked away. If Milo had any thoughts of messing with his ship, he'd have to deal with Quinn anyhow.

Just as Jay and Char were nearing the passageway out of the bay, Milo cried out, "Wait!"

Jay and Char turned and watched the sutac merchant moving not quite at a jog, but with unmistakable haste. When he was before them, Milo said, "Please, please don't go. Despite the hardship this will cause, and the loss I'm going to take due to your time-frame and price, I accept your offer. Even though it will taint my perspective of things and cause my family and my workers some difficulties, it's more important that I get the goods where they need to go."

"You can stop that ploy, too," said Jay. "I checked up on you before I agreed to this meeting. Just like I wasn't born yesterday, neither does a sob story meant to soften my resolve and tug at my heartstrings do anything but make me wonder if the job is worth it. We have a deal or we don't, on my terms or not at all."

Milo looked, as much as Jay could read sutac emotions, crestfallen. His tone changed back to what it had been at the start, but with an air of resignation added. "Very well."

Jay entered the information into the tablet, made a show of checking it thoroughly, then passed it to Milo. The sutac gave it a cursory perusal, then signed his consent and the transfer of the currency.

He passed the tablet back to Jay, saying, "My pallets will be here in two hours."

Jay nodded. "Good. We'll have them loaded and secured within an hour of that, then we'll raise ship and get on our way."

Milo nodded. "Thank you. Safe travels."

The sutac nodded to Char, then walked away.

Jay glanced back to make sure he'd cleared the bay, then started towards the ship.

"I love when you give it to them like that," said Char. "It never ceases to amaze me how many nonhumans think we're idiots."

"We did a bit better than we would have had he not tried to play me," said Jay. "Normally, I'd have accepted another five-hundred over the pallet fees."

Char grinned. "Serves him right. So, rangeen space?"

"Yup," agreed Jay. He looked at the name of their destination again. "I wonder what Ibi Plerum-que has to offer?"

Chapter 12 – We're In It to Win It

Only while he was alone could he admit to how terrified he actually was.

So far, it was all going according to plan. While he was deeply pleased that he'd been utterly correct, a part of him worried that it was only a matter of time before his luck ran out.

Imaro Iwoto had a lifetime's worth of playing it cool, even under tremendous personal or professional pressure. In fact, he prided himself on that. They'd made it to the transport, gotten off the planet, and were still en route to the furthest destination in the rangeen sector the transport was going to, Sovereign Boundary.

What he would never admit to anyone but himself, even Kukeb, was how worried he'd been that they'd only be able to remain on the public transport for two, or at best, three stops, before they'd be forced to flee. However, had Kukeb been aware of how genuinely concerned Imaro had been, he'd have insisted that they bail on the plan altogether.

Granted, Imaro understood Kukeb's reluctance. Imaro's defiance of his father, if he were caught, would come with a terrible price. Of that, he had no doubt. That was his father's nature. Kukeb, however, would be potentially in far more trouble and have it a lot worse.

Overall, Imaro and Kukeb had been keeping to their private cabin aboard the transport. There were no porters to check in on them, as that was done via automated systems that pinged you before each stop to allow you to retain the cabin until the next. Imaro had also learned that the other passengers in the private berths desired as much privacy as he did.

The best thing about it was that Imaro and Kukeb were spending so much time together, privately. That was making the trip quite pleasant. The two might have been lovers for some time, but circumstances had dictated that Imaro and Kukeb could rarely bunk together or even share a room.

As Imaro reflected on that, he realized that other than a stolen afternoon or late-night excursion, they'd never been able to openly be together before. This was the primary reason why Imaro had decided they needed to run away.

Although Imaro and Kukeb were both adults, they were still subject to certain traditions of their births that could not be abandoned. Imaro was expected to marry and father some children, even if he was not heterosexual. His father was aware of his orientation but made it clear in no uncertain terms that Imaro's duty was to obey that and do as expected. The rest of his family and other authorities around them couldn't and wouldn't accept if he had other desires and plans.

Imaro understood but refused to accept it. When he had found Kukeb and fallen in love with him, there was no other option. He didn't care if it would be acceptable for him to maintain a relationship with Kukeb outside of the public eye. He wouldn't live a lie and marry a female for the sake of tradition, family, and expectation. Love, to Imaro, was the most important thing in life that he could possibly have.

It was impossible for Imaro to see a life where Kukeb was only a secret, disconnected part of it. Even if Kukeb might have accepted that place, Imaro did not. That had finally resolved itself, and he and Kukeb had abandoned it all and ran away.

Fortunately, money was not a problem. Imaro had been a wise investor, but also clever enough to put monies in accounts that would be unknown to his father or their accountants, partners, and associates. Via EVILC, it was readily accessible without alerting anyone that it was being used.

The only issue that Imaro was currently uncertain about was what came after Sovereign Boundary. It wasn't the challenge of finding and hiring public transport away from rangeen space troubling him. It was where, after rangeen space, he and Kukeb should go so that they'd be impossible to find.

Imaro knew it would depend, in part, on the ship they hired and its crew. He knew they absolutely could not be rangeen and wouldn't be likely to be sutac nor soetub. While that left many options, Imaro felt his unfamiliarity with so many of the races out there would make it all that much more challenging.

Before he could give it more thought, the door to the cabin opened and Kukeb entered, carrying a box with their meal in it.

"Welcome back," Imaro said as his partner set the box down on the small table that had come up from its hiding spot in the floor. "Any problems?"

"You mean aside from the compartment full of Royal Enforcers? No," said Kukeb.

Imaro was well aware that Kukeb's tone had been teasing. "Cute."

Kukeb shrugged. "I can only be so paranoid, love. Nobody was paying me any mind, and I didn't notice anyone following me back here, even at a distance. If the few authorities aboard this transport have been alerted to keep an eye out for us, they're not working hard at it."

"I'm quite grateful that this ship has very little crew," said Imaro. "It's good nearly everything on board is automated."

"A happy accident," commented Kukeb. "Because I know you weren't aware this was even a thing."

Imaro was not about to admit that. However, Kukeb wasn't mistaken. Rather than say more, Imaro opened the box and started to withdraw their meal.

"Working on the plan for when we get to Sovereign Boundary?" Kukeb questioned.

"Nothing more specific than we had before," Imaro replied. "We arrive, which will be at the end of the day local time, get accommodations for the night, then hire a transport."

"You can't hire a transport now, before we arrive?" questioned Kukeb.

Imaro shook his head. "No. Even if we can access the information, and I know that we can, it won't show us who the crew of the ships are. We need to see them, I think, to make the most informed decision."

"Can we just wander around the commercial part of the spaceport and look for a ship?" asked Kukeb.

"Maybe. I can't say for sure. But I think we'll figure it out and make the necessary arrangements and hire a private, off-the-main-grid starship."

Kukeb sighed. "You sure this part of the plan won't draw unwanted attention to us?"

"I think, so long as the ship isn't rangeen or crewed with any rangeen, no," Imaro replied. "That's part of why this is the best idea."

"Imaro, are you sure that other races visit the outer rangeen worlds? You hardly see anyone who isn't rangeen or roptera on Rangeenavelt. What makes the outer systems more likely for them to visit?"

"Because our people trade with other races, and not just in their sectors of space," stated Imaro. "You and I may never have seen this for ourselves, but according to my business partners, our friends, and our associates, yes. Particularly the worlds like Sovereign Boundary. People can come to rangeen space and trade with us. You know all of the peoples of the galaxy use at least some of our tech."

Kukeb didn't immediately respond, as he was opening his meal. He drew out the utensils and settled himself at the table. He took a bite, chewed it thoughtfully, then looked to Imaro.

"You know I trust you. I believe in you. Crazy as this plan is, so far, it's working. Are you sure public transport out of rangeen space isn't smarter than hiring an unknown, private ship and crew?"

Imaro had opened his box of food. He'd taken his utensils up and was moving around his meal but was not eating it yet. While he was certain it was the best option, he wasn't certain how to do it. However, he wasn't about to tell Kukeb this and feed his paranoia.

Forcing himself to take a bite of his food, he chewed and swallowed it as nonchalantly as he could. Then, he said, "Public transport is a lot more open to search than private. The possibility of Royal Enforcers seeking us there is far, far higher than if we get private passage. While there are a lot of unknowns and uncertainty when it comes to this, it's the best way we stay safe and unfindable."

"By the time we reach Sovereign Boundary, they'll be sure to be looking for us," said Kukeb.

"Looking for us, maybe," conceded Imaro. "But they won't know where to truly begin, and the first places they'll look - once they've realized we're not on Rangeenavelt - will be public transport. We will find and hire private transport, and by the time they realize we're gone, we'll be so far away and so far off the grid that they won't have the slightest idea where to even look for us."

Chapter 13 – Do You Judge a Book by its Cover?

Char and Jay had, in their travels, visited some truly wondrous, incredible, beautiful, and exotic worlds. They'd seen sights that were unforgettable and made their life aboard a starship as their home utterly worthwhile. Thus far, however, Char was thoroughly unimpressed by what she'd seen of rangeen space.

Though Char was always open to new experiences and visited every world with as few preconceived notions as possible, Ibi Plerum-que was one of the most disappointing, ugly worlds she had ever visited.

The first issue was the color of the sky. Char fully understood that the combination of water vapors in the air, plus the color of the local star, plus color wave size, would determine the color of a world's sky. While there were many worlds with blue skies, she'd seen green, orange, purple, and even pink. What she'd never seen was the dull grey that was Ibi Plerum-que's skies.

The white and variably darker clouds that floated by nearly, but didn't quite, provide relief from the monotony of the grey skies that even the sun seemed unable to truly impact.

The second issue was that, like the sky, the color of the waters of Ibi Plerum-que was grey. At first, Char wondered if that was some sort of pollutant, related to the local city. However, on further inspection and checking over local data, she learned it was natural.

Outside the spaceport, which was on the edge of town, there appeared to be relatively wild, unsettled lands. Yet, what little flora she saw out there was dull, muted, drab shades of brown and yellow, offering no relief from the dull, muted, drab grey of the of the waters and skies.

That was the third issue she had with Ibi Plerum-que. The fourth was the city where they'd landed. The tallest buildings were unimpressive, as all the architecture of the city seemed uniform, primarily concrete, shades of cream against the grey of the sky and water. There were no shapely buildings of glass and metal, no interesting angles or unusual, unexpected structures. They were all utilitarian and, frankly, boring to look at. This was apparently the way of things all around the planet, too.

Maybe, Char mused, this was an aesthetic the rangeen, with their naturally bright, almost neon red, green, blue, purple, and similarly-shaded hair, enjoyed. Lack of color opposite their own colorful elements. Char knew next to nothing about the rangeen, and she knew her assessment was likely unfair. What's more, it was based on her emotional response to the uniform dull of the world of Ibi Plerum-que.

Char was sitting on a bench in a park outside the spaceport but within view of it. There weren't currently a lot of ships docked there, and Char could see *Audacia* clearly. While Jay was overseeing the offloading of Milo's cargo, Char had gone for a walk.

Char never minded long periods of time aboard the ship. It went well with her overall introverted nature. However, since her parents' deaths and years of therapy, she knew it was important for her to get fresh air and sunlight. Hence, even a dull world like Ibi Plerum-que invited investigation, since she couldn't, and shouldn't, spend her every moment of her life shipboard.

Fortunately, Jay was a very understanding partner. He usually knew when to push Char and when not to. He respected her introversion and privacy, which she had appreciated right from the start of their relationship. Probably a good part of why she'd fallen for him as easily as he fell for her.

Char found the dull colors of the world were dulling her mood. This was making her easily distracted. She'd been trying to figure out where she and Jay could explore between completing their delivery and arranging their next job. Right alongside the rest of the almost mind-numbing dullness of Ibi Plerum-que, there were no attractions, unique mountain ranges, hot springs or cold springs, healing or stimulating plants, or anything of intrigue.

Char had perked up upon learning that Ibi Plerum-que was a terraformed world. Different races had come to work out their own methods to turn uninhabitable worlds inside the so-called "Goldilocks Zone" of a solar system into living worlds. Various techniques would be used to enrich the atmosphere to make it breathable, cultivate the soil to make it life-sustaining, and introduce microorganisms to alter the planet so it could be occupied.

Some races had created incredible machines to do this. Char had seen a few from the worlds of the various races she and Jay had visited. Unfortunately, even the old terraforming machinery still present and preserved as a monument/attraction was uninteresting. Unlike the other singular terraforming machines others had used to transform their worlds, the rangeen terraforming engines were just low chimneys of what looked to be concrete, with no real design aesthetic to them.

The predominant theme of Ibi Plerum-que, Char had determined, was drab. Like the word itself, it was uninteresting and uninspiring. Char hoped this was not a reflection of how the overall rangeen people were. She couldn't recall if she'd met any before. Hopefully, that wasn't the case because – like this dull world – the impression they'd made had been uninteresting.

Before Char could continue looking for something for her and Jay to do, her 'cator began to signal. To her delight, it was her sister.

Mirella was a few years older than Char. She lived on the predominantly human world of Namurt, one system from where they'd grown up. Mirella and her husband lived there, in part, because it was the first world they could both agree had its act most together, as human worlds went.

When she'd met Jay, Char had lived on the other inhabited world of the same system, Notnilc. Probably the primary reason she'd chosen to call it home was so that she could spend her free time, when not at work, with her nephews.

Jules and Phil had been the main joy in Char's life before Jay came along. Also, she had to admit, before they were nineteen and fifteen years old, respectively. The two teenagers were a handful for her sister. When they'd been younger, Char would take them for a weekend now and then. During that time, she'd feed them all the treats they wanted, spoil them in various ways, then send them home.

Still, Char and Mirella spoke at least two or three times a week. The timing couldn't have been more perfect, so Char accepted the transmission.

"Hi Mirella," she said.

"Hey, Char. You in hyperspace, or somewhere interesting?"

Char snickered. "We're somewhere, but I can't call it interesting. We're in rangeen space on Ibi Plerum-que."

"Rangeen space," Mirella said. "All I know about the rangeen is that they are essential to the creation of all the 'cators in the known galaxy. Even if they don't manufacture a 'cator they supply elements of its components."

"I think I recall Dad saying something about that," Char said. "What's new with you?"

"You will not believe what your nephew did," Mirella began. She could always be counted on to share the shenanigans of her boys, which tended to make her equally proud and exasperated.

"Which one?" asked Char.

"Phil."

"What's he done this time?"

Mirella sighed. "My darling son decided to disassemble our central cold-fusion reactor."

Char snorted. "He did what, now?"

"He told me it was schoolwork. Of course, that wasn't the whole story at all. They were studying, in his science class, the workings of cold-fusion reactors. He got really into it, but then got so distracted by the minutia of it that he failed to turn in his homework assignment related to it. So, Phil being Phil, he figured he had it all worked out, and he could take it apart and put it back together again before Don or I noticed. Meanwhile, he'd record it to get credit for school. Suffice it to say, that did not go as planned."

"How bad is 'not as planned'?" Char asked.

"We needed three days and two separate visits from repair techs to get it all in order again," Mirella said.

"And just how much trouble is my nephew in for this?"

"Probably not as much as he should be," Mirella replied. "Probably, in part, because of Jules being clueless."

"What's he done?" asked Char.

"You know his new band is starting to book gigs and get some traction, right?" asked Mirella. Before Char could respond in the affirmative, though, she went on and said, "So the band gets a gig. However, it's on the space station at L5. Jules didn't bother to ask, he just assumed he could borrow a shuttle from his dad. Don and I are displeased. We want to tell him no, but we want to see this band succeed. So, you know how it gets."

"Jules has always been a wiseass," said Char. She glanced up and saw that Jay was walking towards her.

"Sometimes, I really think those boys will be the death of me," said Mirella. "Or at least the reason I'm going prematurely grey."

Char laughed. "Yeah, that's kids for you. Hey, Mirella, Jay got done offloading, so I gotta run."

"Okay," said Mirella. "You take care."

"You, too. Love you, Em."

"Love you too, Char." And the transmission ended.

Jay stopped before her. "Chatting with your sister?"

"Yeah. You won't believe what your nephews did this time."

"Why are they always my nephews when they misbehave?"

"Because it can't possibly be me who's the bad influence," Char said, teasing.

Jay leaned in and kissed her. "Yes, dear."

"Don't you derisively 'yes dear' me," Char chided.

"That was in no way derisive," Jay said. This was not new banter between them. Jay activated a hologram above his 'cator, showing Char a 'catortext. "Just heard from my dad."

"How's he doing?" asked Char.

Jay's father, Marcus, mostly reached out via 'catortext. He was semi-retired, and not so long ago had relocated with his wife, Simone, to Shinnecock-Dornoch IV.

"Apparently, dad's getting to play one of the newest courses," Jay said. "He also was thanking us for the gift basket we sent for his birthday."

Char liked her father-in-law, even though she'd spent very little time with him. Shinnecock-Dornoch IV, his current place of residence, was known for its elaborate and deeply respected GOLFER courses.

Char didn't care for most sports, but both Calista and Mariska were avid GOLFERs, so Char had a basic understanding of it. Geographic Orientational Loophole Flagged Endgame Recreation – GOLFER – was a game similar to but unlike old Earth's golf. It involved convoluted trick shots with balls and clubs, enormous, well-groomed, engineered courses with elaborate features, and a scoring system she couldn't make heads or tails of.

GOLFERs tended to be fanatical about the game.

"Does GOLFER seem to you like a waste of a perfectly good hike?" asked Char.

Jay laughed. "If you're into it, you're really into it. Didn't Mariska once land a deal because she beat her boss?"

"Yeah," Char replied. The memory of said boss was not a favorite of hers. For the most part, that job had been good. But that boss had been arrogant, misogynistic, and frequently misguided. While drunk during a party that Mariska had persuaded Char to attend, he'd made a clumsy pass at her.

On the plus side, he'd been the main reason Mariska had started their business. Char found that kind of paradox both unsettling and far too common.

"Anyhow," Jay started. Char could see he recognized he'd struck a nerve and was starting a different line of thought. "Have you found anything worth checking out on Ibi Plerum-que? Anywhere we simply need to see?"

Char sighed. "No. It's just an incredibly utilitarian, uninteresting world."

"That's what the buyer was telling me," Jay said. "The only reason her business is based here, she told me, is because taxes and fees are super low, keeping profit margins high."

"Interesting buyer?" asked Char. Given Milo and his attitude towards humans, she'd been wondering who he'd sold to.

"No more so than most others," said Jay. "But, given what you've learned about Ibi Plerum-que, do you think we should leave rangeen space altogether?"

"Not necessarily," said Char. "What are you not telling me?"

Jay grinned. "We have another potential job, but it both requires us to depart Ibi Plerum-que rather quickly and travel to another rangeen world."

Char arose from the bench. "Do tell."

"Uyunu Koptii, the rangeen buyer we just delivered to, got a 'cator message while she was overseeing the offloading of the pallets. Apparently, something's going on with some relative of hers. There's some sort of emergency, and she needs quick passage to another rangeen world."

"Okay, that sounds promising," said Char. "How quick is quick passage?"

"Departure in the next few hours," Jay replied. "For which, by the way, she's offering to pay almost double the normal rate."

Char nodded. "Sounds like the kind of job that we'd be foolish not to take, right?"

"That was my thought," said Jay. "But you know I always want to run these sorts of last-minute jobs by you."

"Which I always appreciate," said Char. "Unless she's giving you a bad feeling, let's take Uyunu Koptii from Ibi Plerum-que to... Actually, to where in rangeen space?"

"Some world called Sovereign Boundary."

Chapter 14 - The Part You Neglected to Tell Us About

Uyunu Koptii was a delightful woman.

Sometimes, those who booked passage on the *Audacia* very much kept to themselves. Other times, they treated the starship like it was an interplanetary bed and breakfast, which, to some degree, it was. Jay and Char were always happy to take meals and spend some of their free time with passengers.

The trip to Sovereign Boundary from Ibi Plerum-que was two days. Relatively short, but in-sector hops were like that sometimes.

There was, however, one small detail their passenger had left out before boarding the ship. It wouldn't have been a problem had she told them beforehand so they could have prepared.

The problem? Uyunu Koptii came aboard the *Audacia* with her pet compsanines.

Compasnines were furred, feathered creatures about the size of a small dog, like one Jay's mother had once called a Bichon Frise. But they also looked like an old Earth prehistoric creature called a dinosaur Jay remembered reading about in his youth.

Unlike spacecats, which were trained to use a waste disposal unit, compsanines needed to be walked and cleaned up after.

The two Uyunu Koptii had as companions were not often quiet, and, like the rangeen, had brightly colored fur. One, which she claimed was her emotional support animal, was brown and neon orange. The other, which she claimed was the emotional support companion for the brown and orange one, was brown and green.

Similar to the space cats, the compsanines used recognizable language amid their chirps and yips. However, the words were in rangeen, which neither Jay nor Char understood.

The compsanines might have been less of a problem, were it not for the fact that their arrival had sent the spacecats, Thalia and Cosima, into hiding. It didn't help that, immediately upon boarding *Audacia*, the pair of compsanines had gotten loose, and, in their race around the ship, had chased the two spacecats.

Uyunu – who insisted they address her by her first name – had apologized profusely and vowed to keep her companions in her cabin. Jay and Char had agreed to that, and all would have been fine, except the clever compsanines had other plans. In the day since their arrival, they'd escaped Uyunu's cabin, not once but twice. The first time, they'd simply run all around the ship, before Char and Uyunu caught them.

The second time, the brown and orange had made its way to the cockpit, where it had found Quinn and hissed at the robot, not stopping until it was scooped up by Char. The brown and green, meanwhile, had found its way into the lavatory, where Jay had been sitting on the toilet. It had, nearly literally, scared the shit out of him.

Apart from close encounters of the compsanine kind, Jay and Char found Uyunu extremely companionable and pleasant. The rangeen woman stood about one-point-eight meters tall, with deep-set, black eyes that featured flecks of metallic red within them beneath her pronounced brow. Her shoulder-length, wavy hair was a bright neon yellow and her skin was brown. She dressed like almost every other business professional Jay had seen elsewhere in his travels.

Still, they learned a great deal about the rangeen people from Uyunu. The first thing being why Ibi Plerum-que was so uniformly dull. Char had worried that her assessment of the world might be offensive, when Uyunu had asked them what they thought of it. Yet the rangeen merchant agreed the world was boringly plain and that it was due to the terraforming never being fully completed. There was air, the planet could sustain flora and fauna, and that was good enough for the terraformers.

On the morning of the second day in hyperspace, Jay and Char had left their deck to have breakfast with their passenger. First, though, Jay had gone to check on Quinn, who proceeded to suggest that the spacecats always left him be, so by his logic, if the compsanines felt the need to hiss at him, there was no reason not to eject them off the ship. Jay reminded the robot no harm had been done, but Quinn remained skeptical.

When Jay joined Char and Uyunu in the galley, they were conversing over coffee. Char had poured a mug for Jay. As Jay sat, Uyunu said, "Good morning, Captain."

"Please, call me Jay. No need for formalities."

Uyunu smiled. "Thank you. I was just telling your lovely spouse about doing business with other races as rangeen while not being involved in manufacturing 'cators or their components."

"Oh?" replied Jay. "I know rangeen are a major supplier of 'cators and their components."

"Not just major suppliers," said Uyunu. "The single largest producer in all of known space. Not a 'cator is made without something from the rangeen."

"Really?" Jay had read an article or two about this, but never paid it much mind. As much as he loved random trivia, the 'cator industry had never piqued his curiosity.

"Yes," Uyunu said. "If the rangeen don't produce the 'cator, we make some of the quantum-microcircuitry that goes into all 'cators or other communications devices. Even those built into starships such as this, planetary systems, space stations, you name it."

"I knew they had a rather broad hand in that," Char stated. "Do you know why and how the rangeen came to be the preeminent makers?"

"Yes," replied Uyunu. "This is because the roptera have a heightened sense of sound in ranges few other races have."

"I've heard of the roptera, but only the name. I don't know a thing about them," said Jay. When Jay later called up an image of the roptera he learned they were also built much like human and rangeen. They were distinct in that they lacked the colorful hair of the rangeen and had bat-like ears and beady brown eyes that – upon closer examination – contained shiny red flecks. They also have vestigial wings but had not been capable of flight for tens of millennia.

"They are a people of our homeworld," said Uyunu. "Another sentient race, though quite different from us. After many years of conflict, our ancestors learned to work together with the roptera, which allowed us to become the producers of 'cators and their components that we are."

"I'm surprised, given that two sentient races emerged from the same world, that you don't have astrobiologists all over your homeworld," remarked Char.

Uyunu laughed. "For reasons I certainly do not know, the roptera have only begun to venture from Rangeenavelt for a few decades. Besides, the king would not be fond of random astrobiologists poking around our homeworld."

"The king?" asked Jay. "Do you mean to tell me the rangeen have a monarchy for their government?"

"Yes," replied Uyunu. "Indeed, we are the only true monarchy in the galaxy at this point. Every other race that had the same long ago relegated them to ceremony and legend. But our king is the head of the whole of rangeen space."

She made a 'tsk' sound, then said in a conspiratorial tone. "He's always on Rangeenavelt, hasn't left in decades, or so they say. Most of my contemporaries are convinced that he's fairly out-of-touch with the workings of the rest of the galaxy."

"Given your people's involvement in creating all the 'cators or their components across known space, you'd think he'd be more savvy than that," remarked Char.

Uyunu made a grunting noise and said, "Some weird rumors I've heard from reliable sources worry me. They say that the wealth of the rangeen from manufacturing the many elements of 'cators has increasingly gone to his head, and that he's got some bizarre ideas to use that to expand his influence. You know how rumors can be, no?"

"Sure," replied Char. "Have you met the king?"

Uyunu laughed. "No. No, I've only seen him on the 'tangle and the MESS-work. This far from Rangeenavelt, the crown's sway isn't so dominant. But it's still felt and still in one's best interest to not be too dismissive of it."

Jay nodded. "Sounds intriguing."

"Jay," Char began, "would you get breakfast started?"

"Of course, my love," Jay replied. He noted that he'd already emptied his mug. "Anyone else need more coffee?"

"Good for now, thank you," said Char.

"No, thank you, Cap...sorry, Jay."

He grinned and headed for the kitchen to prepare breakfast.

Jay loved how traveling across space not only allowed him to see and experience new places but also meet new people.

Then, his foot sunk into something, and a terrible smell immediately reached his nose. One of the compsanines had left a present on the deck that he'd not seen.

Uyunu and her pets were fascinating. Unfortunately, the cleanup after their visit was going to cut into the profit this last-minute trek was earning them. Yes, Uyunu was great company, but as he went to clean up the poop on his deck, Jay again wished that she'd told them about her pets before coming aboard.

Chapter 15 - We're Not in Ranrop-Palast Anymore

With Kukeb at his side, Imaro strode down the ramp and off the transport. They had made it across rangeen space and were now a long, long way from home.

Imaro could not remember the last time he'd left Rangeenavelt, let alone the city of Ranrop-Palast. He had definitely been with more than just a single companion, that much was certain. Yet there he was, further from home than he'd ever ventured before.

Both hearts felt like they might burst in excitement. Despite the nervous jitter he could feel from Kukeb at his side, thus far, it all had gone according to plan.

Kukeb had argued that they should find a way to sneak off the transport. Imaro, on the other hand, felt that if the Royal Enforcers were already on the lookout for them, they wouldn't get past the transport. Thus, they'd join the others disembarking.

It took every bit of self-discipline that Imaro possessed to not stop and stare at all that was around them. Taking it in, he did his best to catalog what was before him and Kukeb.

Sovereign Boundary, even on first view, was nothing like Rangeenavelt or the city of Ranrop-Palast. Though it was only the spaceport in a city that Imaro couldn't remember the name of, the architecture he was seeing was far different than he was used to. Everything appeared to be comprised of concrete, glass, metals, composites, and the like. No stone or brick was visible.

Imaro knew that Sovereign Boundary had not been settled until millennia after Rangeenavelt. Thus, there were no structures predating space flight. Perhaps there were brick, stone, and similar materials used in the architecture deeper within the city. Yet they'd still be thousands of years newer than their counterparts in the rangeen capital.

The other striking difference between Sovereign Boundary and Rangeenavelt was the stunning number of non-rangeen. A quick count told Imaro that there was only one rangeen for every five aliens. What's more, he was seeing alien races in person he'd only ever seen on the ITEM or MESS-work. As he and Kukeb made their way through the terminal, he was elated by all the unusual colors, scents, languages, and unfamiliarity of it all.

Imaro couldn't help but notice that Kukeb was being overly cautious with every rangeen they encountered. Sighing, Imaro said, "We're here, we made it, and we're still well and free."

His partner sighed. "Yeah, yeah, maybe. Sorry, Imaro, I know you're confident. But I'm still nervous about all of this. The aliens here? They're safe. They have no idea that we are a long way from home and might be in trouble for running away from it all. But every rangeen could be keeping tabs on us, reporting us to authorities."

Imaro said, "If there weren't Royal Enforcers or some other rangeen authority checking the passengers as they left the transport, we're safe, Kukeb. I told you nobody who cares would realize we were gone for some time, and even if they have, they'll start by looking for us across Rangeenavelt a while before they start to look across rangeen space. We're a very, very long way from home."

Kukeb nodded and sighed. Imaro hoped his partner would accept his confidence and worry less.

Imaro had his own worries. Despite all his confidence, he knew with zero doubt that, eventually, his father would do everything in his power to find him. Imaro knew that his father wasn't a stupid male and would use every resource at his disposal. Still, he felt that time remained on his and Kukeb's side, so long as they didn't dilly-dally in their next move.

At the moment, however, Imaro was reveling in being on this strange, new-to-him world. He knew that Sovereign Boundary was a relatively wild world. The sky was a sunny, clear turquoise. The air had a dry, earthy but slightly salty tang to it, a smell and taste which Imaro attributed both to the spaceport and the overall atmosphere of the planet. He did note that the air felt cooler than he was used to, and knew the planet was globally chillier than other rangeen worlds.

Sovereign Boundary had no oceans, per se, but a vast number of large seas, deep lakes, long and wide rivers, and countless streams both permanent and flowing only after rain. Between all those bodies of water and others, Sovereign Bounty was seventy-percent water even without oceans.

There had been, in ancient times, long before the rangeen found and settled the world, oceans that had dried up and were now vast, dry salt lands. That was probably where the saltiness in the air originated. The topography of the world was diverse but unusual. The salt lands were almost totally uninhabitable, dipping well below freezing every night, all year round. Meanwhile, they reflected sunlight in a way that could quickly blind and burn the skin of all rangeen people and most other races.

When the rangeen had discovered Sovereign Boundary, the first thing they had detected was its vast, pristine, untouched mineral and ore deposits. Because of the diversity of the planet and its ecosystems, the forests, beaches, and mountains provided many other useful resources for rangeen industry and export options.

Imaro knew that mining operations and their employees, support staff, and families, made up the majority of Sovereign Boundary's population. There was otherwise only one major city on each continent, either in the heart of a mountain range – like the one he and Kukeb were in now – or on a seashore.

Because of the unique wildness of the world and its hospitable, albeit chilly atmosphere, adventurers enjoyed exploring the beaches, wilderness, ranges, and the like. Hence, Imaro knew that the Royal Enforcers spent most of their time rescuing hapless adventurers who got lost, realized the mountain range they were trying to climb offered no forage or was too steep, the insects of a lake or river unexpectedly ferocious, or found themselves unprepared for the always cold nights.

This was one of the many reasons why Sovereign Boundary had been Imaro's chosen destination.

As Imaro and Kukeb reached the edge of the passenger spaceport, they came to a café. Imaro led Kukeb to a table.

"I'm going to get us a drink," he told his companion. "Then we'll figure out our next move."

Kukeb looked about, but as Imaro had already noted, there were more non-rangeen than rangeen in this café. "Okay," Kukeb said.

Imaro went to the dispenser, ordered himself and Kukeb warm drinks, then took them to the table where Kukeb sat, looking only slightly less nervous.

"Here," Imaro said, passing him the drink.

"Thank you," Kukeb said as he took it. After he took a sip he said, "I've been thinking. Maybe we shouldn't press our luck."

"What do you mean?" questioned Imaro.

"Well…" Kukeb paused, looked to make sure nobody was paying them any attention, then continued. "We got here without anyone seeming to be looking for us. Sovereign Boundary is not the kind of world your father would think you would settle on. Let's just find somewhere out of the way and stay here, maybe."

"Kukeb," Imaro cooed. "We haven't come this far to stop in rangeen space. We won't be truly free of our old lives and obligations if we don't leave this sector of space."

"Then what are we waiting for?" Kukeb asked. "Let's find passage offworld and go now."

Imaro leaned back as he savored his drink. The warm beverage was sweet on his tongues and soothed him. The only thing he sometimes found irksome in his companion was his nervousness. "Look around," he said. "We're not in Ranrop-Palast anymore. Nor are we on Rangeenavelt. We are, in fact, on the other side of rangeen space, and we made it here without incident. I know you're worried, but we're fine for a little while longer. Look at this place. Have you ever seen a sky that color?"

Kukeb looked up a moment, and Imaro saw the sky reflecting on his dark eyes. "No, of course not. Not in person," Kukeb said.

"Of course not," Imaro echoed. "We've been sheltered too long, locked away from the lives we've wanted. We left, and though we know that they'll be looking for us, they won't get here for some time. Besides, it's already late afternoon. I think we should get a room for the night, then we'll go to the cargo terminal and look for transport in the morning."

"You act as if your father…"

Imaro held up a hand. "Let's not talk about him. Especially in the open like this. Yes, he'll stop at nothing to find me. Since anything that could track me or you has been removed, altered, or shielded, and we took a lot of precautions, we have time. Stop worrying, love. Let's focus on what's amazing about this and trust one night exploring this place won't be detrimental to us."

Kukeb sighed. "Alright, alright. It's a good thing I love you because you're crazy."

Imaro chuckled. "I know. And I love you, too."

Chapter 16 – Just Your Sponsor Pausing for Another Word

Hi there. This is your friendly neighborhood author, yet again. I know it's kind of weird having the author breaking his own story to talk directly to you. But hey, if characters in TV shows and movies can "break the fourth wall," can't authors, too?

This brings up an interesting question. What do you call "breaking the fourth wall" in book form? It's a book, so you've either got pages or bits and bytes of data in your hand (or my rich baritone in your ear if you're listening to the audiobook version). Still, my question is relevant, right? Is this called suspending suspended disbelief? Interrupting the reader? Writing off the page? Does it involve a window or door instead of a wall?

(For the curious, there is a whole genre of this type of writing called metafiction, though it's more about the character than the narrator. It can also be an "aside", an "authorial interjection," or a transgression of narrative levels called a metalepsis. Good to know, right?) But I digress.

Anyhow, let's talk about interactions between various races. This can be challenging in a world where "race" is a matter of skin color, nationalistic background, type of eye shape, or any other largely meaningless difference in the same race of beings. What happens when we move past that bullshit and start to interact with other sentient races like us but not like us?

Most of the people in the galaxy – and by people, I mean all the sentient beings flying around in ships – are just doing their thing and living their lives. Once they got over however they were initially shocked when they learned they weren't at all alone in the universe, it was much like how normal, peaceful humans of different "races" interact with one another.

Most of the races in the galaxy started out on one world, alone in their solar system. Hi, human race, I'm looking at you. However, then they found their way to orbit and, in time, to other parts of their solar system, which eventually led them to either colonize, terraform, or otherwise establish themselves on other worlds.

Despite the Milky Way being a relatively small galaxy – when compared to other galaxies – it's a big galaxy. There's almost endless variation, and thus little to no one-size-fits-all origin story. There are places where more than one totally sentient race evolved and lives together. Some, like the rangeen and roptera, both evolved on the same world at a similar – albeit somewhat different – pace.

Also, there are many shared worlds that are the result of past invasions or wars from so long ago that the sentient races that call them home have always thought of them as home, even if they were not originally all from that singular world.

Still with me? Good. Okay, so, somehow, almost every race can interbreed. Yes, in addition to most of the sentient races having similar general body types, they can get down and get it on with one another. How the reproductive organs from disparate worlds are compatible is beyond the scope of this book.

Seriously, this is a thing that *Star Trek* has been doing since the 1960s, and everyone accepts it. One of the major characters, Mr. Spock, has a vulcan dad and a human mom. So, I'm just going to accept that if they can do it, I can do it. And plainly, not to put too fine a point on it, but everyone can do it.

There you have it. Let me just conclude by stating that it's easier to tell you these things in this way because they might not be wholly relevant to this story, but I feel the need to put them here all the same. Enjoy!

Chapter 17 – This Book Has a Much Better Cover

The color of the sand was not something he'd ever seen before. It was a vibrant, glossy black with glints of gold and silver in the sunlight beneath the turquoise sky. They were on the eastern shore of the largest inland sea on Sovereign Boundary.

Despite the sunlight, it was too cold to lounge, as it was a chilly four degrees Celsius. Char, always a fan of cold weather, was loving it. Jay, on the other hand, was not so thrilled. He had on one of his heavier coats, as well as gloves and a hat.

They had arrived at Sovereign Boundary without incident. Though they'd enjoyed the company of their passenger, Uyunu Koptii's compsanine companions had made a mess every time they'd gotten out. Fortunately, without them asking, she had paid for and arranged a special cleaner to attend to the *Audacia*.

Jay and Char had gone exploring, leaving Quinn to handle the oversight of the cleaners. Not that Quinn ever left the ship. He didn't.

Jay had always been amused by that. Quinn was not held to the ship, per se. He was free to move about and could request to leave the ship at any time. Maybe it was his inherent programming, or maybe it was something else, but the robot opted to seldom, if ever, leave the *Audacia*.

When Jay and Char had first "acquired" Quinn, they'd made certain the robot understood he was not a servant. While that seemed to work just fine, sometimes his words implied otherwise.

While the *Audacia* was getting a good interior cleaning, Jay and Char were taking advantage and were sightseeing. Fortunately, Sovereign Boundary was a far cry from the incredibly drab Ibi Plerum-que.

This was the third beach the couple had explored. The first had boasted a fascinating neon blue sand with green and yellow muted flecks of color, the second a shimmery silver with pink accents. The waters were largely the same, though the first beach was off of a lake and the second a wide river.

The beaches were all colorful and beautiful. Sovereign Boundary was a very pretty world, and Jay was glad they'd made their way to it.

Jay was standing on the beach near the water's edge. Char had wandered off for a moment, either to take a call from one of her work companions, or perhaps to get them a drink to ward off some of the increasing chill as the sun was starting to go down.

Jay knew that this area was a tourist destination. The beach was long enough that there were other sections where the locals might pay the sea a visit. A world without true oceans but made mostly of water was a fascinating concept to Jay.

There was fish and other aquatic life the locals enjoyed in this sea, and he'd learned that there were some commercial fisheries, as well as a few villages and a town or two with fisherrangeen.

Not for the first time, Jay pondered how all the diverse races, from unique and varied ecologies, were able to share so many interests, foods, and other compatibilities. It wasn't his area of expertise, but it sometimes piqued his interest.

Looking away from the water, Jay observed the food vendors, random stalls selling necessities, and the gift kiosks. It was still bustling with many figures, including numerous non-rangeen, but no other humans that Jay had seen.

Something caught his eye. A figure was approaching him. He was unique, like Jay and Char, in that he was the only member of his race Jay had seen on this beach. He was a kijivu.

When humans had first made their way to space, it would be more than a century before they ventured outside their own solar system. Prior to that, however, many had speculated that humans were probably not alone in the galaxy. Hours after the first hyperspace transit, humanity learned that, indeed, they weren't alone. Jay couldn't recall which race had been the first to welcome humans to the broader galaxy at large.

In the period on Earth called the twentieth century, when most humans still thought they were alone in space, a few people, frequently treated with incredible incredulity, had claimed to have been abducted by aliens.

The kijivu were the grey aliens of abduction drawings who, it turned out, *had* abducted some humans in the Earth's past.

Jay remembered watching a video where an enterprising investigator asked a member of the kijivu government if they had done abductions of humans during the mid-twentieth and early twenty-first centuries on Earth. Surprisingly, they'd admitted that they had abducted some humans during that time, as they were going through a weird phase. As a unified people, they had been debating if they should enslave a race to build up their civilization and exploration fleets. Humans had been considered for that role. However, it was deemed to be too much trouble for reasons not specified, so they'd dropped it.

Jay had met a kijivu a time or two. Large, bulbous heads, big black eyes, long, lanky arms and legs, nostrils but no nose and no ears. They were always male, as for some cultural or biological reason nobody knew, their females never left whatever world they called home.

The one approaching him Jay had seen wandering at both this and the previous beach he and Char had visited. Jay had noticed him in part because he was the only kijivu in the immediate area, and this one had been using an elaborate camera on a tripod, which was also somewhat unusual.

Jay noted that the kijivu was most definitely approaching him. Jay tried to discern if he looked familiar, though he had to admit that telling one kijivu from another, apart from how they might be dressed, was virtually impossible.

"Hello," the kijivu said as he reached Jay. He extended a hand for a handshake.

As Jay accepted the handshake he asked, "Do I know you?"

"No," the kijivu said in a perfectly pleasant tone. "I just wanted to let you know you're an odd-looking fellow."

He released Jay's hand, turned, and walked away.

Jay was flabbergasted. He found he was searching for a response, but none came as the kijivu proceeded to walk away and Char came to Jay's side, holding two beverage cups.

"What's up, hon?" Char asked. "Why do you look so stunned?"

"I just had the weirdest, most bizarre experience," Jay replied, still trying to wrap his head around it as the kijivu merged into the crowd. Jay shared with Char what the kijivu had said.

"That's not normal," his spouse commented.

"You think?" Jay asked, taking a cup from Char. She just shrugged, which more or less was what Jay felt about it, too.

He took a sip and sighed. "Oh, that's lovely."

"Some sort of local specialty," Char said. "Like a hot buttered rum, but no alcohol. So, what do you want to do next?"

"Night is coming on," Jay remarked, glancing up towards the slowly darkening sky. "You have anything in mind?"

"Well," Char began, pausing to sip her drink before continuing. "We could rent one of the bungalows, spend a night here on the beach."

Jay glanced towards the bungalows. "I mean, they're neat looking. But they're not heated, are they?"

Char laughed. "No. I'm told they retain some heat from the day, but they are not heated. The water lapping the beach and the various other natural noises are supposed to be really soothing. And, ya know, good cuddling time."

"Sure," Jay agreed. Then, though, a breeze off the water touched Jay's face, and he shivered. "You do know it's going to be below freezing? I mean, great cuddling, but then we gotta wait for the sun to come back up and warm things up to just above freezing. No offense, love, but no thanks."

"We could, I guess, go back to the ship," Char said. Jay, however, noted the disappointment in her tone, of course.

"Or," Jay began, "we go back to Terminus, and don't go back to *Audacia*. Instead, we get ourselves a hotel suite with various amenities, like a soaking tub for two, massaging shower, maybe a fireplace. We splurge and enjoy ourselves somewhere cozy and warmer than here."

Char laughed. "Or we do that, yes. That's got my vote."

Jay grinned. "Love you."

"Love you too, my odd-looking fellow."

Chapter 18 - Make Like a Tree and - Photosynthesize? Get the Hell Out of Here? Oh, Right, Leave!

Imaro was not about to admit that he had slept poorly during the night. Kukeb, surprisingly, had slept perfectly soundly. Imaro, however, had kept waking up, as every little sound made him hyper-alert.

Maybe, he mused, Kukeb's worrying was wearing off on him. However, he knew himself. When they had been on the transport, he and Kukeb had been able to keep to themselves and escape notice. What's more, there had only been a couple of hundred people on the transport, total. Even when it had made stops along the way, the numbers hadn't changed much. Further, they'd been able to largely stay to their quarters and remain unnoticed.

Now they were on Sovereign Boundary, in one place, with far more people. Granted, there were more non-rangeen than rangeen that they'd seen so far in Terminus. However, he knew that the rangeen were the majority across the planet.

Terminus was an attractive city. On the one hand, the many, many people felt like the kind of crowd Imaro knew he and Kukeb could blend into without notice. On the other hand, however, they were in the open and were more visible than they'd been on the transport.

While the few Royal Enforcers appeared to be minding the aliens more than the rangeen, all of them represented a potential opportunity to get Imaro and Kukeb noticed and caught. Imaro couldn't admit to Kukeb that his own concerns about the chances of their getting caught were increasing.

Still, after he got up, Imaro showered, repacked his bags, and returned to exuding the confidence that he had maintained since they'd launched their plan. Maybe he wasn't entirely feeling it, and he was feeling similar anxiety to Kukeb's, but they'd gotten this far. All they needed to do now was leave the planet unnoticed.

Imaro was still convinced that the best way to do that would be to hire a private transport.

Kukeb insisted that they check on public transport options. Thus, they initially headed for the passenger terminal of the spaceport. Once again, Imaro was impressed by how many non-rangeen he was seeing. So many different races in one place. When he noticed a couple of Royal Enforcers, he also saw they were still far more intent on the non-rangeen.

Imaro and Kukeb approached an automated display. Checking it for passenger transports making their way off-world, two caught his eye. Both were leaving rangeen space from Sovereign Boundary. However, they were excursions that had originated at Rangeenavelt and would be looping back to Rangeen space. That was not going to work for them.

"Alright," Kukeb conceded. "Let's go to the cargo terminal."

The pair departed from the passenger terminal, taking a tramway to the cargo terminal. Fortunately, Imaro noted that there were all kinds of people in the terminal, ranging from businesspeople to dockworkers to transport crews and everything in between. That meant that neither Imaro nor Kukeb stood out.

As they made their way around the terminal, Imaro realized he was unsure of how to proceed.

"Kukeb," Imaro began. "You've made arrangements for transports for work before, yes?"

"Yes," Kukeb said. Yet, before Imaro took comfort from that, Kukeb continued, "This presents a challenge, however. To hire a transport, unless you pre-book matters privately, I'm unsure how to go about that without opening up a contract on the local public MESS-work."

Imaro cursed under his breath. "I hadn't thought of that. What about our fake identities?"

"Those are fine for security checks and the like with locals," said Kukeb, "but they won't get us into the MESS-work unnoticed."

Imaro debated the efficacy of taking that chance. It wasn't like querying the MESS-work would trigger anything. Unless it did. Given the rangeen connection to all the 'cators, it was especially risky. Best-case scenario meant they'd manage to get a transport and depart, but not without giving away where they were departing from.

Imaro looked around the terminal. Now he realized that it was mostly impossible to distinguish transport crews from charters stretching their legs, non-rangeen dockworkers, or anyone else in the terminal. Looking around, he hoped to find inspiration.

Which he did. "Kukeb, let's take a walk into the bays and see what ships and crews we can get a look at."

"I don't know if that's advisable," said Kukeb nervously. Still, without another word, he let Imaro lead him to the portal out of the terminal.

Once they were on the tarmac between bays, Imaro read a few different signs. One pointed to the bulk transport section. That would be where massive freighters were loaded with different cargos, or multiple cargo pallets were put in larger containers to be carried into space for loading on bulk freighters that couldn't land on a planet.

One sign pointed to hazardous material loading. That was something to be avoided. The next sign showed the way to corporate transports. The last sign indicated the way to the private ones.

Imaro found that he appreciated his people's penchant for this sort of organization. He and Kukeb made their way past the corporate transport bays to those for the private ships.

"What do you want to do here?" asked Kukeb as they neared the first. "Inquire about getting passage directly from the crew?"

"Do you have a better idea?" asked Imaro, trying not to be curt with his partner. Kukeb just shook his head.

The duo looked into the first bay. Inside, Imaro noticed a junky-looking, flat, disc-shaped starship with two squarish protrusions off the front and the cockpit emerging from one side. As he took a closer look, not entering the bay, Imaro noticed that there was a discussion going on.

Discussion was not the right term for it. It was an argument. One side of the argument was an alien he believed was called a Korelly-ehn - which were a rarely seen race that looked a lot like humans but weren't - and a tall, massively shaggy creature he could not identify. The other side was a group of tough-looking brutes, a guy in a fancy armored suit, and a shaggy, slug-like, worm-like being he was even more baffled by.

Glancing at Kukeb, he shook his head, and they moved on.

At the next bay, there sat a ship that was quite aesthetically pleasing to Imaro. It had engines that tilted, mounted on the end of stubby wings, and a neck that reached forward to a cockpit high above. Various panels were also present, giving the ship a haphazard appearance.

There were six humans near the ship. Imaro thought they seemed gruff, three women and three men among them. However, what caught his eye most were the numerous, large herd animals they were attempting to corral onto the ship.

The beasts were noisy, smelly, loud, and unpleasant. Also, there was something about the scene, while vaguely exciting, that felt to Imaro like it might lead to an untimely cancellation. He gestured to Kukeb and they moved on.

In the next bay, there was a saucer-shaped starship. Outside of it, a pair of greenish, bulbous aliens with sharp teeth, one light yellow eye, and brown spots on their heads, under clear-domed helmets, were loading cargo. Beneath the domes, they each had multiple tentacles. They were speaking in low tones that sounded like angry proclamations. Kukeb tugged at Imaro's arm and they departed before the pair of kokangdos might notice them.

Imaro was getting frustrated but was not about to show that to Kukeb. The next two bays were empty. As they neared the one after that, they heard two males shouting at one another.

Reaching the bay, Imaro saw a small, round ship that appeared to be home-built, some of its parts looking like garbage receptacles. A door was open, numerous empty glass containers having spilled out. The people shouting were a pair of humans, an old man who belched every few seconds between his words and a boy in a yellow shirt. Imaro and Kukeb walked past without fully stopping.

"We're wasting our time, Imaro," Kukeb said. "We're never going to find a ship this way."

"I'm definitely feeling like this is going nowhere," Imaro conceded. "But I'm not willing to give up."

They reached the next bay. Within sat a starship, a vessel in good repair with clean lines that was rectangular overall but curved to a soft point at the front and featured engines at the rear, high above the bay.

"That's a Han-Mal Shipworks *Baritone* Class multitask starship," commented Kukeb. "Usually, these ships have three decks, can accommodate a lot of cargo or a dozen passengers, but can be crewed by just two."

"How do you know that?" asked Imaro.

Kukeb gestured to a readout at the entrance of the bay. It didn't get past Imaro that none of the other ships they'd looked at had entered their registries. While nobody was likely to look closely, it was still a matter of proper procedure. Imaro made note of that as he read the ship's name. *Audacia*.

Imaro looked into the bay. The ship was sealed up, none of its hatches or bay doors open. Either the crew were not present or they were aboard it and minding their own business.

"Hello!" Imaro called into the landing bay. "Uh, ahoy crew of the *Audcacia*. Is anyone there?"

There was no reply and no movement from in the ship. Imaro sighed. Kukeb said, "Now what?"

"Let's go," Imaro said. He had no idea what step to take next. At least they could still book a cabin on one of the passenger liners. However, he didn't like their chances of getting away on a ship such as that.

As Kukeb and Imaro turned from the bay to head back towards the terminal, a pair of humans approached, leading a hovercase behind them. The man was shorter than Imaro or Kukeb, had salt and pepper hair, a goatee, and was a little chubby. The female was a few centimeters shorter than her companion, had auburn hair down to just past her shoulders, and was wearing eyeglasses, which was not common.

"You two look lost," the male said.

"Were you looking for someone?" the female questioned.

"No, we were..." Kukeb began.

Imaro stepped ahead of Kukeb towards the humans and said, "Not someone, no. What my companion here was starting to say is that we booked passage on a starship a day ago, and they told us to come today to bay seventy-one, and they'd be here. We came and, well, as you might have noticed, there's no ship in seventy-one. My companion thought maybe we misheard, so we were looking into the other landing bays. We never got the name of the ship that I recall, but the captain is a human named Jones. I was hoping we'd find him."

"You didn't get the name of the ship?" the female asked. "Did you pay in full?"

"No," Imaro said, trying not to sound like a complete fool. "That's why I thought everything was set."

"You heard of this sort of thing?" the female human asked her companion.

"Usually, they make you pay it all up-front and ditch, but a clever con might be happy to get half," he replied.

"Sorry, guys," the female addressed Imaro and Kukeb. "There hasn't been a ship in seventy-one since we docked in seventy-two yesterday. Doesn't happen often, but you have probably been scammed."

"I told you this was a terrible idea," said Kukeb.

"He certainly seemed legit," Imaro remarked, unsure if Kukeb was stating a fact or playing along. Looking to the female, he said, "This is our first time leaving the system, and we're going out way past where most of the commercial liners go. So, we thought, for a little added adventure, we'd take a private charter."

"You do get a few around here," the male said. "Though with cargo ships like these, it's a mixed bag."

"Is one of these yours?" Imaro asked.

"Yes," the male replied. He gestured to bay seventy-two. "The *Audacia*."

"We noticed your ship," remarked Iamaro. "It looks like you take great care of it."

"We do," the male said. "Thank you."

"I'm Imaro," he said, offering a handshake.

"Jay."

"Char," the female said when she took Imaro's hand.

Kukeb also shook the humans' hands and introduced himself.

"You know," Jay began. "You should probably report this to the local guild. Whether you were ditched or it was a con preying on people in the terminal, they should know."

"I guess," Imaro said, thinking fast. "Buuut, see, one reason we went through Jones was, uh, the local guild tends to side with non-rangeen. Something about what's best for business, not upsetting commerce, you know?"

"I've never dealt with the local guild," Jay said.

"Oh, don't get me wrong, they do the right thing, most of the time," Imaro felt the need to amend. "They just regard the likes of Kukeb and I, local travelers looking for an unusual way off-world, with little to no interest."

"I've heard of that sort of thing," Char commented.

"Not to be too forward," Imaro pressed, "but is your ship, *Audacia*, for hire?"

"Just passengers, or do you have cargo?" Jay asked.

"Just Kukeb and I."

"To where?"

Imaro was inordinately pleased with himself for doing some research the last few days they'd been on the transport. He had, as such, chosen a destination. "Abigail."

Jay whistled low. "That's a very long way from here. Why Abigail?"

"I've never been to a world not in rangeen space," said Imaro honestly. "But I've read all about lots of other worlds and seen images of many of them. A place so, so far away from here with incredible natural features and impressive cities? I feel the need to see it to believe it."

"You understand that a trip that far is not going to be cheap?" Jay questioned. "We'd be committed to you for something of a long-haul and wouldn't be able to do other jobs."

"I do understand," said Imaro. "Still going to be less costly than a private yacht, no?"

Jay chuckled. "Maybe. One moment." He and his companion stepped away but didn't go into the bay with their ship.

"What are you doing?" breathed Kukeb.

"Hiring a ship to get us out of here," replied Imaro.

Kukeb threw a glance towards the humans. "We only just met them, randomly. While they seem nice enough, I'm not sure this is such a good idea."

"Kukeb, my love. This is our best shot of getting out of here unseen. I think this is how we do it."

Jay and Char were returning.

"We can do it," Jay said. "But it'll cost you thirty thousand sheks."

"We could buy our own ship for that," remarked Imaro. Of course, he wanted to accept and pay; he had the money. But that, he knew, would be suspicious. "Fifteen thousand."

"Flight via commercial transports will cost more than that," said Jay. "Twenty-eight thousand."

"Eighteen thousand."

"Twenty-five thousand."

"Twenty thousand."

"Twenty-two thousand sheks."

Imaro looked at Kukeb, who simply shrugged. "Deal."

"Deal," said Jay. "Half up front, half on arrival at Abigail."

"Kukeb?" Imaro directed his companion. Kukeb got out his tablet. Jay produced one as well. Funds were exchanged.

"When will you be ready to go?" asked Jay.

"Well, given we thought we were meeting a ship in that empty bay there, we're ready now."

Jay looked at Char. "We good to bring 'em aboard?"

"I think so," Char replied. She looked at Imaro and Kukeb. "You okay with herpestelines?"

"I love space cats," said Kukeb.

Jay gestured. "Well then, this way. Let me welcome you aboard the *Audacia*."

Chapter 19 – BREAKING NEWS

"This is RKNN, The Rangeen Kingdom News Network, Channel VX3410.756Q on the Interplanetary Transmission Entanglement Mediascape," the official-sounding, disembodied voice states.

A pair of rangeen are seated at a desk, male and female. The male has deep-set, black eyes with flecks of metallic red within them beneath his pronounced brow. His spiked hair is a bright neon green, his skin brown. A handsome male by rangeen standards. The female has deep-set, black eyes with flecks of metallic gold within them, thick, long, lush neon blue hair, and skin tone similar to the male. A stunning female by rangeen standards.

Behind them is a display with the RKNN logo, and the words "Breaking News."

"I'm Dajan Ibumu," says the male.

"And I'm Laolat Njura," says the female. "We've received word from the Royal Stronghold in Ronrop-Palast that King Nobiri will be issuing a statement of great import."

Dajan says, "And we are going to the Royal Stronghold now."

The image cuts to an opulent room in the Royal Stronghold, where the King or a representative typically makes announcements to the press. An older rangeen male, with deep-set, black eyes featuring flecks of metallic green within them, bright neon orange hair streaked with black, and a wrinkled face, wearing a circlet on his brow, steps up to the podium.

King Nobiri clears his throat, then begins in a measured, pleasant baritone, "My loyal subjects, it is with terrible, unfortunate news that I come before you today. My son has gone missing. Though the circumstances are unknown, as are his whereabouts, my top counselors and I believe that while he might have been kidnapped, it is equally likely he was lured away."

An image appears before the king at the level of the podium. The rangeen male it depicts is in a formal outfit. He has black eyes that feature flecks of metallic green within them beneath his pronounced brow. His long, straight hair is a bright neon orange, pulled back and tied.

"Though I am loath to share any personal matters that the Royal Household might be contending with," King Nobiri continues, "this must be addressed, lest those who have taken or lured my son away think they have gotten away with it. To that end, I am offering a substantial reward to anyone with legitimate, corroborated information that leads to finding and recovering my heir, Prince Imaro Iwoto."

King Nobiri's face turns especially serious. "To any bounty hunters who might see this missive, the only acceptable and payable option is the return of Prince Imaro Iwoto alive and unhurt. Should you capture any companions, complicit in luring or kidnapping him, I would also prefer they be returned alive."

The king pauses, the look on his face softening. "Imaro, if you are seeing this, and you are not hurt, come home."

After one more short pause, the king says, "My loyal subjects, and all others who see this missive, I thank you."

Questions are being shouted towards the podium and King Nobiri from unseen journalists around the camera. King Nobiri steps away from the podium, joined by several other official-looking rangeen.

The image returns to the newsroom.

Dajan says, "We've been told that Royal Enforcers are being reassigned and dispatched throughout rangeen space, as well as to other nearby systems."

"Of course," Laolat breaks in, "the Royal Enforcers will be getting permission to operate in local sovereign territories outside rangeen space to perform any search for the missing prince."

"That's right, Laolat," says Dajan. "Royal Enforcers operating outside rangeen space is not without precedent, though it is expected that multiple ambassadors will be performing shuttle diplomacy to smooth things out and prevent any unwanted incidents."

Laolat says, "Some of you may recall, ten years or so ago, the near-incident where Royal Enforcers pursued a gang of suspected criminals into sutac space. Agreements were reached between both peoples to make certain communications remain clear."

"Yes, indeed," says Dajan. "If, in the coming days, you see a much larger number of Royal Enforcers in public than normal, please do not panic. They are an integral part of the search for the missing prince."

"Thank you, Dajan," says Laolat. "For those who have just tuned in, King Nobiri has addressed the populace to let us know that Prince Imaro Iwoto is missing, and a kidnapping or other nefarious actions are suspected."

Dajan says, "Anyone with information that leads to the return of Prince Imaro Iwoto to his home will be handsomely rewarded. To any who might be responsible for his disappearance, know that you will not get away with taking the heir to King Nobiri Iwoto of the rangeen people. You will be caught, and then you will be killed in some most unpleasant ways."

"That's right, Dajan," says Laolat. "Stay tuned to RKNN, the Rangeen Kingdom News Network, Channel VX3410.756Q on the Interplanetary Transmission Entanglement Mediascape, as we continue to bring you the latest news in this fast-breaking story."

Chapter 20 – Passengers Always Have Interesting Stories

"He didn't!" Char exclaimed.

On her display, Mariska laughed. "Oh, he did."

"While you were working?" Char pressed.

"Oh, yes. He just walked into my office, thinking he'd seduce me, and gave the client a full-frontal view."

"Too funny," remarked Calista from the other display.

"Who was it that saw Wensleydale?" asked Char.

"Oh, just Oppo," said Mariska.

Char nearly did a spit take. "Our naxul client? They must have had no clue what to make of that."

"Given their lack of sex organs and gender, it fell flat," said Mariska. She began to chuckle. "That, of course, didn't help Wensleydale's self-esteem."

"Of course not," said Calista with a chuckle.

Char grinned. "Speaking of self-esteem, have you heard anything new about K's shenanigans?"

"Oh, yeah," Mariska said, her tone becoming conspiratorial. "You know he managed to talk his way out of being forced out. Well, he did so by promising to deliver a certain client the venture capitalists were keen on."

"I'll bet that went well," said Calista sarcastically.

"Of course," said Mariska. "I'm told the only reason he didn't blow it was because Todd stepped in at the last minute to salvage it all. But that's not the best part. What I heard is that they were disappointed that I'm no longer part of the company, and that set K off."

K was their old boss, Kevin. He had sold the company to a venture capitalist firm with a promise that he'd be more hands-off. However, because he was jealous of Mariska, who was far, far more skilled at the same things that K was, he kept interfering. That was part of why Mariska had started her own competing company with Char and Calista.

"Are you thinking about poaching them?" asked Calista.

"No," Mariska said. "K and the venture capitalists are trying to merge the client in. Not our bag."

"Think they'll ever realize that K is a moron?" asked Char.

"No," Mariska replied. "When I left, they struggled a lot. K, helped by Todd, kept most of them from leaving. But you know as well as I do that it won't last."

"We're nearing my estimate," remarked Calista. "I gave it until the end of this year before they shit-can him. What was the bet?"

"The losers treat the winner to a seven-course meal at Remy's Churrascaria on Notnilc," replied Mariska.

Char laughed. "I'm already out. I had K being forced out six months ago."

"Did we ever create a statute of limitations, in case he never leaves, like I bet?" asked Mariska.

"Four years," said Calista. "And if that happens, we just go to Remy's and split the bill."

"We'll see," said Mariska.

"Question for you both," began Char. "Have you ever encountered a rangeen before?"

"Only in passing," said Calista.

"Not that I recall," replied Mariska. "Why?"

"Well, five hours ago, we picked up some passengers from Sovereign Boundary, the world at the edge of rangeen space we were at. They're quite an interesting pair. We met them outside our landing bay, where they claimed they got ditched. Well, they hired us on the spot to take them to Abigail."

Calista said, "Whoa, that's a long way from anywhere."

"Right?" remarked Char. "They're the most adorable gay couple I've ever seen. Anyhow, until we left the planet and jumped into hyperspace, they seemed nervous, a bit on edge and tenuous. At the same time, they were majorly eager to get away."

"Yeah," Calista began. "I once spoke to a rangeen on public transport. Gay couple? The impression I got was that the rangeen are a very repressed society."

"Normally, I'd be suspect of this sort of charter," continued Char. "However, despite them being unusual, Jay and I like them. We made a point of inviting them to dine with us on this first 'night' aboard *Audacia*."

There was a tone, and then a soft, inflectionless voice in the background from Mariska's home office said, "*This is your reminder that Sammy needs to be picked up in ten minutes.*"

Mariska sighed. "Thank you, Alexiri," she called to her household AI. "Not like Wensleydale is too busy to do it, but whatever. Alright, ladies, we set for tomorrow?"

"I leave Ainrofilac in the morning," said Calista. "And I'll be to you, Mariska, in three days."

"And I'll remote into that meeting with you while she's in transit," added Char.

"Sounds good," said Mariska. "Okay, have a good night, ladies."

Char waved at the displays, and then they winked out.

Char had nothing pressing remaining, so she arose from her desk. Cosima, sitting on the loveseat across the office, merped at her. Char was fairly certain the space cat had said, "Leaving?"

"Yes," Char told Cosima. "You can join me. I'm meeting Jay and our passengers in the galley."

When Cosima chirped, Char was convinced she was saying, "Okay." As she left the office, Char waved a hand over the panel at the door jamb to turn off the lights and set her office cabin into standby mode.

Char made her way from the upper deck to the *Audacia*'s mid-deck, Cosima in tow. The ship was classified as a medium-sized transport by its builders, but it was plenty spacious for Jay, Char, the space cats, and Quinn.

Because Jay and Char's upper deck of the ship was limited to just them, and secured by biometric systems when they had passengers, it felt as homey as any immobile domicile Char had previously occupied. The bonus was that they could take home with them wherever they cared to travel.

The mid-deck was the muted, matte, metallic grey of the hulls, punctuated by colorful abstract artworks. Overall, it was neutral, as Jay and Char both saw great value in keeping a space that would be inoffensive and appealing to a wide range of races.

As Char went towards the galley, Thalia popped out from a side cabin. She chittered at Cosima, who chittered back. This went back and forth a couple of moments, then the pair of space cats bounded away.

"Okay, you two," Char called after them. "Play nice. And don't go getting into our passenger's things."

She shook her head and continued to the galley. Once she arrived, she found Jay doing the meal prep. Quinn was standing near him, which was unusual. Quinn was rarely anywhere on the ship other than the cockpit or engineering.

"No," Char heard Quinn saying. "As I do not eat, I do not find it necessary that I should join you and your guests at supper. Do you really want me to just stand at the table and observe you?"

"Of course not," Jay replied. "But you're part of the crew, and I don't want to exclude you just because you don't eat. On a trip this long, going this distance, you will encounter our passengers along the way. I just think it might be best to introduce you at the start of the trip."

Quinn buzzed in a way Char knew was disapproval. "You know I appreciate that effort, Captain. But if it's all the same to you, I shall meet them at another time. Maybe bring them to the cockpit tomorrow."

"Okay, I can do that."

Quinn looked at Char, bowed, since he had no head to nod, and headed back to the cockpit.

"Done with work I see," Jay addressed Char.

"Yes. Trying to get Quinn to be more social, still?"

"Always," replied Jay. "It's not just because I strive not to treat him like an emotionless automaton as much as it's including him as part of the crew."

"I know," said Char. She walked behind Jay and looked at the pan he was working with. "Pasta al la Baylin?"

Jay smiled. "Yes."

Char smelled the garlic, onions, and the large root vegetable that looked nothing like, but smelled and tasted exactly like, peppers. Jay was mixing that with the sausage and sauce in the pan. It would be more than enough food for the four of them, plus leftovers for a future lunch.

Because the *Audacia* sometimes carried passengers, the galley was equipped with an autocooker. One of the advances that the various spacefaring races shared was food preservation. Meals could be contained in shelf-stable suspension, lasting for years. That meant you didn't need to waste space and power for refrigeration to preserve food.

Jay and Char kept a wide range of foods for their passengers and themselves. They always made a point of letting their passengers know that there were plenty of options, as well as snacks to be had and a variety of beverage choices. They carried a few items that they knew held less appeal to humans, but were preferred by other races, usually rumel-approved, since Jay's brother-in-law was rumel.

Usually, Jay and Char would take at least one meal with their passengers. They always treated the *Audacia* as not just a transport, but something of an interplanetary bed and breakfast.

Jay was adding more sauce as Char said, "It never ceases to amaze me how food is food. Despite all the different worlds we come from and the other unique elements of our anatomies, all sentient races have a similar palate that includes sweet, savory, salty, bitter, umami, and gaushemaque. Yet, at the same time, some eat anything strictly for the caloric intake and fuel while others savor food and are choosy about what they consume."

"Yeah," Jay said. "Of course, this is also true among humans. My stepdad only eats like five different things, total, and that's it. He loves them, but none are all too exciting."

Char chuckled. "Yeah, fair. You and I have always loved food."

Jay stirred the pasta and remarked, "Another really unusual thing to me is how every race in the galaxy has at least one form of pasta. A starchy carb in noodle form, no matter where they come from. So weird."

Char heard the pair of rangeen coming into the galley. She grinned at how they were clearly a couple but were still somewhat closeted about it. They were, as she'd told Mariska and Calista, the most adorable gay couple she'd ever seen.

"That smells wonderful," said the green-haired, lighter-skinned Kukeb. "What is that?"

"It's a pasta dish that I invented for me and my sister when we were kids," Jay said. "After my parents divorced, Mom would be busy, so I learned to cook. One night, there were only a few items in the house, so I invented this. It's a favorite of my family."

"Are human families close?" asked Imaro as he and Kukeb took seats at the table.

"Some yes, some no," replied Char. "The definitions are pretty variable. Jay and I, for example, come from very different families with different cultural backgrounds."

"Have you found your stateroom adequate, gentlemen?" asked Jay. Char grinned at her husband's hospitality. He took his duties as captain and host very seriously.

"Oh, yes," replied Imaro. "Do you transport passengers more than cargo?"

"No," said Jay. "But when we do take on a charter for transporting people, we want them to be comfortable."

"I've seen some private vessels with less impressive quarters for guests," said Kukeb.

Jay had set the table before Char's arrival and was now dishing up the pasta for everyone. Char had gotten water and wine out on the table. "If you have another drink preference, let me know."

"This is wonderful, thank you," said Imaro. Jay set the skillet in the center of the table. As he and Char sat, Imaro asked. "Do you always ask your passengers to have meals with you?"

"At least once during the trip," Jay said. Both Imaro and Kukeb tried the food, and Char was gratified to see both expressing their approval and then digging in.

"Now, Captain," Kukeb began.

"You can call me Jay. I don't feel the need to be all that formal."

"Very well, Jay," Kukeb continued. "So, do you both own the ship?"

"Yes," replied Jay.

"But," Char took up, "this is his ship. We both own it, yes, but I have a totally different job. Jay and Quinn do all the work with and for the *Audacia*."

"What sort of work do you do, Char?" asked Imaro. "And is your name really Char, or is that short for something?"

Char grinned. "It's short for Charlotte. Just like Jay is short for Jason. And I love my job." Char went on to tell the rangeen couple about her company and the work she did with Mariska and Calista.

The rangeen couple asked several more questions about the ship, Quinn, their travels, and more. It was a very pleasant conversation, and Char found them both quite easy to talk to.

"So," Char said as Kukeb was helping himself to seconds. "What do you two do?"

They exchanged what appeared to be an uncomfortable look between them. Then, Imaro said, "Oh, well, I'm an executive for one of the largest businesses in rangeen space. There are a lot of, shall we say, traditions, expectations, and obligations that come with my job. It's a family business."

"Oh yeah?" remarked Jay. "You like a second, third, or older generation in?"

"Oh, quite old, yes," said Imaro wistfully. "I think I'm around the fifteenth generation. Maybe older? My, uh, father runs things."

"Interesting," said Char.

"I'm a special secretary to Imaro and some of the other executives," said Kukeb. For some reason she could not put her finger on, she felt that that was a forced statement. Like he'd made it up and spit it out before he might forget it.

"If I may," Jay began. "No offense, but couldn't you have acquired a more, shall we say, glamorous transport?"

"Yes," said Imaro. "But, we, uh... Well, that is to say, while we could have, we... Yes, we wanted to not make a big deal of it. I mean, the moment you take a corporate trip via a fancy yacht a great distance from home, people get nosey."

"Right," added Kukeb. "Too much attention and other weirdness and..." he trailed off.

Imaro added, "It's a circus we both prefer to avoid."

Char felt that the pair were holding something back and being somewhat evasive. Still, though, she was certain it was nothing malicious. Maybe it was a rangeen thing? She knew some races were not comfortable sharing things like certain personal and semi-personal matters with members of other races.

"I know that the rangeen are a big part of 'cator manufacturing," said Jay. "Both components and whole 'cators. Is that your business?"

"No, no, it's not," said Kukeb in a way that Char found odd.

"Though we are involved in other elements related to 'cators," Imaro amended. Char saw him pass an odd look to Kukeb, before adding, "The rangeen crown is actually the majority shareholder of all the 'cator manufacturing companies. They have a hand in mining the materials, distribution, and other aspects of the business. They have made their fortune on this tech and its continued use, deployment, and employment across space."

"That's interesting," said Char. "We were told by another rangeen we transported recently that the king is the leader of the rangeen. Did the crown have a hand in the making of 'cators from the start?"

"Oh, there's some fascinating history there," said Kukeb. "There is a resource in rangeen space with unique and fascinating temporal properties. I don't know what you call it, and it's a name only pronounceable by rangeen with our two tongues. It resonates with hyperspace in a way that allows it to work with and through hyperspace. It somehow defies surreal parsecs of distance for instant, interplanetary communication. We learn in school that before the rangeen met other space-faring races, communications were delayed and limited."

"Yes," agreed Char. "We learned that early spacefarers from Earth had real problems with that. Some other race, and I don't recall which, helped."

Imaro said, "Though we rangeen take credit for the 'cators and all their elements, the technology is also attuned to frequencies that are unique to the roptera. They have the most amazing aural range and understanding, which is a part of their natural biology. What's more, the hard-won symbiotic relationship between rangeen and roptera is how we worked out combining the frequencies and our unique resource to develop the quantum-microcircuitry that drives 'cators."

"Wow," said Char. "You know a lot about 'cators."

"Rangeen of our... status, all learn this. It's important for diplomatic and business reasons," said Imaro.

Jay was nodding his head. Then, he asked, "Now, if it's not too personal of a question, can I ask? What's the deal between the rangeen and the sutac?"

Again, Char saw an uncomfortable look pass between the rangeen couple. Then, Imaro replied, "Well it's... It's sort of a combination of discomfort between the roptera and sutac. Whenever sutac have visited Rangeenavelt, they always get into altercations with the roptera. Like they're natural-born opposition to one another. Yet, the more pressing issue seems... Well, rather, the king has made multiple attempts - failed attempts - to acquire certain sutac resources. In fact, said resource, far as I know, from various rumors I've heard, he believes, would supposedly expand 'cator tech and the rangeen dominance, or rather, sorry, hold, over it."

It did not escape Char that Imaro had appeared increasingly uncomfortable talking about the matter of the crown and another sovereign people. Maybe, she presumed, it was a natural reaction not to want to badmouth one's leaders or government to near-total strangers.

The rest of the meal passed with a bit more small talk. Then, with a great deal of thank yous, Imaro and Kukeb retired to their quarters.

Jay and Char cleaned up. As they did, Char said, "Did you get the sense there was stuff they intentionally weren't telling us?"

"Yeah," Jay said without hesitation. "But, I mean, maybe it's because they're heading so far from home with non-rangeen. Remember the first time we took nonhuman passengers on?"

"Oh yes," Char said. "First time I've ever been in close quarters with kijivu. It was uncomfortable for most of the trip."

"That might be it," said Jay. However, Char knew his tone. Like her, he suspected there was more to it.

"Still," Char went on. "I like them. They seem like decent beings. It was a nice meal and good conversation."

"Even if they were uncomfortable about... something," Jay remarked. He shrugged. "They're odd, but then, my love, so are we."

"Yes, we are," she agreed.

Placing the skillet in the wash-cycler, Jay added, "But this isn't the weirdest job, nor are they the strangest passengers we've ever taken, by any stretch of the imagination."

Chapter 21 – Things That Go Bump in the Night That Shouldn't

Jay awoke with a start. Where was he? What was going on? Why did he feel panicky?

It was the middle of the night cycle, and he was completely disoriented. Why did he think he'd heard something make a loud noise? How come he was certain that he'd felt the bed shake, and not because Char had moved beside him? After a few more moments of disorientation, Jay got his bearings and recognized he was in his cabin lying next to Char.

"Jay?" she queried softly.

"Yeah?"

"What was that?"

Jay rolled over and sat up. "What do you mean, what was that?"

Char propped herself up on an elbow. "I felt something. If we were planetside, I'd have thought it was an earthquake."

"Okay, yeah," Jay confirmed. He was both glad and worried that he'd not just been imagining something was off. He listened to the *Audacia*, listened for the normal sounds of the powerplant humming, air processor cycling, and engines rumbling. He knew what was wrong. "We're not in hypserspace anymore."

"What?"

Jay arose and went towards the shelf on the wall opposite the bed and grabbed comfy pants, boxers, and a t-shirt. "I can feel it. Hear it." Pulling on his shirt, he went to the viewport and opened the digital "shades." As they cleared, what he saw were stars. However, it should have been the blurred lines of stars as they were passing by in hyperspace.

Char sat up and looked out the viewport. "We were nowhere near a destination, right?"

"Right," Jay agreed. "I'm heading to the cockpit."

Jay left their cabin and made his way to the middle deck. Passing quietly along the corridor, he entered the cockpit.

Quinn looked at him as he entered and said, "There you are. What kept you?"

"Why didn't you use the 'cator to contact me?" Jay asked.

"I figured the bump woke you up."

"Yes, it did. What happened?"

Quinn turned back to the instruments and their screens. "For reasons I cannot explain, the *Audacia* has shifted out of hyperspace."

Jay frowned. "What? That's impossible. The only way that could happen is if the Phased Reality Drive completely shuts down, and the failsafe kicks in to drop the ship out of hyperspace into a safe area in normal space."

"Exactly," Quinn concluded.

"Okay." Jay was at the pilot's station and was activating screens and displays to look everything over. "So why did the Phased Reality Drive shut down?"

"I have no idea," replied Quinn.

"Well, I'm here now," said Jay. "Go back to engineering and look at the drive itself. See if you can make heads or tails of it."

"Yessir," said Quinn in his usual manner. Without another word, the android left the cockpit.

Jay tapped the part of the screen to activate the internal 'cator. "Char? You should come join me down here."

"On my way," she replied.

Jay started to look at the readouts to see if anything obvious stood out. This, he knew, was a largely pointless exercise. Quinn would already have examined this. If the 'bot had no idea from the data available on the flight deck, Jay wasn't going to glean something new.

Jay sensed someone poking a head into the cockpit who wasn't Char or Quinn. He turned and found Imaro there. "What's going on?" the rangeen asked.

"Everything is okay," Jay began. "But there is something wrong with the Phased Reality Drive. There isn't any damage to the ship. All other systems are functioning normally. Quinn is back in engineering looking into it."

"Does this sort of thing normally happen?" Imaro asked.

Jay sighed. "No, it most certainly does not. We'll get underway again as soon as we figure it out. However, we're not in any danger. The failsafe puts us in open space away from any problem areas. Sorry for the inconvenience."

"Thanks, Jay," Imaro said. Jay could see that the rangeen had relaxed as he went back to his quarters.

Char arrived in the cockpit a moment later. "What happened?" After Jay explained the unusual and unexpected Phased Reality Drive shutdown, Char asked, "Did we miss some sort of maintenance or put off something we saw as a minor problem for another time?"

Because he was still sleepy, rudely awakened by his ship, he hadn't checked that. Jay called up their meticulous maintenance records and looked them over. With relief, Jay was able to say, "No. We're up to date on everything."

"Captain," Quinn's voice came from the bridge speaker as the robot reached out via the internal 'cator.

"What's the verdict?" Jay asked.

"The Phased Reality Drive is fine. It is undamaged. There are no problems with it. All indicators show its operations should be normal."

"Good," Jay said. "So, what's wrong with it?"

"It has switched off," Quinn said.

"How is that fine?" Jay almost shouted.

"It is undamaged," Quinn said again. "Nothing has blown up. There are no obvious issues with the Phased Reality Drive. It is simply non-functional."

"Why?" Jay asked. "It can't be fine but non-functional at the same time."

"There is no known reason," Quinn stated. "The diagnostics have produced no results. All connections between the Phased Reality Drive, engines, and power systems are as they should be. It has simply shut down."

Jay sighed. "Did you do a restart?"

"Of course I did," Quinn replied. "It did not restart."

"Can it be jumpstarted somehow?" Jay asked.

"No," Quinn said. "To all intents and purposes, according to all readouts and diagnostics, it should be working. But it is not."

"So, we know nothing more than the Phased Reality Drive should be working, but it isn't, and there is zero known reason why that is," Jay summed up. "Quinn, can you download additional data on the specific Phased Reality Drive that we have aboard *Audacia*? See if there's something about this particular unit that you're not already familiar with?"

"Yes," Quinn replied.

"Do so, please," Jay requested. "See what you can do from there."

"Yessir," Quinn replied. The 'cator signal cut off.

"Now what do we do?" Char asked.

Jay tapped at his screens and called up star charts on the display. "Well, let's start by figuring out where we are."

He looked at the charts and groaned. "Great. We are in the very definition of the middle of nowhere."

He tapped a control, and a 3D image of the space around the *Audacia* appeared in the center of the cockpit behind the pilot and co-pilot's seats. A small, digitized image of the ship was in the center of the chart.

Jay explained, "Here we are. We're on the outskirts of a solar system with no planets. As you can see here, this is an old star and a lot of asteroids that might have been planets long ago."

He zoomed the image out further until a solar system with planets appeared in the hologram. "We're about five lightyears from the nearest civilized world."

"What system is this?" asked Char, pointing. "Who claims it?"

"The nairodna," Jay said.

"That's a good thing," Char said. "The nairodna tend to be pleasant overall and are neutral in most things."

"I really hate to do this," Jay said. He tapped a control on his screen. "Activating the distress beacon."

"You don't want to start flying towards that system?" Char asked.

Jay chuckled, but he was not feeling any humor. "Between the more than five-year trip in normalspace and the various navigational hazards of this system we're in? No, thank you. We're much better off just staying put."

Jay sighed again as he switched off the holographic star chart. "If Quinn can't fix the drive, we're going to need a tow."

Chapter 22 – Pretend We're Not Really Here

Imaro slowly became aware of his surroundings. He'd been sleeping soundly when the *Audacia* had jolted and whatever had made a loud noise in the middle of the night cycle awoke him. After a visit to the cockpit and Jay's reassurance that all was well, he'd returned to the stateroom and climbed back into bed beside Kukeb.

Surprisingly, he'd gotten decent sleep after the incident. Kukeb was still asleep at his side, which made Imaro grin.

He glanced towards the viewport and, finding the remote on the nightstand, he tapped the control to open the digital "shades." Outside, there were stars. Not the starlines of hyperspace, however.

Imaro groaned, and Kukeb stirred. Sleepily, he asked, "What's wrong?"

"We haven't returned to hyperspace," said Imaro.

Kukeb was upright in the bed, as if he'd been shocked awake. "What do you mean, we're not in hyperspace?"

Imaro explained what had happened, which Kukeb had slept through.

"You're sure it's a malfunction, and not the captain stopping so that Royal Enforcers can come collect us?" asked Kukeb.

"Yes," Imaro replied. "First, they don't know anyone is looking for us. Second, they don't know who we are. Third, I saw Jay in the cockpit. He was clearly frazzled, and Quinn, the 'bot, was in engineering. This is not intentional. This is a problem."

"If I didn't think that Jay and Char were honest and earnest, I'd wonder," said Kukeb. "Let's go see what's going on."

The two rangeen got dressed. They left their cabin, but Imaro felt it would be better to go to the galley than the cockpit. This turned out to be wise, as both Jay and Char were there.

"Good morning," Char addressed the pair.

"Morning," replied Imaro.

"What happened?" asked Kukeb without preamble. "I notice we're not in hyperspace."

Jay said, "No, we're not. The Phased Reality Drive isn't working."

"Isn't working?" asked Imaro. He knew nothing about the tech, but he thought it was built with numerous redundancies so that it wouldn't fail, especially during faster-than-light travel. The condition of the *Audacia* spoke of a crew that cared for their ship and didn't skimp on maintenance.

Jay shrugged. "That's all we know. Quinn is working on it, but he's not found anything that can explain why it's not doing its job."

Char added, "The Phased Reality Drive isn't driving, or phasing reality."

"That's not helpful," remarked Jay.

Char grinned. "You're just annoyed because I beat you to it."

"Pardon me?" Kukeb began. "But what happens if it can't be fixed?"

"Well," Jay replied, "the distress beacon is active. Given that our night cycle is synched to Consistent Galactic Time-Code, I expect it won't be long before someone picks it up and comes to check on us."

Looking concerned, Kukeb asked, "If we're not in hyperspace, and we're not in an inhabited solar system, won't the beacon attract pirates?"

Jay chuckled. "Nah. Between the rangeen and the nairodna, pirates don't stand a chance."

"The rangeen?" asked Imaro, feeling some of Kukeb's concern in his chest. "I thought after the number of hours we were in hyperspace before the trouble with the Phased Reality Drive, we were a long way from rangeen space?"

"Well, yes," replied Jay. "But also, relatively speaking, no. Though this part of space is nairodna space, rangeen space is the next occupied sector nearest where we are now."

Kukeb nervously asked, "Might a Royal Enforcer from rangeen space respond to your distress beacon?"

Jay didn't take long to give it much thought before saying, "It's possible, I suppose. But we're deep enough into nairodna space that I expect it's the nairodna who will likely find us."

"Uh," Kukeb began. Imaro saw how flustered and obviously worried Kukeb had become, and before he could interrupt, Kukeb continued, saying, "Whatever happens, whoever shows, could you pretend that Imaro and I aren't here?"

"What?" Char questioned. "Why?"

"Well, you see," Kukeb choked out. "This close to rangeen space, the nairodna have a problem with rangeen. It has nothing to do with Imaro or me; it's just an old dispute about a, uh, asteroid field or Oort cloud or some such thing between our people. Yeah."

That, Imaro knew, was a lie. There were no issues whatsoever between the rangeen and the nairodna. Still, Kukeb had started a lie and Imaro wasn't about to toss him out the airlock. "It's quite recent and almost exclusively between the nearest sectors of each. It ties into some other trade issues between nairodna and rangeen, and there are varying and lesser degrees of issues over this. So, as Kukeb was asking, can you pretend – whoever shows to help – that we're not here?"

Jay looked confused, and if Imaro didn't know better – which, really, he didn't – he looked somewhat irked, too. Jay said, "You do know that most starships have sensors that detect life forms on other ships? They'll know there are four of us. Six, if their sensors also read the spacecats."

"Interesting," remarked Imaro, trying to salvage the situation. "How good do those sensors tend to be? How good are yours?"

Jay just shrugged. "Never needed to know more than if there were life forms somewhere or not. Char, you know something about this from your work, right?"

"Yeah," Char responded. She arose from the table and went to get a beverage while she said, "Most aren't sensitive enough to distinguish one life form from another. Not unless they differ considerably, such as if they breathe oxygen or nitrogen, there are massive variations in body temperature, and so on. However, most races run so similar that we're mostly indistinguishable from one another on sensors. There are exceptions to the rule, of course, but that's some majorly specialized equipment only surveyors tend to use. Not even militaries tend to have them."

Jay was nodding at that. As Char brought a mug to him, he looked at Imaro and Kukeb and said, "I know this might seem to be prying, but is there something that you're not telling us?"

"No, not as such," said Imaro with more confidence than he felt. Jay was eyeing him in a way that he knew said the human captain wasn't entirely buying it. Cautiously, Imaro added, "Kukeb and I aren't in trouble with the law, fugitives from justice, or anything like that. We just really need to stay hidden. It would be for the best if we could avoid being identified by anyone, nairodna, rangeen, or otherwise. Trust me, we didn't bring legal or ethical trouble onto your ship."

A look passed between Jay and Char. She had not resumed her seat, and he stood up. "Give us a moment to talk about this."

Imaro nodded, and the human couple left the galley.

"What do we do?" asked Kukeb.

"What can we do?" Imaro replied with his own question. "I don't think they're going to throw us out an airlock or jettison us in an escape pod. We just have to hope they will agree to keep us hidden."

"What if they don't?" Kukeb breathed.

"We tell them everything," replied Imaro. He held a hand up to forestall more from Kukeb and said, "Which we'll have to do anyhow."

Jay and Char returned to the galley. Imaro realized he couldn't read either of them, so he had no idea what they'd decided or what their attitude towards him and Kukeb was, now.

"Alright," Jay said. "I am not fond of this in the slightest, and I don't like that you're asking us to keep you a secret. But Char and I think you both mean well and that whatever the issue is, you're not about to cost us our livelihood. So, here's the deal. Take some food and drink, then return to your quarters and stay there until we come for you when it's safe."

"How do we know you're not selling us out?" asked Kukeb. Imaro had an unusual urge to slug his companion.

Char replied, saying, "We're trusting you, and I don't think it's too much to ask you to trust us in return."

"Agreed," said Imaro, looking coldly at his partner. Kukeb subsided and nodded.

"Know this," Jay added. "You had better be prepared to explain yourselves once we get rescued."

"Yes, Captain," replied Imaro. "Thank you, Jay. Thank you, Char."

Neither of the humans responded. Kukeb and Imaro gathered some food and drinks, then left the galley to return to their stateroom.

"They don't know who you are," said Kukeb when they were back in their cabin.

"Until we get rescued, that's probably for the best," said Imaro. "I just hope that our problems truly won't become theirs. I like Jay and Char. They seem like decent people, and I do not wish any ill to befall them."

"Guess all we can do is hope for the best, then," said Kukeb.

Chapter 23 – What Seems to Be the Problem?

"What the hell have we gotten ourselves into with this one?" questioned Char. She knew that her ire came through as she sat sulkily in the co-pilot's seat.

Quinn remained back in engineering examining the Phased Reality Drive, but still found nothing. Jay, meanwhile, was seated in the pilot's seat beside Char, brooding.

It wasn't often that her spouse was in such an obvious, foul mood. She suspected that part of it had to do with their passengers and whatever it was they were hiding. However, more than that, it was the state of their ship, their home.

"Jay?" Char prompted.

"I must have missed something," he said, sounding both dejected and irked at the same time. "This makes no sense whatsoever. For a Phased Reality Drive to just fail like that? This sort of thing doesn't happen. Clearly, I missed something. Must have been a maintenance or other technical check I didn't have done. Stupid."

"Jay, my love, you are blameless here," said Char as reassuringly as she could. "These things happen. You are always fastidious about ship's maintenance. You didn't miss anything that should have been done. This is a freak occurrence."

Jay growled, which Char recognized was a release of his displeasure over what was going on. He said, "It makes no sense. I should really have put more time and effort into studying ship systems. Gone for some lessons in maintenance and repair. If I own my own ship, it behooves me to be a better mechanic."

"That's what Quinn is for," said Char. She reached out to put a hand on Jay's cheek. She gently pressed to turn his face towards her. "You never neglect this ship, just like you never neglect Quinn or me. This was not your fault, Jason Baylin. Shit happens. We're safe, and we have more than enough funds to do any repair work that will come of this. You're an excellent captain, so stop this nonsense."

He sighed. She stuck her tongue out at him. Then she crossed her eyes. Jay rolled his eyes, but a grin began to touch his lips. Char leaned in and nibbled his lower lip, then kissed him.

"Okay, yeah, thank you, my love," Jay said.

"Brooding depressive doesn't fit you, ya know," Char commented.

Jay harrumphed softly. "You're so lucky you didn't know me in my twenties and early thirties."

"So you've said," Char remarked. "Now, what do you think about our passengers?"

"Imaro and Kukeb don't strike me as criminals," said Jay. "But they are definitely avoiding something. Maybe running from something? I don't know. It wouldn't matter, except now that we're in this position, and we need help, they want to avoid recognition?"

"Maybe it really is a cultural thing?" mused Char. She shrugged. "Still, they're not the weirdest or most secretive job we've ever taken."

Jay snorted. "You mean that mess with the gorlek and the not-weapons we were transporting for them?"

Char chuckled. "Among other things. Actually, I was thinking about -"

An alarm went off, interrupting her. It only took Char a moment to realize that it was the proximity alarm as Jay silenced it. If the *Audacia* wasn't in motion, which it wasn't, that meant a ship was on approach and closing.

Char looked at the display as Jay did. He tapped a few spots on the screen on the console in front of them, and the approaching ship was now actively viewed by their sensors. Char read that it was a frigate of the nairodna Civil Defense Fleet.

Jay looked at a display, and Char knew without him saying anything that he was checking the time. Glancing herself, Char realized it was about four hours into the day cycle according to the Consistent Galactic Time-Code.

Before Char could comment, they received a 'cator signal. "Unidentified ship," a female-sounding voice addressed them, "we have received your distress beacon. Standard identification, please?"

Jay tapped the screen to reply and said, "This is the starship *Audacia*, OVERLORD standard registration Bravo-Five-One-One-Five Delta-Four-One-One *Audacia*."

There was silence for a moment, and then the female voice returned and said, "Registration confirmed. What seems to be the problem, *Audacia*?"

"We were traveling through this system in hyperpace when we experienced a total shutdown of our Phased Reality Drive. It is offline, but there's zero reason why that should be, and we can identify no problem with it."

The female voice from the nairodna ship said, "That's not possible."

"Oh, we know," Jay said. "Believe me, we're well aware it's not possible. But here we are, and we cannot get our Phased Reality Drive functional."

"One moment, *Audacia*," the voice said. "Please be aware we'll be performing a thorough scan of your ship."

"Understood," Jay replied.

Char and Jay sat in silence. The scan from the nairodna ship was silent, of course. What's more, there would be no sensation as the other ship used various sensors to explore the *Audacia* and probe for obvious issues, violations, and certain contraband.

Char was always amazed by how OVERLORD had both created and maintained so many standards. More than that, it amazed her that all the variable races abided by them. It definitely made trade, commerce, travel, and communications far easier than they would otherwise have been.

The voice was on the 'cator again and said, "Our scan is complete. We note that you have four humanoid and two non-humanoid lifeforms."

"Correct," Jay said. "My wife, two passengers, and two herpestelines. No cargo at this time."

"Destination?"

"Abigail," Jay replied.

"That's a very long ways away," said the female on the 'cator. "We cannot take you that far."

"Oh, we certainly would not expect you to," Jay assured her. "However, if you could give us a tow to the nearest inhabited world or full-service space station or platform, that would be greatly appreciated."

"Before we can agree to assist with a tow," the female on the 'cator began, "we need to ask a few questions. Do you have any hazardous materials on board?"

"Apart from fuel, no," Jay replied.

"Weapons?"

"No projectile weapons and the ship is unarmed."

"We know from your registration that you and your wife are human. Where are your passengers from?"

"Strelizia," Jay replied without hesitation.

Char tensed. She didn't like to tell lies to any authorities. Fortunately, Jay had chosen to claim their passengers were people from a destination they knew well. Also, he had not specified their race.

She didn't know if it was real or if she was imagining that it was taking what seemed like a long time for the nairodna to respond. Then, finally, the female voice on the 'cator said, "Have you been to rangeen space recently?"

"Yes," Jay replied. Char was gratified that he sounded utterly unperturbed by that question.

The nairodna representative asked, "Are you aware that the rangeen prince is missing?"

Char and Jay exchanged a confused look. Then, Jay said, "No."

"Don't you watch the ITEM?" questioned the nairodna.

"Of course we do," Jay said, slightly exasperated and as confused by the line of questioning as Char was. He continued, saying, "The *Audacia* isn't just our ship, it's our home. We have no strong ties to any one world, and we tend to avoid watching news programs like the ITEM First News Network or any local news networks. We figure if it's something important and might have an impact on us, we'll get news from our friends or via the MESS-work."

"But you have recently visited rangeen space," pressed the nairodna representative. "And you claim your passengers are from where?"

"Strelizia," Jay said. "Look, if it would help, I'm more than willing to transmit my ship's logs to you."

"Proceed," the female voice on the 'cator requested.

Jay leaned in and tapped at a screen or two, which Char knew would transmit the ship's log to the nairodna.

She gestured toward the speaker to make sure they weren't transmitting on the 'cator anymore. When he indicated they weren't, Char asked, "Uh, Jay, my love, won't sending them our log tell the nairodna that we acquired our passengers on Sovereign Boundary in rangeen space?"

"No," Jay answered. "I'm only sending the logs that any authority can request and expect, which is the ship's location beacon logs. Volunteering that info tends to go a long way. And it will show that we visited Strelizia, but not when. No authority can request anything more thorough without a warrant of some sort."

"Clever," Char said.

"Keeps all kinds of obnoxious activities by local authorities from happening," Jay said.

Char wasn't entirely sure what Jay meant, but she could guess. Local authorities, with access to more comprehensive data, might abuse it to set up unnecessary quarantines, demand payment on some obscure regulatory matter, or confiscate a cargo for spurious reasons.

"*Audacia*, we've reviewed your log. Everything looks good," the voice came across the 'cator. Char let out a breath she'd not realized she was holding. "Prepare to receive an attractor stream to tow you."

"Thank you," Jay said.

Yet the nairodna on the 'cator had more to say. "You might or might not care to know, but there's a rather hefty reward being offered by the rangeen crown for any information that leads to finding their wayward prince."

"If we had such information, that would be good to know," Jay said.

After another moment, the nairodna female said, "We are transmitting a recording to you with a more detailed explanation from the rangeen. Meanwhile, we'll be towing you to the Rodna Bazaar space station. You should have no problem getting help for your ship there."

"Thank you," Jay replied.

"We will be towing you," the female nairodna said via the 'cator, "after you transfer one thousand EVILC to us."

"Agreed," Jay said.

As he started tapping at the controls to initiate the transfer, Char balked and said, "That's hyperspace-way robbery! A thousand EVILC is a ludicrous amount for a tow."

Jay sighed and said, "Yeah, well, normally I'd agree with you. At the most, a tow should only run a hundred to two-fifty. But we're in the middle of nowhere and have no better options. So, it's pay the exorbitant fee or float until who-knows-when."

Char shook her head as Jay completed transferring the funds.

"Positioning for tow now, *Audacia*," the nairodna transmitted. Jay did not respond.

Char was bothered by the info from the nairodna, especially given the attitude that Imaro and Kukeb had presented with their need to avoid being seen. "I have a bad feeling that our passengers had something to do with the rangeen prince going missing."

Jay grunted, then said, "They seem like really nice guys. Neither strikes me as being the kind of person who might harm anyone. I really hope you're wrong. But I can't deny I'm concerned, too."

There was a slight lurch as the nairodna frigate engaged its attractor stream with the *Audacia*. A few moments later, the female voice came across the 'cator again, "Attractor stream engaged. Contact confirmed. Prepare for hyperspace."

Another moment passed, and then there was a slight sensation of acceleration as the nairodna frigate towed *Audacia* back into hyperspace.

"How long to the bazaar?" asked Char.

Jay checked on the charts, then said, "Looks like about forty minutes or so."

"Shall we see what the nairodna shared?" asked Char.

Jay nodded. He tapped some controls, and the overhead display flashed a moment, then showed a banner claiming they were watching the Rangeen Kingdom News Network.

Chapter 24 – The Spacecat's Out of The Bag

Kukeb was pacing around their cabin. Imaro felt like doing the same, but Kukeb paced sufficiently for them both. He was aware that a ship had arrived to respond to the distress beacon. What that would amount to remained to be seen.

Imaro recognized that Jay and Char were displeased, knowing he and Kukeb were hiding something from them. He knew the story he and Kukeb had told them stretched credulity and that they suspected the rangeen had left something important out of it. Now, all they could do was wait. Imaro hoped the rapport he and Kukeb had with the human couple would be sufficient for them to protect their identities.

If not, then what? Imaro suspected whoever had arrived in response to the beacon would come aboard and remove the rangeen couple. Perhaps before that happened, however, he'd get a chance to explain their situation.

They had only been aboard the *Audacia* a short time, but Imaro rather liked Char and Jay. They were pleasant, friendly, and welcoming. They either didn't notice or didn't mind that Imaro and Kukeb were more than just friendly companions.

There was a slight sensation of acceleration, and a look out the viewport showed they were back in hyperspace. Imaro breathed a sigh of relief and said, "Kukeb, look."

Kukeb stopped his pacing and joined Imaro beside the viewport. He sighed and said, "That's a good sign, yes?"

"Yes," Imaro agreed. He sat on the edge of the bunk, realizing his muscles had tensed up while Kukeb paced. It was as if an unseen pressure that had been bearing down on him was gone.

Kukeb was leaning into the viewport to look out towards the fore of the starship. "The ship towing us is much larger than we are. I think it's nairodna ship. Frigate, or destroyer, maybe? Either way, not rangeen."

"Good to know," said Imaro.

The speaker for the internal 'cator system became active, which Imaro could tell by a slight shift in the ambient sound of the stateroom. Char's voice came over it, saying, "Gentlemen, you probably noticed we're back in hyperspace. Please come to the galley now so that we can talk."

Imaro noticed the tension in Char's voice. "We're on our way," he said to the air.

Kukeb looked to his mate with a nervous grin. "What do we tell them?"

Imaro didn't reply, but he stood up from his seat on the bunk and left the stateroom to make his way to the galley. Kukeb followed. When they arrived in the galley, both Char and Jay were seated and awaiting them.

"Please," Jay gestured for them to also sit down. Imaro wordlessly obliged, followed by Kukeb. It didn't take a mind reader to note that both Char and Jay looked displeased.

"So," Char began without further ado, "one of you is the missing rangeen prince?"

"What?" Kukeb sputtered. "A prince is missing? What... Whatever do you mean? We're just... That is, my companion and I are just..."

Imaro placed a hand on Kukeb's upper arm to get his attention, and he went silent. Then, plainly, with no emotion in his tone, Imaro stated, "That would be me. I am Prince Imaro Iwoto."

"What the hell?" asked Jay. His tone wasn't unkind, more exasperated and displeased. "We saw one of the transmissions from your Rangeen Kingdom News Network. They're telling everyone who tunes in that you've either been kidnapped or lured away. What's the deal with that?"

Imaro sighed. There was no point in obfuscating or avoiding the truth. It was time to lay his cards on the table, as he'd heard the phrase went. "My father is quite set in his ways, and he has never understood me or my desire for how I'd like to live my life. Kukeb here neither lured me away nor kidnapped me. No offense to Kukeb - but he couldn't kidnap a beverage out of a refrigeration unit without alerting half the galaxy by opening the door. I left of my own accord."

"But why?" asked Char.

"As prince, and heir to the throne, I am expected to follow certain traditions. I was presented with no options but one, and no matter what I desired or sought to do for myself, there was only a single path available to me. It is not the path I want for my life, but my father is forcing me to accept it. I won't be forced to be somebody that I am not. I can't and won't give in to my father's wishes."

Jay said, "I mean, sure, I can understand that. I have never done what my mother wanted or expected of me. Still, doesn't being prince mean that while you might need to give in to your father's wishes now, he won't last forever? And then, when you take the crown, you can change it how you want?"

"Yeah," Char added. "Sure, I get not wanting to do what's forced on you. I had plans for post-secondary education my parents wouldn't allow. But I made an alternate choice that worked out well for me. Since your only option, I'm guessing, is to follow in your father's footsteps to eventually take the throne, wouldn't it behoove you to become the ruler of rangeen space?"

"That's not the main issue," Imaro admitted. "I have been raised my entire life to one day succeed my father. I've held numerous leadership positions to prepare me and hone my skills to that end. It's that I've been putting off one of the most expected – and, I'm told, most important - duties laid on my shoulders. And that has caught up to me. It's a step that I am being given no choice but to take."

"What would that be?" asked Char.

He glanced towards Kukeb, who was maintaining a stoic gaze into nowhere, and said, "I am being forced to marry a rangeen woman, one from a noble family of my father's choosing, and must create an heir as soon as practicable."

"Ah," said Char. "I get that, since you and Kukeb here are clearly lovers."

"What?" scoffed Imaro out of force of habit. "That's not it at all. You see, Kukeb is my closest advisor and personal secretary, and he's not my -"

Char held up a hand to forestall him and Imaro felt compelled to stop. Char then said, "Imaro, you're a terrible liar. You and Kukeb look at each other in a way only lovers would. You might not be human, but it's so, so obvious. There's no need to hide or deny it. I've had gay friends all my life."

"It's true," Jay added. "She even tried to out me as gay when we first started dating."

Imaro saw Char throw a loving glance towards her spouse before turning back to him and saying, "It's utterly clear that you and Kukeb are a loving couple, and your aversion to being forced to marry is perfectly natural."

Maybe he shouldn't have been surprised, but Imaro felt the need to remain cautious. Thus, he asked, "Homosexuality doesn't offend you?"

Jay broke into laugher. "No, not at all. Love is love. If anyone gets offended by that, they need to stop worrying about the lives of other people and look inwards at themselves."

"Besides," Char added. "I'm bisexual. And Jay and I maintain a non-monogamous, polyamorous relationship."

Imaro had read about various forms of sexuality among the races, and one thing that had always struck him was how open they were to all kinds. Biology versus culture could be curious. That was the main issue Imaro had faced all his life. He said, "Thank you. Overall, homosexuality is common and normal in rangeen society. But that's among normal, everyday rangeen people. Among nobility, and certainly with the royalty, it is unacceptable. To carry on the line, noble or royal, it is imperative that you do your duty and do the needful thing, accept heterosexuality and produce offspring to maintain the bloodline and the leadership therein."

"My family are lesser nobility," said Kukeb quietly. "I have several older siblings, which is why I was sent off to work for the royal family at a young age. Imaro and I were paired long ago, and over time we realized that we felt more than kinship and friendship for one another."

"So," Jay started, "you couldn't accept having to give up this relationship and marry a female, let alone produce an heir with her. You ran away, and here we are."

"Which we get," Char took up. "We've known people who made choices others didn't want them to. But why not stick it out? Could you not put off the need to marry, play the long game, and change things when you ascend the throne?"

"Sadly, no," Imaro replied. "As I stated before, I have done that for as long as I could get away with it. Time has run out, as King Nobiri, my father, has chosen a bride for me."

"And," Kukeb added, "Imaro is to espouse her before the end of the month."

"Why now?" asked Jay. "Some sort of ritual thing? A holiday of some kind?"

"No, nothing like that," Imaro replied. "My father has a big plan afoot. He has a whole project that he's about to set into motion, which will massively increase the influence of the rangeen people. It's complex and will have broad implications for more than just the rangeen. But before that happens, he wants my marriage secured. The king clearly needs to know succession is in place."

"Do you know what it is he's planning?" Jay asked.

"Yes," Imaro answered. "You see…"

Before he could say more, the *Audacia* lurched slightly. Glancing toward the nearest viewport, Imaro saw that they had dropped out of hyperspace.

"Captain," the ship's robot, Quinn, called via the 'cator. "The nairodna frigate attractor stream has disengaged."

"Thanks, Quinn. On my way," Jay called. He arose and looked at Imaro and Kukeb. "I need to go to the cockpit to land the ship."

Char also stood up, saying, "And I need to go over with Quinn all the details about the problem with our Phased Reality Drive, so that we can figure out who on this station might be able to repair or replace it."

"This discussion is not over," Jay said. "However, we need to pause it. For now, you can remain with me and Char while we get the ship repaired."

"But we will need you to tell the rest of this to us," Char said. "If we're going to take you away from your duties and obligations, we need to fully understand what implication there might be from that, not just for you, but for us."

"Thank you," said Kukeb, nearly in tears.

"I understand," said Imaro, feeling relieved. Despite their deception, Jay and Char wouldn't abandon them. They were still safe and free, for now.

Chapter 25 – I Need to Repair My Ship Not Change My Career

Char was in the cockpit with Jay and Quinn. Fortunately, the rest of the ship's engine systems were functioning perfectly. Once the nairodna frigate had disengaged their attractor stream, Jay and Quinn had flown to their assigned bay and landed.

The trio had remained in the cockpit. While the nairodna had been towing the *Audacia,* Quinn had found information that was useful to their situation. Now that they'd landed and were settled in the bay, Jay was going over it.

Char, meanwhile, was researching the Rodna Bazaar's hypermedia network. It had been easy to learn who the local ship mechanics were, as well as whether they'd be able to repair or replace a Phased Reality Drive. There was more to Char's search than just the basic information and capabilities of these technicians.

She was also reading reviews about them via the broader MESS-work, their work ethic or lack therein, how honest or dishonest people found them to be. While the info on the local hypermedia network was more sanitized, the wider Multimedia Establishment Synchronized Systems network tended toward greater frankness. Char would get a better understanding of if people avoided or used any of the mechanics.

Jay grunted from the pilot's seat. Char knew immediately why he was annoyed and not repressing it. Char had already read what Quinn found and understood Jay's reaction.

The issue with their Phased Reality Drive was an almost ludicrous problem. What had occurred was something that should never have occurred. Fortunately, the safety systems had done their job. They also knew that while it wouldn't, by any stretch of the imagination, be free to fix; but neither would it break their savings.

Despite what she'd read, Char had no idea what the problem was. Neither Jay nor Quinn could explain, as neither could fully grasp the meaning of the issue as it was presented. The gist, according to Jay, was that "an impossible cascade failure of multiple redundant systems within a component of unknown origin" had occurred.

Whomever they hired to do the work, Quinn would remain onboard the ship to assist. Despite the person they would hire being an independent, it was a normal practice for a ship's mechanic or captain to assist. Given that Quinn was more or less wired directly into *Audacia*, he'd be best suited to not just give insight, but valuable help.

Jay groaned. "This is insane."

"To what are you referring, dear?" chided Char.

Jay turned his seat to face her. "I dunno anymore. A Phased Reality Drive failure that should be utterly and completely impossible, our passengers, maybe both?"

Char sighed. "Yeah. How in the universe did we wind up with a renegade prince and his lover?"

"Luck?" Jay questioned. "I mean, arguably, luck. The unanswered question is if it's good or bad."

Char chuckled. "Fair enough. They seem like perfectly decent beings, right?"

"Oh, absolutely," agreed Jay. "You could add them to your collection."

"The rest of my gay friends are human," said Char. "But I'm open-minded."

"Yeah. Well, hopefully, since we're already out of rangeen space, the rest of our voyage will be uncomplicated once the ship gets fixed."

"Sure," Char agreed.

Jay's face broke into a rueful grin. "Of course, we both know that's seldom, if ever, how our lives go."

The 'cator signaled that a transmission was incoming. As if they needed another complication, it was Jay's mom.

"Oh for the love of..." Char started, cutting herself off. "Really, Sindi? Now? Just ignore her, Jay."

Jay sighed. "Normally, I'd agree here. But it's been more than a week since we last chatted, and if I keep blowing her off, the next time we do chat will be far more unpleasant. Face it, this is as good a time as any to deal with her."

Char had had a largely good relationship with both of her parents, prior to their passing. They'd been married for nearly fifty years, and though they had not always understood Char, they'd supported her. Jay's family dynamic and childhood were so vastly different from Char's that it was nearly alien to her, in multiple ways.

Jay touched the appropriate control and said, "Hi, Mom."

"Hi honey," his mom's voice came across the 'cator via the cockpit speakers. "I hadn't heard from you in a while and wanted to reach out."

"Yeah," Jay said. "Char and I have been in motion a lot. We have visited a whole bunch of places that were totally new to us, in fact."

"That's nice," Jay's mom replied. Char would have expected her to ask Jay to elaborate on their travels, but instead, she said, "Did you read the article about your old friend, Gary?"

"No, Mom," Jay replied. "You know I don't read the news and haven't been in touch with Gary for over thirty years, right?"

"Well, still, I thought you might like to know he's now the leading attending physician at his hospital."

"Good for Gary," Jay said, his tone ever-so-slightly disinterested. Char saw him roll his eyes. "How are things with you and Bob?"

"We had lunch with our new friends, the rumel couple who moved in next door, Oxonor and Ptanga," she replied. "They treated us to Hyperspace Harold's. You'd like them; they've traveled a lot. We're good. How are you and Char doing?"

Char saw Jay contemplate his response before saying, "We're good, except the *Audacia* had a weird systems failure. But we're making arrangements now to get everything fixed."

"Oh, well then," Jay's mom's tone immediately made Char's hackles rise. "Then this is the perfect time to share. It's why I called now, really."

"What's up?" asked Jay. Char noted that he did a valiant job of not putting any ire into his tone.

"You remember my friend Joan? Well, it seems her brother's son is looking for a new manager for his company, and I couldn't help but think about you, Jay. With all your skills and how quickly you learn, you'd be perfect. The job is three systems over from us on Sona-Dhoop Prime."

"Is that so?" asked Jay.

Char was sure his mother had missed his displeased tone, as she continued, saying, "Oh yes. I told Joan that you'd be just perfect. All you'd need to do is work on a couple of certifications, which you'd have no problem getting, and she agrees the job would totally be yours. Also, the pay and benefits are so amazing. I really think it would be perfect."

Jay was silent for a moment, and Char knew he was completely taken aback. Char was doing her damndest to hold in her own ire over this. Why was his mother so hell-bent on Jay getting a conventional job? How did she not recognize that it was never the right fit for Jay?

"Mom," Jay began, "I said that I needed to repair the ship, not change careers. I don't know why you can't seem to understand that I'm perfectly happy with my life as it is. Starships have a lot of moving parts, and some of those parts break sometimes. You don't just walk away when that happens. Also, *Audacia* is my home. I feel no need whatsoever to settle down on one planet, let alone Sona-Dhoop Prime of all places."

"Oh, sweetie," Jay's mom began. "I can't possibly believe that Char is really content flying around to who-knows-where, moving random cargo and various passengers all the time. Doesn't she want you both to have a set place you call home, on a world where you see the sun every day?"

That was more than enough for Char. Before Jay could reply, she spoke up and said, "I'm right here, Ma."

"Oh, hello dear," Jay's mom said.

Before she could utter another word, Char said, "You seem to forget that buying the ship and traveling across the galaxy was *my* idea. Though it was something Jay had long wanted to do, I'm the one who decided that we should do it. Also, for the record, I'm not the fan of sunlight that you are. The stars are more my speed."

"I mean, you know," Jay's mom was sputtering. "You've changed careers and homes so often, I figured eventually you'd want to make a place, one place, home, and settle down. I can't imagine living on a ship with no place but that vessel to call home."

Jay sighed. "I'm well aware of that, Mom. But I can more than imagine it. I live it. And I love it. So does Char. She doesn't do something just because I want to do it. We're an equal partnership and always have been. Also, please remember that I might be your son, but I'm a fifty-year-old man who has a great life and the most amazing companion he could possibly have imagined. I'd really appreciate if you'd accept that Char and I are happy, and that you'd stop trying to find me different employment."

After a moment of silence, Jay's mom said, defensively, "You know that I just want what's best for you, Jay. And you, Char."

"Really?" Jay asked. "Then, if that's the case, how about you listen to what we're saying when we tell you we are happy, and stop questioning my life choices?"

"That's not a very nice thing to say, nor very fair," Jay's mom sounded hurt and indignant, but Char wondered if that was legit, or an act.

"You're absolutely right, Mom," Jay agreed. "Also, maybe you should heed that for yourself."

"What?"

Jay sighed. "Sorry, Mom, but I gotta run. I need to go see a man about a Phased Reality Drive. Love you."

Jay tapped the control to cut off the transmission, then fell back into his seat, releasing a deep breath. He sat like that for a moment, and Char was worried that his mother's call might have left him unable to cope.

Before Char could say anything, Jay shook his head, leaned forward, and said, "Right. You were right. I should have ignored her call."

Char reached out, and Jay took her hand. "You do your best, my love."

Quinn, who had been silently running diagnostics on the ship through it all, said in his deadpan, emotionless tone. "Yes, maybe now I understand why you goad your mother, after all."

Chapter 26 - We Don't Define Fair the Same Way

A few hours later, Jay and Char addressed Imaro and Kukeb.

"Here's the deal," Jay explained. "You should remain on the *Audacia*, for now. I think you are better off just staying here, until we've hired the mechanic to fix the Phased Reality Drive and we all need to get off the ship so they can work."

"We agree," Char began, "that it's probably better you two not be seen wandering around the bazaar."

"Especially as close to rangeen space as this is," Jay concluded.

"I have no problem with that," said Kukeb.

"Perfectly reasonable," agreed Imaro.

"Great," Jay said. "Pack what you need for a couple of nights, and we'll all go to a hostel once the plans to get repairs done are in place."

"We'll be back once we have someone hired, and we'll take it from there," Char said.

"And don't worry," Jay felt the need to add. "We're not going to sell you two out."

"I trust you," said Imaro. He was looking at Kukeb as he said that, and his companion nodded in agreement.

Jay and Char told Quinn to let them know if Imaro or Kukeb left the ship or if anyone paid their landing bay a visit.

Jay was not pleased with any of what was going on. He knew enough not to blame himself for the failure of the Phased Reality Drive. It wasn't something that could have been accounted for. Still, he was unhappy. Overall, the *Audacia* had been a mechanically sound starship.

When they'd decided to buy the ship, Jay had initially looked at used ships. Char, however, had felt that it would be best to get something new. First, starships tended not to lose all that much value when you bought them new. A well-maintained, two-year-old starship saved only a small account of EVIL-C over a new one. To save on a ship, you had to get something at least five years old.

Which was the second reason Char had insisted on buying new. Unless otherwise specified, all the components would be new and under warranty. Thus, you could expect at least five years without needing to spend money on more than standard maintenance and upkeep.

Unfortunately, the Phased Reality Drive wasn't under warranty, as the *Audacia* was just over five years old. It was possible, because of the nature of the failure, Jay might get some sort of partial reimbursement from the manufacturer. However, it would have to be done after the repair was complete, or else they'd be waiting a very long time. If it was even doable.

Jay trusted Char and her knack for finding excellent service people. Thus, they were now heading across the bazaar to visit the mechanic she'd determined was the best. He was a nairodna, with a reputation for being an ass, but otherwise being fair, efficient, and reputable. Unfortunately, he was also highly likely to overcharge them.

They left the landing bays and entered the main bazaar itself. Both Jay and Char paused.

The space was immense. It was divided into "streets", the outer walls lined with shops that were three or four stories tall. Each "street" was a mix of metal and composite "buildings" often made of repurposed bulk shipping containers, open stalls, or arrangements of shelving, brackets, and other assorted means to display goods.

The top of the space was open to the stars through a transparent metal or composite, probably thirty meters above them. A cacophony of sounds and smells reached Jay, some pleasant and some distressing. He could see a lot of different races represented. It was almost overwhelming.

"This is very people-y," remarked Char.

"I'd heard of the Rodna Bazaar Space Station," Jay said. "And I knew it was gargantuan. But this is really extra."

Char led them to the location of their chosen mechanic. It was on the outer wall, which made sense, as that probably allowed better access to the landing bays. The front of the shop was an open space with shelves full of small starship components. Moving inwards, there was a nairodna male standing at a workbench, tinkering with some sort of component or other Jay didn't recognize.

"Ah, humans," the nairodna greeted them. "Welcome to Basa's shop. How can I help you?"

"We understand you repair starships?" Jay queried.

"Basa repairs starships," he replied. "Basa can repair anything. What's your trouble?"

"We had an unexpected, and frankly impossible, total failure of our Phased Reality Drive. Safeties all kicked in and we were dropped out of hyperspace in the middle of nowhere. But there was no getting the drive functional again, and we had to hit the distress beacon and got a tow here."

"Oh, that's not good. What kind of drive?" Basa asked.

Char passed Jay her tablet. Jay saw she'd called up the specs for him. "It's a Blue Sun, Falcon M Class Phased Reality Drive."

"Point five or point two-five?" asked Basa.

"Point five," Jay replied.

"Oh," Basa remarked. "You have one of those."

"Yes," Jay agreed.

"Those are the ones with a one in two-hundred and fifty-thousand chance of total catastrophic cascade failure."

Jay sighed. "Yes, so it would seem. And that's the problem."

"Basa knows this issue. The problem has to do with a faulty part manufactured by some third-party that Blue Sun has never been able to identify."

"Yes, my 'bot and I got that far," agreed Jay.

Basa continued, saying, "That component, whatever it is, however it's flawed, can fail, even in hyperspace. Which should, of course, be impossible."

"Yes," agreed Jay through gritted teeth.

As though Jay hadn't replied, Basa continued with, "So, that failure leads to an improbable cascade failure of nearly every component of the drive, which then tends to cause a total shut down."

Jay sighed again. "Trust me, I'm all-too familiar with this. It's why we're here."

"Why," Char began to ask, "if this is a known issue, didn't Blue Sun issue a recall?"

Basa chuckled. "That's because when you sell a minimum of two million Phased Reality Drives per year, and only a total of eight might fail, you don't recall all of them."

"Okay, I get that," said Char. "Do you have one?"

"Yes," Basa agreed. "It's six thousand nairodna credits for the drive, plus labor."

Jay knew that was a twenty-five percent markup over the normal retail cost of a drive. He decided to apply logic and see how Basa responded, saying, "If this is a known problem that you are aware of, Basa, and we need to replace the drive entirely, you should be able to trade the faulty one you take from my ship back to Blue Sun."

"Your point being?" questioned Basa.

"You should only charge us the cost of labor."

Basa shook his head and opened a panel in the workstation to meet Jay and Char on their side, saying, "If we were closer to any Blue Sun manufacturing plants, you'd be right. However, we are a long way from the nearest. And even if I can trade out your busted drive for another new one, I pay fees to restock."

Jay looked at Char, and she shrugged. Jay looked at Basa and said, "Is that why you are charging so much more than standard for this Phased Reality Drive?"

"Come now, Basa isn't gouging you," the nairodna mechanic said. "Restocking fees are legit, plus the logistics of trading a busted Phased Reality Drive with Blue Sun takes a lot of time to navigate. And if you want to try to file a claim with Blue Sun because of this impossible failure, you need to exchange one for one. Basa knows he gives you the best deal in the bazaar."

"Fine," Jay replied. "Six thousand nairodna credits for a Blue Sun Point Five Falcon M Class Phased Reality Drive. How long will it take to get the job done and what will labor run us?"

"Basa will need a week, and I'll do the job for six thousand five hundred credits."

"Seriously? A week?" Jay demanded. "That's ludicrous."

"Not so," Basa said. "First, there is the disconnection and removal of the old drive, multiple diagnostics, then the seating and calibration of the new drive, and other potential challenges you might experience along the way."

"We can help expedite some of that," Jay said. "We have a robot who will assist you, who is not just well versed mechanically, but also fully familiar with all ship functions. He's the co-pilot. He can do much of the preliminary prep and diagnostics, which should mean you'll need way less time than a week."

"A robot assistant familiar with the ship is always appreciated. But Basa has jobs in my queue ahead of you. A week is the best that I can do."

Jay sighed, then said, "Let's clear a few things up here, okay? I'm no mechanic, but I'm well-versed on what it takes to do work on my ship. At most, the removal, replacement, and recalibration of a Phased Reality Drive should only take two days."

Basa grinned. "Are you offering to incentivize me to put you at the front of my queue?"

"Sure," said Jay. "You get to keep the drive you take off of my ship, which you can replace with Blue Sun, even though that might be troublesome. Or, you can repair it and sell it used."

Basa chuckled. "You know that the drive can't be repaired."

"Oh, I know that it can be, but only if you want to take months tearing it apart to locate the initial faulty component that caused the cascade failure, then replace it and any adjoining failed parts. At least, a mechanic with your degree of skill, Basa, would be able to, yes?"

"Well, yes, you are correct," Basa agreed.

"Here's what we're willing to offer," Char began, taking the tablet from Jay. "For the drive and labor total, getting the work done in two days, we'll give you eighty-five hundred nairodna credits, and you get to keep the broken drive you replace."

"Thirty-five hundred for labor?" scoffed Basa. "No. Twelve thousand credits total, and the broken drive, yes."

"No," Jay said. "That's insane, and you know it. You might be the best mechanic on the Rodna Bazaar Space Station, but not the only one. No matter what, you get the broken drive to trade out or fix. Let's get more reasonable here. Nine thousand nairodna credits."

"Tell you what, human. Basa likes your moxie. Eleven thousand."

"Ninety-five hundred," Jay countered.

"Basa sees that you know how this is done. Ten thousand."

"Ten thousand," Jay agreed. "We pay you half now, and you put it in writing, guaranteeing two days to complete repairs, or we take away a thousand credits every day you run longer than that and let it be known across the MESS-work that you're not good for your word."

The nairodna mechanic chuckled. "Yes, Basa does like your moxie. How about you trust Basa, pay it all now, and Basa will start repairs tomorrow morning?"

"Given the hour, that's fair," agreed Jay. "Except we pay half now, after you sign the agreement, and the rest once our robot confirms installation is complete and the new Phased Reality Drive is in working order."

"Basa understands your caution, but that's hardly fair. You worry Basa won't do the work. But what if you just leave and stiff Basa?"

Jay snorted. "Leave and go where, and how? My ship hasn't got a functional Phased Reality Drive, and we can't get anywhere without one. So, do we have a deal?"

Jay extended his hand as Char held up the tablet. Basa took his hand saying, "Yes, we have a deal. Basa will repair your ship."

Chapter 27 – And Now Yet Another Word from Your Sponsor

Hi there. This is your friendly neighborhood author once again. I thought this would be a really good place to insert some potentially very useful information about some of the background aspects of Jay and Char's era that I've touched on but haven't necessarily explained.

I've used several acronyms and made references to things without providing an explanation. It occurred to me that, as we've just been witness to a lot of trade and commerce, I should detail some bits.

Trade is of vital importance to everyone. The main reasons for any race to leave the cradle of their civilization are usually twofold. First, to seek out others and confirm if you are or aren't alone. Second, to learn what they have that you don't – and what you have that they don't – and get to trading.

In a purely barter system, this is easy. In time, and when the valuation of thing 'X' is greater or lesser than thing 'Y', you need money.

Imagine if the American dollar, Euro, Yen, Peso, and the like, weren't just the product of different nations and banks, but whole other races that are not from your planet. How do you equalize things? What's more, who is responsible for making that happen?

Somewhere along the way, and nobody can really remember when or where, a committee of members of the various spacefaring races – now realizing they were not alone and wanting to trade things with one another – was formed. They'd come to the realization that establishing protocols and processes that would benefit everyone was probably a really good idea.

Just establishing these things would be hard enough. Without oversight and maintenance, it would be easy for disputes, disagreements, and misunderstandings great and small to wreck everything. Given the premise that the second most desirable reason for a race to leave its cradle is to establish trade, everyone wanted to avoid that. For the record, this would involve everyone who found their way out of their own solar system, if they desired trade. And all of them did.

So, a committee of rotating representatives from participating races across the galaxy – which, again, is all the races, since they all desire to trade with each other – formed the Organization for Verification of Extraplanetary Rules and Logistics for Overall Referential Definitions (OVERLORD).

OVERLORD would establish numerous universal protocols and practices. Yes, there were pockets of resistance to this, usually in the name of maintaining sovereignty or racial/species purity, and the like. This, however, always collapsed when trade got underway and the promise of new expansive resources was realized.

OVERLORD and its rotating committee maintains oversight of many accepted galactic standards that make interaction, trade, and other matters happen with far greater ease. This includes such things as the Consistent Galactic Time-Code. Like Greenwich Mean Time, this is how spaceships and space stations establish a similar rotational clock for the purpose of keeping track of hours, days, weeks, and so on, while in the void.

OVERLORD also sets the standards that allow for intergalactic communications and entertainment. This includes the interplanetary version of the World Wide Web. I guess you could call it the Galaxy Wide Web. This is the Multimedia Establishment Synchronized Systems network (MESS-work). Via the MESS-work, there is the equivalent of social media, called the communal hypermedia (since it can travel faster-than-light). The MESS-work is part of how communications are nearly instantaneous, despite mind-boggling distances of many, many, many parsecs.

Video and audio transmissions of news and entertainment are broadcast via the Interplanetary Transmission Entanglement Mediascape (ITEM). The other name for ITEM is the 'tangle. That's where the Rangeen Kingdom News Network, Channel VX3410.756Q on the Interplanetary Transmission Entanglement Mediascape can be accessed alongside tens of thousands of others.

With apologies, I can't fully explain the math or science behind the workings of the MESS-work or ITEM. That's beyond the scope of this book, likely would be boring and uninteresting to most, and would be an utterly unnecessary digression.

That written, let's address the most confusing element that OVERLORD oversees. Money.

Money is issued by planets, governments, corporations, and the like. Take every type of currency you can think of, then add in Monopoly money, Disney money, cryptocurrencies, seashells, and anything else. Now imagine that every single type of currency is accepted and valued somewhere by somebody. They might be a solar system, a mining conglomerate, Google, take your pick.

Let's say you want to buy a pair of shoes. They are $50 American dollars. Rather than being able to work with a common exchange, like Euros to American dollars, you normally deal in seashells. How in the hell do you find and create the equivalency from seashells to American dollars?

Enter the Enigmatic Valuation Institute of Leveraged Currency (EVILC, usually just called EVIL). Under the auspices of OVERLORD, they've created an exchange that allows for one-to-one commerce transactions. That's why, if you recall chapter 2, Jay was dealing with the bullshit of that buyer trying to cheat him by using EVILC to swap rumel chits for kukacoin.

Allow me to explain that a bit more clearly. Imagine you're on a station, platform, or moon that doesn't use a form of currency that you have. Let's say, to keep this a bit simpler, that you have rumel chits and they deal in kukacoin. Since this place is a hub of commerce frequented by multiple races - each with different money - rather than having to use elaborate conversion tables or sophisticated AI to handle exchange rates, the rumel chits and kukacoins, as EVILC, are one in the same. Easy to track, and you're not frequently being forced to swap currency and do regular exchanges as you travel.

While, overall, this is a great system and simple, it's imperfect. It's fine in space, where dealing in no specific denomination benefits everyone, like on platforms, stations, and many moons, where there's no set currency type. However, this can be troublesome when one thousand rumel chits – which will buy you a full meal on any rumel world – translates to one thousand kijivu dollars – which will buy you a cup of cofveina (a drink close to, but not exactly coffee with twice the caffeine per cup) on any kijivu world.

For travelers like Jay and Char, this is a sometimes annoying but relatively minor nuisance and inconvenience. It's only a problem if you're stranded on a rumel world with a pocket full of kijivu dollars and not much of a taste for cofveina. And now you know.

I hope this hasn't thrown you too far off and helps you feel less lost when I drop common acronyms on you.

Thank you for reading. Now, back to our story.

Chapter 28 – This Might Complicate Things

Upon returning to the ship, Jay and Char packed their things for two nights at a hostel.

The trouble with the Rodna Bazaar was that, as a trading outpost, there were no hotels or similar accommodations. Most crews visiting the bazaar would stay aboard their ships. The only reasons they'd not stay on their ship were if they were transferring from one ship to another and had an overnight layover, needed repairs that it was best they leave the ship while they were being made, or were hitchhiking or otherwise errantly traveling across space.

Hostels were far more utilitarian than hotels. They were less about providing a base of operations and more about providing somewhere you could sleep. The most basic hostels were single and double bunks you could rent, stacked one atop another, with communal restrooms and large common spaces, if any. Others were closer to hotels and had fancier accommodations but with more of a bare-bones approach, like being pre-fab constructs, former shipping containers, and the like.

That was what Char had located for them. She'd found a hostel where they had adjoining rooms that shared a restroom and a common room. Jay paid for the room for two nights, in advance, through the business account he'd established – *Audacia* Transport – rather than in his or Char's name.

There were a couple of reasons they chose that hostel. First, because booking adjoining rooms would protect the identity of Imaro and Kukeb. Secondly, Char had explained that several of the other hostels on the station with any modicum of privacy were attached to brothels, casinos, and other secondary establishments. All of which, she had concluded – and Jay agreed – were more likely to attract crowds the rangeen wanted to avoid.

Jay made certain that Quinn was set. He had several jobs, including guarding the ship, assisting Basa with the replacement of the Phased Reality Drive, and making certain Basa didn't cheat them or break something on the ship that might then also need replacing. Robots like Quinn were better at those jobs because, even with their limited AI personality, they were considered a neutral party.

Finally, with everything set, Jay led Char, Imaro, and Kukeb off the *Audacia*. They made their way smartly across the landing bay. The challenge was trying to avoid being seen while not looking like trying to avoid being seen.

They paused from time to time to allow groups to pass, and Jay was careful to avoid some of the busier streets and avenues. He and Char had carefully mapped their way from the landing bay to the hostel before leaving the ship. There would be no way, given where the hostel was in relation to where the ship was, to completely avoid people.

Jay was no expert, but he never got the impression of anyone paying them much mind. The four of them reached the hostel without incident. It was a group of converted shipping containers around a central "courtyard" featuring a few vendors selling food and trinkets. At the entrance was the nairodna who ran it. He talked to Char, and then they got the codes for their 'cators to access the rooms.

The space they'd rented at the hostel was a large former container. When the door on the side opposite the courtyard opened, they entered a common room featuring a couple of couches. Across from the entrance was the kitchen and a door to the restroom. Jay presumed the placement of these spaces corresponded with water access under the courtyard.

To the left and right were the bedrooms. Jay and Char went right. The room featured a space for their suitcase, a double bed, and a nightstand. Not very exciting but adequate for a couple of nights' sleep.

There wasn't much more involved in them getting settled in. It was "morning" local time – which, fortunately, was Consistent Galactic Time-Code – and Basa should be arriving at the *Audacia* shortly. Quinn would inform them when he did.

Jay looked to Char and said, "Shall we go check on our passengers?"

"Let's do that," Char agreed.

They returned to the common area and found the two rangeen already there.

"It's amazing," Kukeb started, "how different things are on a space station versus a planet. And yet, the open space is almost treated like a city. Avenues, buildings, it's quite a strange combination. I wonder if the need to create this kind of space is universal among sentients? I've not traveled much, but how common is the Rodna Bazaar?"

"Well," Char replied, "truth is, the Rodna Bazaar is unique. Most of the other stations I've been on are less haphazard and more intentionally constructed. Spaces are erected and rented out, rather than having been built, removed, replaced, or dragged such as we've seen here."

Jay sat on the couch across from the rangeen. "Before we talk more about mine and Char's travels, I did ask that, as a condition of not giving you away, you finish the conversation we'd started en route to the bazaar."

Imaro and Kukeb exchanged a look. Kukeb had a look in his eye that Jay would call pleading if he didn't know any better. Imaro, looking at Kukeb, said, "They will be far more willing to help us if they know everything."

Kukeb nodded at Imaro.

Looking towards Jay and Char, Imaro said, "I thoroughly appreciate that, even after learning who I am, and that it could be problematic, you are still protecting me, us. Keeping us with you and bringing us here with you while the ship gets fixed means a lot."

"Yes," Kukeb agreed. "It really does. We cannot thank you enough!"

As Jay nodded, he said, "You're welcome."

"Now then," began Char, "you were explaining to us how your father is forcing you to marry against your will. Also, you're in love with Kukeb here and that's not something he'd abide. The immediacy of this, you stated, is being motivated and influenced by something he's setting into motion that will potentially increase the wealth and influence of the rangeen people overall. Is that correct?"

"Yes," agreed Imaro.

"What is it?" asked Char.

Imaro leaned back into the couch, closing his eyes a moment. Then he said, "You're aware that the rangeen have a hand in the production of every single 'cator used in the entire galaxy by every race, because of the quantum-microcircuitry utilizing the resource unique to our sector with its distinctive temporal properties?"

"Yes, we are," replied Char.

"Good," said Imaro. "Let me illuminate some further history and information about that resource. It's believed that this singular resource is only found in rangeen space. That's been part of what allowed the rangeen royalty, my family – who's the majority shareholder in everything having to do with the resource – to become wealthy and powerful."

"Admittedly," Char said, "very little is known about how your government works. It's not a surprise that your family is connected so directly to commerce."

"In so many ways," remarked Kukeb.

"Well," Imaro began again, "research has been ongoing to see if the unique temporal properties of the resource might be applicable to more than just communications and 'cator systems. Between the roptera and rangeen engineers and scientists, we have hope for some wider-spread applications. Unsurprisingly, that would mean more opportunities to increase the wealth and power of the rangeen people, but more importantly – to his mind – my father, the king."

"Before you comment," Kukeb interrupted. "Imaro, as the son of the king and his heir, is hugely wealthy, and would be more so from this. However, wealth has never driven Imaro. For King Nobiri, it's his everything."

"That's an understatement," added Imaro. "In fact, it's truly an obsession for him. He's always cared most about his wealth and power over all else, including family. Whatever it takes, no matter how underhanded or unethical, he will do almost anything to hold and increase it. And that's the problem."

He arose and began to pace, saying, "According to recent reports, the soetub and sutac have discovered the resource – previously only found in rangeen space – in parts of *their* space. This would mean it's not a rangeen-only resource. The exclusivity would end, the market could become flooded, and/or someone else would have access to the resource – the raw resource – beyond rangeen control to potentially expand its use. Someone not rangeen might come up with new ways to expand their wealth, power, and influence from it before the rangeen might. It could be potentially devastating."

Jay asked, "Realistically, how finite is the resource, even in your territories?"

"Truly? It's not so rare," admitted Imaro. "Not at all. There is an entire moon made of the resource. Even if the need for it expanded exponentially, in all probability, it would be available for a million years or more."

"The issue is not how finite and rare it is," said Kukeb. "The issue is that the resource being available in soetub and sutac space means the exclusivity is gone. Now, a once-protected resource loses its value as a rare commodity. Competition emerges. And competition means less profit and less power."

"That's where my father's obsession becomes dangerous," stated Imaro.

"Wait," Jay said. "Does that mean the king is planning an invasion of one or both territories?"

"No," Imaro said. "The rangeen only have the Royal Enforcers. They have a small fleet, but nothing sufficient for an invasion or attack. They're largely concerned with policing matters within and very near to rangeen space. What my father plans, instead, is to create a situation that will start a war between the soetub, sutac, and humans, too."

Jay and Char exchanged a look. Jay could see his concern mirrored in Char's eyes. "How would he do that?" she asked before Jay could pose the question.

Imaro looked sheepish. Jay wasn't entirely sure how embarrassment looked on a rangeen, but he guessed that was the expression Imaro was wearing. "As mentioned before, you know that the rangeen have a hand in creating every single 'cator in the known galaxy. A small part of that technology includes an undetectable transmission at a frequency nobody other than the rangeen and roptera would detect. What it does is record everything that goes through every 'cator."

"Everything?" asked Char.

Imaro looked even more embarrassed now. "Yes. All the messages, texts, images, voice transmissions. All of it. There is a database somewhere in rangeen space – even I don't know where – that stores and catalogs all of it. Even with all the privacy settings on the various 'cators out there, this algorithm code digs out, records, and shares them to our database."

"Wow," Jay breathed. "I once watched, when I was having trouble sleeping one night cycle long ago, a program on the ITEM this notorious conspiracy theorist put on. They claimed that the rangeen embedded secret coding in the tech they manufactured for every 'cator to spy on everyone. They even faced a panel of skeptics and made some totally plausible, but highly suspect and circumstantial, arguments in favor of his theory. But all the experts claimed that there was no way that could be possible, given the scale of the number of 'cators out there, coupled with how many beings use them, and the almost unimaginable parsecs of distance involved."

"Oh yes," Kukeb said. "I'm familiar with that. It caused a stir in the rangeen bureaucracy and diplomatic corps. Did you know, Captain, that the proponent of that theory of which you speak rather mysteriously died?"

"Yes, I did," Jay said. "It was dismissed as coincidence."

"Well, it was neither a mysterious nor coincidental matter," remarked Kukeb. Jay could think of no cogent response to that.

"Imaro," Char began, "let me make sure I'm perfectly clear about this. What you're saying is that your father is planning to use secret data he should not have – that, really, nobody should have – to manipulate the soetub, sutac, and humans into going to war with one another?"

"Yes," Imaro confirmed.

"And then what?" asked Char. Jay could see that she was becoming tense.

Imaro dropped back onto the couch, saying, "With everyone distracted, fighting against one another, the rangeen should be able to go into their systems and take the resources from the soetub and sutac. And that will preserve the source of the rangeen's and my family's wealth and power."

Char arose abruptly. "That's what King Nobiri is doing? He's planning to create chaos among other races just so he can rob them of a resource?"

"I mean, yes?" replied Imaro in a questioning tone.

Char turned to him, and Jay saw her angrier than he had in a long, long time, and never towards him. Char said, "Does your father have the slightest idea how dangerous this notion is? Does he have the slightest inkling of where this could lead? Do you?"

"I...I don't know," said Imaro. "What... What are you on about, Char?"

"Starting a war between soetub, sutac, and humans won't just cause an easy distraction to take advantage of," Char said in a cold, dark, unrelenting tone. "It will lead to galactic interplanetary warfare and the collapse of the entire galactic economy."

Chapter 29 – It's Worse Than You Think

Char couldn't decide if she was flabbergasted, flummoxed, enraged, terrified, or some combination of them all. That the rangeen king had such a ludicrous and dangerous plan in mind was unbelievable to her.

She had stalked away from the trio on the couches, trying to contain her wildly emotional response. If she didn't, she'd be unable to explain to the rangeen what they needed to be aware of.

Jay knew her well enough to let her pace, and she'd noticed him silencing Imaro and Kukeb when they'd attempted to ask her what she was talking about.

Gaining clarity was necessary because she needed Imaro to recognize and understand the significance of the danger his father's plan posed. It was something she understood far too well, thanks in part to her work and being a longtime student of history.

Finally getting control over her emotional reaction, Char moved back towards the couches. As she did, she said, "Imaro? What do you and your people know about interplanetary politics?"

Imaro and Kukeb exchanged a look. Then, Imaro faced Char and said, "We know the basics. The rangeen don't live in a bubble, per se, and we're well aware of OVERLORD, the MESS-work, ITEM, and the like."

Kukeb added, "Beyond that, however, the rangeen people tend to stay away from interspecies and interplanetary politics. We deal almost exclusively through matters with OVERLORD concerning trade, EVIL, and such."

"That's bad," Char said without adding the many expletives she wanted to.

"Why?" asked Imaro.

Char started to pace. "Why? Because getting the soetub, sutac, and humans to go to war with one another won't stay confined to those three races alone. It'll spread way, way beyond that. In very little time, it'll spread like an exploding star out of control, consuming everything in its path."

"What?" asked Kukeb as Imaro almost simultaneously asked, "How can that be?"

Jay saved Char from having to calm herself again to explain coherently by replying, "Why do you think it's been so long since there were any real conflicts between various races? Because a war will draw in double or triple the number of races due to alliances, shared territories, mutual defense pacts, and the like. For example, the rumel and kijivu will almost certainly join humans, which means the rest of their allies will feel obligated and will also get involved."

Char was able to join the thought and said, "The sutac and soetub have numerous alliances as well. Their allies, like the allies of the humans, will come in to fight to aid them."

"And then," Jay started, "at least three warrior races, such as the ajerari, gorlek, and naxul – who need little to no excuse to get involved in a fight – will jump into the fray and kill and destroy without pause, making the whole thing that much messier."

Char felt a sense of dread worse than anything she'd ever experienced before, concluding with, "Before long, the entire galaxy will be at war without even knowing why."

"That... I mean, that has to be the worst-case scenario," said Kukeb softly.

"No," Char said sternly. "You're not getting it. That's almost certainly the outcome."

"But the galaxy hasn't been conflict-free," pleaded Kukeb.

"Maybe so," Jay said. "There's no question that there are any number of skirmishes, disputes, disagreements, and some fights between various races – and within different groups of various races – with regularity. Also, the warrior races sometimes contend with a group, a world, another species, or other warrior race to stay sharp or some such. But there hasn't been a full-on war between any two or more races in centuries. That's because one of the big deterrents to outright war has been the alliances everyone has, and the knowledge that if a real war starts, they'll drag others in."

"What's more," Char added, "for the most part, the skirmishes have been either exclusively military, or involved terrorists, marauders, pirates, or others who may have been civilians but were still troublemakers. Full-on war tends to involve everyone, no matter who they are."

"Imaro, this is important," Jay said, leaning towards the rangeen prince. "Is your father, the king, planning to start a war or just get those three races into a skirmish with one another?"

"Oh, no," Imaro said, sounding horribly lost. "War. That's the word he used. I also remember, more than once, my father remarking that there hasn't been a true war in far too long."

"This is all supposition," said Kukeb. "It's the worst possible outcome and not certain. You're just being paranoid. I mean, you must be exaggerating. How bad could it really get?"

Char was ready to get in the rangeen's face and scream at him, but Jay, with more calm, got there first and said, "Are you serious? This isn't a worst-case scenario we're presenting you here. This is how a real war will go down. If a real war breaks out, billions, if not trillions, of lives will be in danger. I can't state enough just how an all-out war would be very, very bad."

"It's even worse than that," said Char, doing her best to remain calm.

"How?" asked Imaro.

Char replied, "Because such a war would collapse the galactic economy. War would disrupt commerce on all sorts of levels, manufacturing across many races would turn to wartime goods, and a whole lot of things we all take for granted would crash."

"Won't OVERLORD intervene?" asked Kukeb.

"No," Char said. "Because OVERLORD only provides a framework, administration, and oversight. That won't matter when war overtakes all reason. So not only will King Nobiri not increase his wealth and power, but likely, he will find it won't be long before he's drawn into the war in some way, too."

There was silence for a time. Char could feel her heart pounding. The ignorance of Imaro, Kukeb, and King Nobiri sickened her. She had preferred to believe that such a level of willful, arrogant ignorance was largely a thing of the past. Clearly, that was not the case.

Finally, as if coming out of a stupor, Imaro said, "I... I had no idea the ramifications of this. I didn't think something so horrific could happen."

Jay said, "Kukeb stated that you were to espouse this woman your father chose for you before the end of the month. This month, as in less than thirty days from now, right?"

"Yes," replied Imaro.

Jay arose. "Then you have to do something to stop him, and stop this lest it all comes crashing down."

Imaro wore a very sad and humorless smile as he said, "Once my father gets an idea in his head and sets things in motion, he tends to be unstoppable."

"You're his son," said Char. "The heir to the throne, right? Can't you stop him?"

Imaro shook his head. "Not likely. The only thing I can think of, and it's a long-shot, would be for me to accede to my father's demands and marry the girl to get into his good graces. But I ran away to avoid that. Yet, perhaps if I were to go back, apologize, play meek, that might open some way for me to get access to his advisors or find some way to force him to yield or even abdicate. But I've no idea how that could be done."

"At the least, can you delay him, try to reason with him, or do anything to disrupt his plan if you return?" questioned Char.

"Perhaps," Imaro nearly whispered.

"Well then," Jay said. "Now that we know this, and how much danger everyone is in, once the *Audacia* is repaired, can we take you and Kukeb back to rangeen space and Rangeenavelt?"

"No!" cried Kukeb, leaping off the couch. Though Char half expected the rangeen to attack her or Jay, instead, he turned to Imaro and cried out, "No! We've evaded them all this time! We've come so far! If we go back, we can't be together, and your father might banish me, or worse. Imaro, please, let's just slip away and leave this all behind."

Imaro arose and placed his hands on his partner's cheeks. "Kukeb, my love, you mean the universe to me. But knowing what we now know, we have to go back. This is not just about the rangeen, my father, an unwanted arranged marriage, or other petty things. There are too many innocent lives at stake if my father carries out his plan. And you know that he will."

Char watched as Kukeb started crying. Imaro took him into his arms, allowing Kukeb to weep. Char looked to Jay and saw the resolve in his eyes.

After a few moments, Kukeb leaned away from Imaro. Though still lightly sobbing, he said, "It's just not fair. But... But I know we have to do it. I know."

Jay caught Char's eye, an unspoken question there. She knew what her spouse was thinking, and she nodded ever so slightly, imperceptible to all save Jay.

Jay stepped up close to Imaro and Kukeb. "You're not alone. Char and I will help you in any way that we can."

Chapter 30 – How To Escape Notice Without Escaping Notice

Jay was not used to feeling anxious. A few times in his life, he'd experienced it. Asking Char to marry him. Waiting for the results after completing flight certification training. Finding and buying *Audacia*. Then, getting the first client and completing the first transport run.

Learning the truth of Imaro's father's plan and knowing how disastrous it would be if he executed it was one thing. Awaiting the completion of repairs on *Audacia* was another. To top all that off, there was also keeping Imaro and Kukeb safe, so that they could return them to Rangeenavelt and maybe stop King Nobiri before he did unimaginable harm.

Jay hoped that the two rangeen had not drawn attention to themselves in some way. Granted, during the two days they had been at the hostel, neither had left it. Yet he still was concerned, and it added to the anxiousness he felt.

He was sitting beside Char in the common room on one of the couches, reading a book on his tablet. The rangeen were in their room.

The 'cator alerted him to a signal. "Hi, Quinn," he said on accepting it.

"Captain," Quinn said. "Basa has finished replacing the Phased Reality Drive. I have run full diagnostics, as well as a static test on the new drive, and it is operating within expected parameters. Or, in less technical terms, it works as it should."

"Thank you, Quinn," Jay said, ignoring the barb. Sometimes he found Quinn's sarcasm entertaining. This was not one of those times. "Please request launch clearance so we can go as soon as we get back aboard the ship. You have authorization to pay any fees."

"I will take care of that," the robot replied. "See you soon."

The transmission ended.

Jay looked at Char. "We're packed. Would you please let our companions know it's time to go while I pay Basa?"

Char set down her tablet. As she stood up, she said, "Yes. Love you."

"Love you, too."

Jay moved towards his and Char's sleeping room. He entered the code into the 'cator to reach Basa.

"Yeah," the mechanic replied when Jay's transmission connected.

"My robot tells me you finished my ship," Jay said.

"Yeah, Basa got it done, with time to spare," the mechanic replied smugly.

Jay didn't care at this point. He tapped the screen of his 'cator. "Thank you, Basa. I'll write a glowing review when I have more time. For now, I'm transferring the balance of what I owe you."

There was a moment of silence while Jay presumed Basa was checking his 'cator. Then, the mechanic replied, "And Basa has been paid. Pleasure doing business with you, Captain."

"Thank you," Jay said. He ended the transmission as Char entered the room.

"All set?" she asked.

"Yes," Jay replied.

He and Char had each brought a duffel, which they'd packed after waking that morning. As she took up hers, Jay slung his over his shoulder.

"We're all paid up," Char informed him. "And I transmitted from the company account that we're heading out in the next hour."

"Good thinking," Jay said. "Ready?"

"Let's go."

As they entered the common room, Jay saw that Imaro and Kukeb were there with their things. Kukeb still looked despondent.

"Hey," Char said, taking a step towards the rangeen. "I understand that this is not at all what you wanted. Going back to Rangeenavelt is what you've been avoiding. You must understand, Kukeb, this really is important. If King Nobiri carries out his plan, the galaxy is in deep shit."

"Yes," Kukeb said, resignation practically oozing from his tone. "I just... I just wanted to be with Imaro."

"I know," Char said, putting a hand on Kukeb's shoulder. "This really is for the greater good. But you know what? There must be a way, through all of this, that you and Imaro can remain together."

"We'll do whatever we can to help," added Jay. He had no idea what that could possibly be, but he meant it.

Kukeb sighed dramatically. Then he looked up at Jay and Char and said, "Thank you."

"Well," Imaro said. "I guess we'd better be going, then."

"Remember to pull up your hoods before we step outside," Char reminded them. To help blend in, Jay and Char wore hooded coats, too.

The four of them departed from the hostel. It was late morning, local station time, but they did the best they could to avoid notice as they threaded through the streets, between booths, stalls, and makeshift buildings. They were more or less reversing the route they'd taken to get there from the ship two days prior.

Jay, taking pains to glance around them as they moved, noticed a couple of people more than once. He shifted the group to a slightly different route, and still caught sight of them.

"Damn," he said through gritted teeth. "We're being followed."

"What?" squeaked Kukeb.

"Shh!" Char hissed. She had her tablet in hand and was calling up a map of the internal layout of the Rodna Bazaar. A line appeared, leading from where they were to the ship. She pointed, saying, "It's a more circuitous way around, but these couple of switchbacks will hopefully lose anyone trying to follow."

"Let's keep going," Jay urged. "Imaro, Kukeb, act casual. And don't run, people."

They shifted from one "avenue" to another, doubled back a couple of times, and made their way out of the main market area. Once or twice, Jay still caught sight of someone he was certain was following them, but after a quick check on Char's Rodna Bazaar station map, he'd change their direction.

They had reached a staging area just outside some of the docking bays. The path toward the *Audacia* lay before them, but as Jay started that way, a gang of seven people merged together to block them.

Jay could feel Char tense at his side, and he heard either Kukeb or Imaro take in a sharp, hissing breath. He thought about turning, but there was nowhere to go. Then, he recognized a member of the gang and knew it was their leader.

That was because Jay had met him before. "Jergo Ceolhe," he called.

"Ah, if it isn't Jay Baylin and his lovely bride, Char Danella," Jergo said almost pleasantly.

Jergo was a rumel who might or might not have been one of this brother-in-law Exeter's cousins. Or maybe he was a second cousin? Or the son of a third spouse, twice removed, of an uncle? Jay always got confused by Exeter's absolutely enormous family. Despite the danger, Jay found himself remembering how both he and his father had asked for a diagram from Essie of her then-soon-to-be-spouse's family to help understand who everyone was.

Jergo was a bounty hunter by trade. He had a crew of three humans and three rumel, all holding guns, whom Jay knew Exeter considered "brutes". Maybe, just maybe, this would leave room for negotiation.

"So," Jay started, doing his best to be casual and nonchalant, "what brings you and your crew to nairodna space?"

"We made our way here to deliver a bounty to the authorities on Rodna Onu," Jergo replied. "It was an especially challenging quarry, so I brought everyone to Rodna Bazaar to treat them to some well-deserved fun."

"Ah, a visit to the brothels," Jay said. He recalled that when not bounty hunting, Jergo's favorite pastime was sex.

"Oh yeah," Jergo remarked lewdly. "Nairodna women are particularly freaky, ya know."

"No kidding," Jay said. "I'll have to remember that. So, this is a surprise. Not sure why you all are here, now. Is there something I can do for you?"

"Yeah," Jergo said. "You and Char can step aside and let me and my boys, here, see if one of these rangeen accompanying you is the lost prince."

"What lost prince?" asked Jay.

One of Jergo's thugs held out a device, and a holographic projection of Imaro appeared. Jay glanced back at the hooded rangeen, knowing that while it was clear what race he was, his face would not be visible.

"No idea who that guy is," Jay said. "These two are just passengers we're taking to their preferred destination. And, no offense, but we're running late and need to get back to the ship."

"You can go. After they drop their hoods and we get a look at them," stated Jergo, pointing.

"That's rude," said Char. "They have an unusual skin condition they're embarrassed by, so they stay hooded for that reason. Move along, Jergo, we've places to go."

"Ah, Char, you're such a sweet talker," Jergo chided. "But, no. They take down their hoods, or we get closer and take them down for them."

"No," Jay said. "Go on, go look elsewhere for bounties and leave us be."

Jergo clicked the safety off his pistol, and it made a low humming, hissing noise as it became active.

Jay felt his pulse quicken but didn't let it show. "You'll draw a lot of attention if you start shooting, don't you think?"

Jergo smirked. "Bounty is only good if we bring 'em in alive. So we're just gonna stun ya. I'll pay the fine if it comes to that. You gonna be smart here, Baylin?"

Jay removed the cylinder from his belt and flicked it. The 'lectro-bo staff extended to its full one-point-eight-two meters total length. With a slight shake, Jay activated the stun capability of the weapon.

"Is that all you got?" asked Jergo, snickering.

"Since we both know stun is a clumsier mechanism of your gun than kill, my staff isn't so ridiculous."

Jay knew that it was, in fact, fairly ridiculous. Yet it had the effect he'd desired and was giving Jergo pause. That provided more time for him or his companions to work out an escape.

"Are you kidding me?" Kukeb half-hissed, half-squeaked. "Why in the fires of the stars don't you have a gun?"

Without turning to look at Kukeb, Jay said, "I don't like guns. I'm not a fan of largely lethal weapons. My 'lectro-bo staff is nonlethal."

"At least, when used to stun," added Char. "I'm not a fan of guns, either."

"Jay, Char, let's be reasonable here," Jergo said in a provocative tone. "I know you know how to use that thing, Jay. But we've seven guns to one staff. Surrender your rangeen companions and we can avoid this turning unpleasant or messy."

Before Jay could say anything more, he heard a new group coming up from behind them. From the looks on the faces of Jergo's brutes, they had their attention, too. Turning, Jay saw a group of fourteen similarly uniformed rangeen.

"Prince Imaro," a rangeen in a slightly different, slightly more official-looking uniform addressed them. Jay guessed he was an officer. The rangeen officer went on to say, "We've found you. And don't try to pretend you're not Prince Imaro Iwoto, Your Highness. We've been watching for you and have matched your gait and body profile to a ninety-eight percent probability. So, you can surrender and come with us the easy way or resist and come with us the hard way."

Imaro reached up and lowered his hood. Jay heard Jergo hiss, "I knew it!"

Imaro addressed the rangeen officer. "Sorry, Captain, but no. We will not be joining you either way."

The rangeen soldiers produced stun batons, and with a click, hiss, and sensation of electrification and a whiff of ozone, they activated them. The rangeen officer said, "This is your last chance, Your Highness."

"Wait one damned minute," said Jergo loudly. "Hey, my crew and I found your prince, here, first. You paying out on the bounty?"

"I beg your pardon?" the rangeen officer questioned haughtily. "We found him without your aid, bounty hunter. There will be no bounty paid."

"Is that so?" demanded Jergo. "Because if that's how you're gonna be, you won't be taking him. We will be."

"We are rangeen Royal Enforcers," stated the rangeen officer. Jay could almost see the stick up his ass become extra rigid. "He is the rangeen prince, and we have the authority here."

"No, you don't," said Jergo. "This is the Rodna Bazaar space station in nairodna space. You have no authority here."

"We have the legit claim to take our prince home, as the enforcement agency of rangeen space," stated the officer.

"And I am a licensed bounty hunter in pursuit of an OVERLORD-sanctioned bounty," said Jergo. "So, my claim is just as legit, if not moreso, than yours."

"We are rangeen Royal Enforcers. Ours is the recognized authority."

"In rangeen space, absolutely. Here? No. My license makes my authority in nairodna space greater than yours."

"You seriously believe..." the rangeen officer barked, but Jay tuned the rest out. He noticed that the Royal Enforcers and Jergo's brutes had turned all their attention to each other. As their argument continued, all eyes were on the bounty hunter and the officer.

Char was still beside him. Jay let go of his 'lectro-bo staff with his right hand and tapped Char's hand. When he caught her eye, he ever so slightly gestured towards the landing bay. She gave an almost imperceptible nod.

Char reached back to touch Imaro or Kukeb and get their attention. Though he was not paying attention to it, the argument between the bounty hunter and rangeen officer continued, gaining in pitch. Char tapped the top of Jay's hand to let him know Imaro and Kukeb were with them.

Slowly, cautiously, Jay took a step away from the bounty hunter's crew and the rangeen Royal Enforcers. Char, Imaro, and Kukeb also began to move slowly away from the two arguing parties. At this point, Jergo and the rangeen officer were nearly shouting at one another, and the tension between the parties was almost palpable.

It would take the slightest spark to get them fighting. Jay deactivated the electrified stun capability of his staff. With care, he shifted his weight and stance and chose his target.

Jay placed the staff at the back of a member of Jergo's brutes and shoved him into a pair of rangeen soldiers across from him.

Jergo and the officer's shouting match was joined by a cacophony of shouts, cries, and curses as the rangeen Royal Enforcers and Jergo's brutes began to shove, punch, and fight one another.

Jay and his companions were out of the fray. Turning, Jay shook his 'lectro-bo staff to return it to its collapsed state. He took off towards the landing bay at a run, Char, Imaro, and Kukeb racing away from the fighting parties with him.

Chapter 31 – Back on Track, Albeit Backtracking

The stars accelerated past the forward viewport, becoming less distinct starlines. The *Audacia*'s Phased Reality Drive had done its job, and they were back in hyperspace.

Jay could not have been happier to depart a place than he was to leave the Rodna Bazaar Space Station. Under other circumstances, it might have been a perfectly nice place to visit. It had not ended well.

Jay and company had gotten away from the bounty hunters and Royal Enforcers without further incident. Quinn had already gotten clearance, and he and Jay had gotten the ship off the landing pad and back into space.

Without waiting to see if either of their pursuers had realized they'd evaded and left the station, Jay had flown them away.

Now that they were in hyperspace, Jay finally let out a sigh of relief. He'd been tense since boarding the ship and getting them away from the Rodna Bazaar. Once a Phased Reality Drive transitioned you to hyperspace, any pursuit could be evaded.

A ship could be tracked through hyperspace. However, a precise pursuit was impossible. Jay knew enough to know that it had something to do with drift, temporal eddies, spatial anomalies, and other sci-fi-esque bits that he didn't know or much care to.

Jay had sunk back in the pilot's seat. He felt as if he'd just run a marathon. That was in part because he, Char, Imaro, and Kukeb had run all the way to the ship from where they'd been confronted. Without rest, Jay had let the adrenaline carry him to the cockpit, where he and Quinn had gotten the ship underway.

Jay looked at his robot co-pilot. "Quinn, thank you."

"For what, Captain?" asked the robot in a curious tone.

"For helping Basa get the ship fixed so fast. I suspect that, without supervision and assistance from one like you, he's the type to take advantage of his employers. At least, enough to keep a good rating while still taking more time and EVIL."

"You are not wrong," stated Quinn. "Basa likes to talk while he works. Me being a robot, even a mostly-sentient one, he was comfortable sharing certain things with me. For example, like many non-humans who infrequently interact with humans, Basa thinks humans are easy to get one over on. I explained that you and Char are not normal humans, as you travel a great deal outside of human space. I informed him that you are not the simpletons he's accustomed to encountering among humans."

Jay often wondered if Quinn shared Basa's assessment. He appreciated that Quinn had been so complimentary and said, "I very much appreciate you saying that to Basa, Quinn."

"Of course. I also shared that, if you were smarter, you'd be a better mechanic."

That was the sort of thing Jay expected from Quinn. "That's what I keep you around for," he said.

Quinn made an electronic buzzing, fizzling noise Jay knew was the equivalent of a 'harumph' or similar grunt. Quinn followed it with, "I do appreciate that you appreciate that of me. Also, I hope you know that it's a good thing that you treat me with respect. Or else you and Char would be up star's nebula without a Phased Reality Drive."

Jay chuckled at that. He felt the tension easing, along with the post-adrenaline-crash exhaustion. "I can't argue with that, Quinn. Thank you. Any concerns about our new Phased Reality Drive or Basa's work?"

"No," Quinn said. "Basa is quite an excellent engineer. He might be overly expensive and do some shady things to get more EVILC in his pocket. But his reputation is more precious to him than a few extra nairodna credits to sell shoddy parts or materials. He's well aware that he's not the only mechanic on the Rodna Bazaar, and a good reputation gets you more business than a bad one does. So, he's on the level with his work."

"Good," Jay said. "Thank you, Quinn, for staying on top of him, and for being a most excellent proxy in my absence. I think it would be a good idea, nonetheless, to keep an eye on the Phased Reality Drive more closely than normal, at least for the next few transitions."

"Agreed," said Quinn.

Jay arose. "Thank you again. You got things in hand here?"

"Always."

"Okay," Jay said. He left the cockpit and went aft to join the others in the lounge.

Everyone was seated around the central table. They all looked both as relaxed and exhausted as Jay was feeling, and they were not currently conversing. Each had a drink. Cosima was curled up in Char's lap.

Jay went to the adjacent galley and got himself a drink. He sat on the small couch beside Char and Cosima. Thalia leapt up on his lap, nearly causing him to spill his drink.

"Hey, Thalia," Char said. "Miss me?"

The spacecat merped, chirped, and softly yowled something Jay was rather sure translated to, "Why didn't you take us with you, thumb monkey?"

"I knew Basa wouldn't disturb you like he'd have disturbed us," Jay said.

"Cosima was equally indifferent," remarked Char. "But she also said they played a game of trying to get Basa to notice them."

Before she settled onto his lap, Thalia mrrped and buzzed what Jay thought he heard as, "Yeah, whatever."

"How well do you understand your spacecats?" asked Kukeb.

"Depends on if they want to be understood," Char remarked.

Jay chuckled. "Yeah, they choose at will if they care to be understood or remain aloof. Someone once claimed that our understanding of them and their language is a telepathic thing, but that's never been scientifically proven."

"Interesting," remarked Kukeb. "I know that some of our people keep herpesteline as well as compsanine pets. But I don't know anyone that talks about understanding them."

"Any comment, Thalia?" Jay asked the spacecat in his lap. She was purring and said nothing.

"Is everything running okay?" asked Char.

"Yes," Jay said. "Quinn says it all went smoothly, and Basa did a good job. We made it to hyperspace without incident or pursuit. So, we can breathe for a bit."

"I can't tell you that last time I had to run like that," Char commented. "In fact, the last time might be never."

"We exercise and spar semi-regularly," said Imaro. "But run? No."

"I'm not a runner," Jay stated. "But when I needed to run, I'm glad that I could. Still, that was intense. Imaro, did you know that Royal Enforcer? You addressed him like you did."

Imaro took a drink, then said, "Yes. He's a part of the Crown Protection Division, so I know him."

"Of course he is," Jay remarked.

"Captain Diwat is one of those ass-kissing suck-ups who will do anything to advance himself, striving for a promotion," Imaro continued. "Of course, while some of the officials and functionaries are taken with him, his superiors are not, and my father can't be bothered. Captain Diwat is an arrogant blowhard. He probably leapt at the chance to come out and find me, figuring that bringing me back would get him the promotion he's always seeking. Truth is, this might have been the kind of thing he needed to land that."

"There is something of an upside to Diwat being outside rangeen space," added Kukeb.

"What's that?" prompted Char.

"If Diwat got sent outside rangeen space, then they didn't expect us to head out of rangeen space. He'll be screaming for reinforcements now that he's seen us, so that means he'll draw the better Royal Enforcers away, since they won't expect us to return."

"True," affirmed Imaro. "The better Royal Enforcers who'd been within our space will now be heading out to supplant Captain Diwat. That could buy us some time."

"Well then," Char began, "now that we have that out of our way, I'd like some more details about just how King Nobiri plans to get the sutac, soetub, and humans to go to war with one another."

"That's a fair question," replied Imaro. "I know that it doesn't involve the Royal Enforcers. Not, that is, until everyone else is busy fighting each other and they can escort in those who can claim the resource. I have some guesses as to what is intended, but not the specifics. I do know that whatever it entails, the necessary assets are in place and awaiting whatever order or signal will start things happening."

Jay looked more closely at Imaro. "If the Royal Enforcers, or some other rangeen agency, isn't performing some sort of invasion or guerilla strike, what do you think King Nobiri intends to do?"

Imaro took a draught from his drink, set it down, and said, "You're familiar with the soetub and that they have wings?"

"Yes," replied Jay.

"You also know that they can't fly?"

"Yes," Jay answered again.

"Did you know that that's only on worlds that are not their own? That on their homeworld they can, in fact, fly?"

"I'd heard that or read that somewhere," Char responded. "It's something that's been speculated for as long as the soetub have visited other worlds. Nobody seems to know why they can't use their wings to fly on any world that's not their homeworld."

"That's true," agreed Imaro. "However, the roptera have a theory that the rangeen have never shared, because the roptera have only ever shared it with us. The working theory on their part is that their ability to fly is tied to energy frequencies. These energy frequencies, as far as anyone knows, are unique to the soetub homeworld. The roptera can easily see them in a way we don't even think the soetub can."

"How can that be used against them by your father?" asked Char.

"Since the roptera can see that energy frequency, they know how to disrupt it," said Imaro. "Disrupting it disrupts their ability to fly. I presume whatever my father plans involves doing just that but then getting the sutac blamed for it. Since the sutac and soetub have never been overly friendly towards one another, and even expressed outright dislike, that might do it."

"Also," Kukeb added, "the sutac have a little-know racial fear of the soetub. I think they resemble ancient predators that the sutac survived long, long ago, to become the dominant species on their world. If they feel sufficiently threatened by the soetub, they'll be more inclined to fight them."

"Sure," Jay said, considering what Imaro and Kukeb were suggesting. "A little manipulation and disruption on the soetub homeworld, manipulation and rabble-rousing on the sutac homeworld, and with the right push they fight."

"There's history behind that," said Imaro. "It's not common knowledge, but when they first encountered one another, they fought constantly. There are still skirmishes between them every couple of years. They're usually minor and nobody gets killed. My father knows that and the history around it rather clearly."

"That explains how the rangeen will get the sutac and soetub to fight one another," started Char. "How does King Nobiri think he can draw humans into this, too?"

Kukeb and Imaro exchanged a glance. Then, looking away from Jay and Char sheepishly, Kukeb said, "Well, it might not exactly apply to all humans, but as a race, you tend to be easily swayed by your emotions. It's a known fact that strong emotions, both good and bad, can get your kind riled up sufficiently to do damage and cause harm."

Imaro coughed, then took up the conversation, saying, "Yes, well, with that in mind, and the rangeen connection to all 'cators everywhere, and the human connections to their 'cators and how they use them sometimes to excess, a service disruption of their functions will evoke anger. Constant disruptions, false information, and fake data created to put the blame with the soetub, sutac, or both, and humans will be primed for a fight."

Jay tried to look at that as a racist, alien perspective. However, he admitted that he couldn't. Humans would fight each other over strong emotions and lose control all too quickly. The right set of circumstances and annoyances, alongside a disruption of their 'cators, could work.

Jay sighed and said, "I wish that wasn't true. Frankly, I hate that it is. But it is."

"So," Char began to summarize, "King Nobiri's plan involves manipulating the sutac, soetub, and humans into going to war with one another, all so that he can claim a resource in sutac and soetub space. Never mind that because of their alliances, this will expand to a much broader and more devastating conflict."

"That's what it is," agreed Imaro.

Jay was shaking his head. "We gotta stop this. Before it even gets started. It's going to take us a few days, even at best speed and the most direct route possible, to reach Rangeenavelt. In the meantime, we should all get some rest, recover from our way-too-exciting escape from the Rodna Bazaar Station, and figure out what options are available to us to stop King Nobiri."

"Before he causes the galaxy to be ripped asunder by an out-of-control interplanetary war," added Char.

Chapter 32 - The Selfish Fantasy

It was "night" aboard the *Audacia*. This was after what had been an especially long day, which had included a convoluted attempt to avoid notice and evade followers, a confrontation with Captain Diwat and his unit of Royal Enforcers, a run across the docks to the ship, and then further explanation of King Nobiri's convoluted and increasingly unhinged plan.

Imaro was, unfortunately, exhausted to the point of being restless and wired. Sleep would not come for some time, as his mind was racing faster than the speed of light. He was troubled and disturbed by both the revelations of the danger of his father's scheme and turning around to confront him rather than continuing to run away from him.

If Imaro was restless, however, Kukeb was positively agitated. Imaro's partner was pacing around their stateroom, pausing only to rant about how everything had gone wrong and plead with Imaro to find some magical way to undo it all.

Imaro had half-tuned out Kukeb's rants. Yet he knew he couldn't disregard them because they were an expression of Kukeb's feelings. Currently, Kukeb was feeling scared, hurt, confused, and even angry.

Imaro was sitting on the edge of the bed, following Kukeb's pacing. When he started to rant again, Imaro gave him his attention.

"This is not how things were supposed to go," Kukeb ranted. "In fact, this is the exact opposite of what we'd meant to do. Going back to Rangeenavelt means we return to the lives that neither of us truly wants. The expectations of our families are unfair, and this is not how it should be."

As Kukeb's ranting became more frenzied and incoherent again, Imaro found himself drifting to other thoughts. This included Kukeb's family.

The Nwomga family were nobility, though there was no specific title they carried with that. Most nobles of the rangeen people had nonspecific titles, unless the crown gave one to a particular individual. That was how Kukeb had wound up working for Imaro's family.

While noble families tended, like Imaro's, to arrange marriages for alliances and the like, and Kukeb's was no different, his parents were far less vested in him being heterosexual and producing an heir. That was because Kukeb had three older siblings.

Imaro was sympathetic. The last thing he wanted to do was return to Rangeenavelt to confront his father. Calling their relationship strained was an understatement. They seldom spoke, and when they did, his father tended to be highly critical, insulting, and harsh. Imaro had no illusions about their relationship. King Nobiri had fathered children only so he had an heir to satisfy the rest of the nobility and leadership of the kingdom, not because he desired to have children to love.

Imaro was the eldest son, and rangeen law and tradition gave him special status as prince. But that also forced obligation on him, which his father determined could not be neglected, avoided, or denied. That was why he'd be forced to marry a female. Escaping with Kukeb and leaving it all behind had driven him for a long time.

Yet Imaro knew that what Jay and Char stated was true. His father's plan would not just open the way for him to lay claim to the resource that was no longer exclusive to the rangeen. It would spark a war across the entire galaxy that would easily rage out of control and cost uncountable lives and EVILC.

Imaro knew that, like his father, he had selfish tendencies, and as the prince of the rangeen people, he was spoiled. He had a degree of privilege very few across the galaxy did. Yet he was not so arrogant as to deny that the threat his father's plan represented could be ignored for his own needs.

Kukeb had not reached the same conclusion, however. Imaro tuned back into his lover's ranting.

"Why? Why do we need to go back to Rangeenavelt? What do these humans know? It's speculation that war between the sutac, soetub, and humans would spread quickly and become intergalactic. They're exaggerating. That's so far-fetched."

Initially, Imaro had thought the same thing. "Kukeb," he interjected, "they're not. I ran several different info searches across the MESS-work, and they're completely right about those alliances each race has. If the sutac go to war for real, their allies will jump in. Same applies to the soetub and humans. It won't just be these three races, but dozens, and it will escalate too swiftly to be believable. Jay and Char are right. It would be disastrous for everyone."

Kukeb made a noise that Imaro knew was one of frustration and distress. "It's not fair!" Kukeb practically whined. "We got away. We'd done it! We'd evaded the Royal Enforcers and got away from rangeen space. Then we ran away from them and escaped again. And where are we going? Back to Rangeenavelt. Back to the lives neither of us want. Going back is going to suck!"

"Probably," Imaro said with little energy.

"Okay, okay." Kukeb suddenly straightened up, as if he'd reached a decision. He stopped pacing and turned to face Imaro. The look on his face was deeply serious. "I've got it. Here's the plan. We get Jay and Char and that robot, Quinn, to meet us in the cockpit. But then, we storm the cockpit and take them hostage. With them as our hostages we can force Quinn to fly us to Abigail just as we'd planned."

"With what guns?" asked Imaro, trying not to sigh at the desperation of his lover. "We have no guns. And we know that there are no guns on this ship. What's more, Jay has his 'lectro-bow staff, which is one more weapon than we have."

"We can take it from him," said Kukeb. "We're both trained martial artists."

"By the time we were close enough to get his 'lectro-bow staff away from him, he'd realize we're a threat and stun us with it."

"Yes, yes." Kukeb seemed to concede. But then, he stood up straight again and said, "Okay, new plan. We still storm the cockpit, but since we can't take Jay and Char hostage, instead we threaten to do something to damage the ship, something that won't get us killed that we can utterly control and use to get them to see that they have no choice but to take us to Abigail."

This time, Imaro could not hold back the sigh. "Kukeb, my love, that's an empty threat. You know it, I know it, they know it. We have no idea how to do anything to the ship that would have that impact, let alone force them to take us to Abigail."

"We could reprogram Quinn," Kukeb suggested.

"How? Neither of us has that level of robotic understanding."

"Yes, yes." Kukeb began to pace again, then turned excitedly back toward Imaro and said, "Right, so, we seal our cabin and then flood the rest of the ship with a knock-out gas of some kind to incapacitate Jay and Char. Then we tell Quinn we won't revive them unless he takes us to Abigail."

"Short of killing our hosts," Imaro said, watching Kukeb flinch at that, "we have no way to keep them unconscious. Quinn is a smart enough AI that he will revive them and get in our way."

"We remove Quinn somehow?" questioned Kukeb. Imaro could see he was on the verge of tears.

"Honey, can you fly the ship?"

"No," Kukeb practically sobbed.

"Neither can I."

Imaro arose from the bed and took Kukeb in his arms. Immediately, his partner began to cry.

"I know," Imaro began in a calming, loving, reassuring voice. "I know us getting away and being together, escaping our duties and our stations in life, is a far more fun and desirable fantasy. And if matters weren't so dire, we would still be on our way. But you know as well as I do that the right thing to do is the right thing. That means we have to turn back, go home, and stop my father and his endless greed from selfishly destroying the galaxy."

Chapter 33 – Do You Even Hear Yourself Speaking?

The *Audacia* was still a day and a half away from Rangeenavelt. They had no problems with their new Phased Reality Drive, and there was no sign of pursuit - not that you could give chase in hyperspace.

Despite a great deal of thought on the matter, and working through multiple angles and ideas, Jay had no idea whatsoever how to get to the king without getting arrested and denied any opportunity to show him the greater danger inherent in his plan.

He and Char had discussed it at length, and she was equally unsure of what they could do. However, she agreed that they had to do something and needed a plan to back up and support Imaro and Kukeb.

So it was that Jay and Char were in their lounge, on their private deck of the ship. They'd been taking meals with Imaro and Kukeb and discussing things with them. Now it was mid-afternoon, ship's time, and both couples had opted for alone time.

Each of them was sitting in their favorite chair with a spacecat beside them. They'd been going over all the information they could find to familiarize themselves with all the players. If they were going to come up with a strategy to help stop King Nobiri, they needed to know as much as they could.

They'd begun by reading up on the rangeen, roptera, sutac, and soetub. The MESS-work was a truly spectacular compendium of knowledge, and they were able to learn some useful things about each race. Such as the roptera were utterly dependent on the rangeen and were never seen outside of rangeen space. Though one could claim a symbiotic existence between the two races, it was still clear that the rangeen controlled the roptera.

They'd also confirmed that, not only did the soetub and sutac have issues with one another, but both races also had problems with the rangeen. It would take very little to get them to fight one another.

Whatever the king was planning, starting a war between the soetub and sutac would have been ugly on many levels. Adding in humans would be the equivalent of turning an amplifier up to eleven.

After that, both Jay and Char had been studying up on King Nobiri. Everything they learned made the same points. Nobiri Iwoto was an arch-conservative, held onto his power with a relentless iron grip, and all the researchers and biographers agreed that he was the most brutal ruler of the rangeen of his family line in centuries.

Jay was no psychologist. Also, xenopsychology was complicated because what made one race tick wasn't necessarily what made another. Yet it took no stretch of the imagination to presume that King Nobiri was likely a narcissist, an egotist, and firmly believed in his own superiority over everyone.

The king had married a noblewoman, but she was not Imaro's mother. His mother was one of a dozen handmaidens that King Nobiri kept as consorts in addition to his spouse. The practice was not polyamory but instead, state-sanctioned polygamy with a heavy emphasis on male domination.

Jay could not find out why the consort had not been the mother of Imaro or his siblings, but there was only speculation, rumor, and gossip to that end, with no solid information. He suspected this was not a topic Imaro would care to discuss, but also didn't think it was important.

"You know," Jay began, feeling the need to share his thoughts with Char. "I totally get why Imaro ran away. When faced with an implacable force like King Nobiri Iwoto, even the most hearty and tough individuals would be hard-pressed to stand against him. Everything I'm reading makes it clear that when he wants something, he gets it, and nothing gets in his way. That includes no leeway for his children, especially his heir."

"Oh yeah," Char agreed. "I can't fathom how the son of a male like that managed to not follow in his footsteps. King Nobiri must be a terrible example of self-righteousness and probably has servants leaping to his every beck and call. How Imaro isn't selfish and equally entitled and arrogant is a hell of a study in nature versus nurture."

Jay snorted. "Yes. I don't get it either."

"King Nobiri might as well be a burning star," Char continued. "How do you get a force like that with that much power to shift? Or else, how do you get it out of your way?"

"There's plenty in rangeen history about coups and assassinations," Jay said. "Only with the right manipulations and usually only by the hand of the heir or a noble that can take his place, would that not lead to total chaos. And there is no way that Imaro or Kukeb could or would kill King Nobiri."

"No, not at all," agreed Char. "Neither of them could do such a thing. But it's going to come down to one or both of them confronting him. How they're going to convince him to abandon his plan is going to be a hell of a challenge at the least."

"How did we get ourselves mixed up in this insanity?" asked Jay.

"Because we convinced them to abandon their abandonment of responsibilities and feel responsible," replied Char.

Jay grinned and, with a shake of his head, remarked, "That sounds like something I'd say."

"I felt the need to beat you to it," commented Char.

The intercom pinged, and Quinn's voice came to them, saying, "Captain, your mother is calling on the 'cator."

Jay exchanged a look with Char as he debated ignoring his mother. That, however, would lead to other issues he'd prefer to simply avoid. Since nothing was pressing now, but likely would be soon, he answered.

"Hello, Mother," Jay said as the 'cator transmission connected.

"Hello dear," his mother began. "So, did you get your ship fixed?"

"Yes, I did, thank you for asking," Jay replied.

"That's good," Jay's mom said. "I'm glad. So, I called because I wanted to let you know that your stepfather and I have booked a Five-Nebulae cruise on a starliner."

"Yeah?" Jay asked, feigning interest.

"Yes," his mom continued. "Bob and I will be taking a month-long journey on the luxurious Trans-Planetary Interstellar Cruise Ship *Star Seeker*."

"That sounds delightful, Mom," Jay said. She and Bob loved to go on starliner cruises. Seeing the tourist sites, the attached kitsch, and the often-overhyped attractions suited them on many levels. Jay wasn't going to bother to mention that he and Char had seen all those sights themselves from far better vantage points and more interesting perspectives beyond the limited trappings of a luxury starliner. Starliners also tended to seldom get especially close to those attractions, unless you paid extra, and even then, it was the parts everyone saw and knew about. "When's the trip?" he asked.

"Well, Bob managed to get us a fabulous deal, so it's in two weeks," Jay's mom said.

"That sounds really nice, Mom," Jay said. "I know how much you and Bob love to travel."

"Very happy for you, Mom," added Char.

There was a moment of silence, and then Jay's mom said, "So, anyhow, now that your ship is fixed, we'd really be grateful and appreciate, to save us a bit of hassle, especially with only two weeks, if you'd come get us and take us to the home port for the *Star Seeker*."

Jay looked at Char. She raised her eyebrows. Jay said, "And where is *Star Seeker*'s home port?"

"Vanitas Primus," Jay's mom said.

Jay was absolutely stunned. He wasn't sure where to begin - the distance from where they were now to there, let alone the time involved, or the fact that saving them a hassle would be a hassle for him. Remaining as calm and collected as he could, Jay said, "Well, Mom, I'd love to help you out. However, Char and I are currently at least a week away from you, and we're in the middle of a job. Then, on top of that, Vanitas Primus is a good five-day travel from Magoonay, so there's almost no way we'd be able to get there in time to take you. Oh, and I should probably mention that Vanitas Primus has one of the highest docking fees in the galaxy."

"Jay, honey, you can't just do us this favor?" his mother asked.

"Are you for real?" Jay could not hold back. "Let me repeat, we are in the middle of a job and can't just drop it to come to you. Also, even if we could, we're probably too far from Magoonay to get to you then get you to Vanitas Primus in time for you to catch your starliner. Not to mention that between their ludicrous docking fees and what it would take to travel to you from here, the cost would be obscene."

"If it's the cost, honey, we'd pay for the docking fees, I guess," Jay's mother said. He could hear her wheedling tone, and the hint of guilt at him inconveniencing her.

"Mother," Jay started. "No offense, but I don't have a starship for ferrying my family. My job, my career, is using my starship to carry cargo and passengers who pay for my services to transport them. This is how I earn my living, with the added bonus that Char and I get to travel and see the galaxy along the way. Also, again, we are in the middle of a paying job and can't drop it to come there to transport you for your vacation."

There was a moment of silence, and Jay had hope that he'd gotten through to her. Then, his mom said, "It's just one favor, Jason. You can't shift your priorities to do this one favor for your mother and stepdad?"

Jay couldn't help himself and began to laugh derisively. "You don't hear yourself at all, do you? You keep telling me in no uncertain terms how you think I'm wasting my potential, despite me doing what I love. *Audacia* is more than my starship, it's my home. This is where I want to be. Yet when I'm doing the thing that I do for the money you think I should be making more of than I am, you want me to drop it and come do a favor for you, for free. Even if I was willing to come help you out, I can't. Because, as I've said, I can't just drop my paying client in the middle of a job."

Once more, Jay's response was met with silence. As it went on, he thought, hoped, that maybe, just maybe, she'd heard him. Maybe his mother would realize how unfair she was being, and maybe even how hypocritical. Did she really expect him to quit doing the job he was doing just to come to her and do the thing she criticized?

Yet her next statement told Jay all that he needed to know. His mom said, "I'm very disappointed in you, Jason. I don't ask much of you, but when I do, you refuse to lend me a hand and be here for your family. I ask so little of you, son, and yet..."

"Sorry, Mom," Char interrupted her. "We were right in the middle of something when you called, and we have business to take care of that we can't put off any longer, lest Jay disappoint his paying client. Sorry we can't come help you and Dad out at this time."

"Well, Charlotte, I.." Jay's mom began.

"Yeah, Mom, sorry again, but we gotta go," Jay interrupted her. "Love you. Bye!"

Jay tapped the screen on the tablet to end the transmission. The silence that followed was abnormally still and somewhat tense.

"The audacity of that woman never ceases to amaze me," Char said, breaking the sense of tension in the air. She added, "How do you think she'd feel if she knew that you named the ship *Audacia* for her?"

Jay chuckled. "I love her, but she'd never get it. I didn't name it *Sindi's the Best Mom*, and if she realized I called it *Audacia* because *chutzpah* was too on-the-nose, she might even be outright offended."

"So, you *should* have named the ship *Chuzpah*," Char stated.

Chapter 34 – BREAKING NEWS

"This is RKNN, The Rangeen Kingdom News Network, Channel VX3410.756Q on the Interplanetary Transmission Entanglement Mediascape," the official-sounding, disembodied voice states.

A pair of rangeen are seated at a desk, both male. One has deep-set, black eyes with flecks of metallic red within them beneath his pronounced brow. His spiked hair is a bright neon green, his skin brown. A handsome male by rangeen standards.

The other has deep-set, black eyes with flecks of metallic green within them beneath his pronounced brow. His well-coiffed mane of hair is a bright neon blue, and his skin tone is similar to the other male, also handsome by rangeen standards.

Behind them is a display with the RKNN logo and the words "Breaking News."

"I'm Dajan Ibumu," says the first male.

"And I'm Unbussu Wifali," says the other. "We've received word from the Royal Stronghold in Ronrop-Palast that King Nobiri will be issuing a statement of great importance regarding missing Prince Imaro."

Dajan says, "As you may recall, King Nobiri Iwoto has been searching for his heir for several weeks. We are going live to the Royal Stronghold now."

The image cuts to an opulent room in the Royal Stronghold where announcements to the press are made. King Nobiri Iwato has just stepped up to the podium. He looks either concerned, angry, or quite probably both.

After a moment's pause, he begins, saying, "My loyal subjects, I bring news about my son. After a long and exhaustive search throughout rangeen space, forces were deployed to explore beyond our border. Why Prince Imaro Iwato might desire to leave the borders of his home sector is a mystery that remains disturbing and unresolved.

An image of Imaro appears before the king at the level of the podium. He continues, saying, "Prince Imaro has been sighted in nairodna space. Although a squad of my Royal Enforcers valiantly attempted to bring him home, their efforts were thwarted. What's more, we have learned that Prince Imaro might be the captive of humans."

The image of Imaro vanishes from the screen, the camera zooming in for a closer view of King Nobiri. There's no missing the ire in his bearing as he says, "Hear me now, all. If any harm comes to my heir, you will pay a terrible price. Certain information that I cannot fully disclose at this time has come to light regarding a possible conspiracy against myself and the rangeen people. This points to meddling on the part of other sovereign governments, though I will not state more at this time."

His face gets decidedly angrier and more serious as he says, "The consequences of this action will not go uninvestigated. Any members of any race that move against the rangeen in any way will find that we are not to be trifled with. What's more, messing with the affairs of the royal family will not be to your benefit."

The King pauses, the look on his face softening only a little. "Imaro, if you are seeing this, and you are not the victim of a kidnapping, it is imperative that you come home."

After one more short pause, the king says, "My loyal subjects, and all others who see this missive, I thank you."

The image immediately cuts away from King Nobiri and the royal stronghold back to the newsroom and the rangeen anchors.

Dajan says, "RKNN has learned from reliable sources that it was the Royal Enforcers who positively identified Prince Imaro in nairodna space, although they would not disclose the precise location where he was seen."

"That's right. Dajan," says Unbussu. "What's more, multiple government officials, when questioned, have alluded to the prince's disappearance perhaps being tied to a foreign plot to negatively impact rangeen business and internal affairs. Though none would speak on the record, like King Nobiri's statement just moments ago, more than one hinted at a conspiracy on the part of foreign powers to potentially discredit the royal family in some way or to otherwise do harm to the rangeen economy."

Dajan picks up the narrative, saying, "For more on this, we go live to Laolat Njura, currently at Royal Enforcer headquarters."

The image shifts to show the stunning female rangeen reporter.

"Thank you, Dajan," she states. "I've been interviewing multiple Royal Enforcer officials since word of the king's press conference was made public. Though none would go on record, I can confirm that they believe the prince to be a captive, possibly of these humans. There was, however, hits of potential involvement possibly tied to either the soetub or sutac, though no clear statements to the effect were made on or off the record. But the mere speculation is worrisome."

The screen splits, showing Laolat on one side and Dajan and Unbussu on the other. Unbussu says, "Laolat, has there been any indication of increased Royal Enforcer activity on rangeen borders that might offer more information?"

"No, apart from the search for Prince Imaro, there has not been any increase in Royal Enforcer patrols or presence that might correspond to issues the rumors and speculation we're hearing might raise."

Dajan asks, "Have any Royal Enforcer officials indicated where the search for Prince Imaro might take them?"

"Well, Dajan," Laolat begins. "They were being evasive about that, possibly to avoid alerting any bounty hunters, as rumor has it the reason the Royal Enforcers failed to retrieve the prince was due to bounty hunter interference. However, based on off-the-record remarks, it does appear that the search for Prince Imaro will continue to extend further outside rangeen borders."

The split screen resolves back to the anchors in the newsroom. "Thank you, Laolat," says Dajan. Then, he continues with, "That was Laolat Njura, bringing you exclusive coverage from Royal Enforcer headquarters in Ranrop-Palast."

Unbussu says, "As previously mentioned by King Nobiri, there will be a reward for any credible information that leads to the whereabouts of Prince Imaro, or any information about his disappearance, kidnapping, or those who might be involved."

"Well, Unbussu, I'd hate to be responsible for this incident," states Dajan. "The king has made it abundantly clear that those responsible will suffer even more horrifically than previously promised."

"No question, Dajan," replies Unbussu. "King Nobiri is not one to make threats lightly. If those responsible do not come forward, there's no doubt what might happen next will be thoroughly unpleasant."

The camera returns to Dajan. "Right you are, Unbussu. Stay tuned to RKNN, The Rangeen Kingdom News Network, Channel VX3410.756Q on the Interplanetary Transmission Entanglement Mediascape, as we continue to bring you the latest news in this increasingly mysterious and troubling story."

Chapter 35 – This Was a Very Bad Idea

It was, relatively speaking, an unremarkable world. The land masses were predominantly brown and blue, the sky green, with orange clouds drifting at various altitudes. There were obvious cities below, masses of metal glinting in the sun. The world had satellites and docks orbiting around it, as well as a variety of different starships.

The *Audacia* had reached Rangeenavelt a few hours before. Now, they orbited the planet on a prescribed path, claiming to the authorities that they were awaiting word from their contact as to where they should land.

Meanwhile, Jay, Char, Imaro, and Kukeb were in the ship's mess, debating how to approach landing on Rangeenavelt. The trip had been uneventful, and it appeared as if the Royal Enforcers either had not marked their ship or didn't expect them to be there.

Quinn was maintaining their orbital path while the others decided how and where to land.

"The *Audacia* is a standard, medium-sized Han-Mal Shipworks *Baritone* Class multitask starship," Jay started. "Our registration should be clean, and thus far it looks like we have no pursuers. So, I think we should land like any freighter at the starport in Ranrop-Palast. Once we're settled, we get transport into the city proper and then access the palace that way."

Kukeb said, "Even though we've not had the Royal Enforcers take notice of us thus far, and they might not know your ship, they're surely on the lookout for Imaro and me."

"I don't think that's all that likely," Jay remarked. "We all watched that RKNN broadcast. The authorities have never mentioned you and have made it abundantly clear they believe that Imaro is heading away from rangeen space, not into its heart. Rangeenavelt, and Ranrop-Palast, are the last places they'd expect you to turn up."

"I agree with Jay," said Char. "However, I do think that you two need to exercise considerable caution. It's best that you both remain as inconspicuous as possible."

"Disguises?" asked Kukeb.

"Yes," replied Char. "Nothing too outrageous, just keeping you both hidden in plain sight. It's always the more elaborate disguises that never work."

"Maybe," conceded Kukeb. "I see the logic of this approach, I do. But I still worry that crossing Ranrop-Palast from one of the spaceports is highly likely to expose and draw attention to us."

"If it wasn't clear that they're not really looking for Imaro here, I'd agree with you," said Char.

Jay looked toward Imaro. The rangeen male had remained silent thus far, observing the back and forth between Jay, Char, and Kukeb. Even in the short time that they'd been together, Jay knew that it was not his usual practice.

"Imaro?" he coaxed. "Any thoughts on this?"

Imaro didn't immediately respond. Jay saw his eyes were cast down at the table where he was sitting. Finally, he looked up and said, "I think, rather than take a circuitous path, we should contact the palace and arrange to land there directly."

"That is an awful idea," stated Kukeb.

Imaro arose and began to pace. He said, "Here's how I see it: if we do this Jay's way, if we're caught, the odds are far too high that Jay and Char, and frankly you, Kukeb, will all be killed on the spot. The Royal Enforcers, you know all too well, Kukeb, have a reputation for tending to shoot first and ask questions in intensive care. With the official story being spun that I've been kidnapped or otherwise coerced to leave, that will redouble their resolve."

Jay found that unacceptable. "Yes, well, that would not be the desired outcome. But will the Royal Enforcers allow us to land at all, if they know you're aboard?"

"I believe that they will," Imaro said. "Also, I have no intention of going through standard channels to get us landing clearance at the palace. That would just invite more chaos. No, if we take this route, it begins with going directly to my father."

Jay had no response to that. Ultimately, he knew this would end in a meeting with King Nobiri of one sort or another. Was walking through his front door the best option, or a recipe for disaster?

Char, unsurprisingly, was thinking along the same lines as she asked, "Is it safe? What if they just shoot us down when they know where we are?"

"I'm rather certain it'll be safest for several reasons," began Imaro. "First, we'll head into the atmosphere when we send our 'cator signal to my father. Boarding a starship in atmosphere isn't an option. Secondly, King Nobiri has made it abundantly clear that he wants me home. Thus, if I make contact with him to let him know I'm coming home, I should be able to dictate the terms for my voluntary return."

"Sorry, Imaro, but I think you're wrong," said Kukeb. "I'm not so sure your father will negotiate in good faith."

"What about the rest?" asked Imaro, ending his pacing to stand beside the seat where he'd begun.

"As to that," replied Kukeb, "no, they won't just shoot us down. As much as I hate everything about this, you're right that landing at the palace reduces the risk of landing at the spaceport and being spotted and killed in the streets."

Jay felt uncomfortable about the whole thing. He wondered, for the briefest moment, if he and Char had gotten in too deep and made a mess of everything. Still, there was no going back. "Well," he said. "I don't care to die, and that certainly sounds like the most likely outcome if we go with my plan. So, let's do it your way. But I want to be present when you have your conversation with King Nobiri."

"Absolutely," replied Imaro.

"Quinn," Char spoke, activating the intercom, "what's the approximate local time in Ranrop-Palast?"

"Approximate or precise?" remarked Quinn.

"What time is it there, Quinn?"

"Fifteen-hundred twenty-three hours, forty seconds," replied Quinn. "Mid-afternoon."

"Thank you," said Char.

"Okay," started Jay. "Let's take this to the cockpit."

With Jay and Char in the lead, the foursome made their way across the ship to the cockpit. Once there, Quinn said, "You couldn't have waited to come here and ask me about the time?"

"If it had been the middle of the night, we'd not be making our next move," remarked Jay.

"But we are making a next move?" asked Quinn, and Jay recognized the added note of irksomeness in his tone. "You see, port control has placed a time limit on how long we can remain in open Rangeenavelt space without requesting a flight path to land, and ours is running out."

"And you were going to bring this to my attention when?" asked Jay.

"In seven hours, when we had only one hour left," said Quinn.

Jay didn't roll his eyes as he said, "Well, you needn't worry yourself about our time to remain in orbit running out. We're here to arrange our landing. Get a flight path to Ranrop-Palast and start taking us into the atmosphere as soon as Imaro starts his 'cator transmission."

"Yes, Captain," replied Quinn.

Jay gestured to the port-side seat, and Imaro sat. The rangeen prince activated the holographic image mode and started transmitting to the palace.

A rangeen female, with bright, neon-orange hair and black eyes featuring flecks of metallic silver appeared on the holographic screen. "Authentication?" she asked.

"I am Prince Imaro Iwoto, Firstborn of King Nobiri Iwoto, son of Mosfun and heir to the Crown. Authentication Prima Secunda, Zero-Zero-Two, Bravo One. No more questions. I demand that, without further delay, you put me through to the king at once!"

The female rangeen in the hologram looked nervous, but said, "Y-yes, Your Highness. One moment." A royal crest that Jay presumed represented the Iwoto family appeared in her place.

A moment later, the visage of King Nobiri Iwoto appeared in the hologram. The king of the rangeen appeared calm, but the set of his shoulders told Jay that he was seething with anger beneath it. His eyes, even via hologram, were not kind."

"Hello, father," said Imaro.

"Son," replied the king with no warmth in his voice at all.

"Please allow me to speak my piece, without questions," started Imaro. King Nobiri gave a slight nod of his head in response. "First, and foremost, I ran away. I was not kidnapped, coerced, or otherwise persuaded or forced to leave. I departed of my own volition. Secondly, where I have been is not important to this conversation, nor is where I was going after my departure from Rangeenavelt. At present, I am on a human-built and captained transport currently entering the atmosphere. Which brings me to my third point. I would request permission to land, unobstructed, at the palace. Lastly, I request that no harm come to any of my companions aboard this vessel, either on our approach or once we have landed."

Jay noted to himself that Imaro made no mention of Kukeb at all.

King Nobiri was silent for a time. Jay could tell, however, that he had tensed further throughout Imaro's demands. After he'd not spoken for an uncomfortable amount of time, he said, "I agree to your request. You will be allowed to land unobstructed, and no harm will come to you or any of your companions."

"Swear to me in a solemn vow, Father," demanded Imaro.

King Nobiri's look hardened and he tensed ever-so-slightly more, then said, "I swear on my crown, on the reign of my ancestors, and on the life of all my family that you will be allowed to land unobstructed, and no harm will come to you or any of your companions."

"Thank you," said Imaro.

Without a word from King Nobiri, the transmission ended.

"We've just received clearance to land and coordinates," said Quinn.

Jay climbed into the pilot's seat. As he did so, he asked, "Imaro, is your father narcissistic and above every aspect of the law?"

"Yes, yes he is," replied Imaro.

Jay proceeded to take control of the flight from Quinn and flew along the prescribed flight path over the sea. The city of Ranrop-Palast became visible from hundreds of kilometers away. It was a huge city, dominated by all sorts of tall buildings with oddly wide tops, comprised of metals, glass, and various composites, ever-increasing in height moving towards the city's center.

At the center of the city stood a walled complex. The palace absolutely dominated the capital city of Rangeenavelt. The tallest structures in the city were contained within the opulent, unnecessarily tall walls.

"Incoming," remarked Quinn, having only moments ago resumed the co-pilot's seat after taking care of an errand for Jay.

There were numerous starships and other flying vessels in motion all around and through the city becoming visible as they neared it. On the scopes, however, a half dozen small, fast craft were approaching the *Audacia*.

"I thought he was going to allow us to land unobstructed," remarked Kukeb.

"Unobstructed, yes," said Imaro. "Unescorted, no."

The fast-moving craft swiftly resolved into sleek fighters. They passed the *Audacia* then looped around and took up a formation alongside the ship.

"Starship *Audacia*," a signal transmitted to them on the 'cator. "We will escort you the rest of the way in. Any deviation from your course will result in us firing on your ship."

"Acknowledged," replied Jay. His heart was pounding in his chest. Jay was not liking any of this plan.

"They're not obstructing us, just threatening us," remarked Char.

"I chose the words I did to meet my father halfway," stated Imaro. "This was not unexpected."

The path over the city was clear of any ships. Jay wasn't sure if this was a standard matter, or if traffic had been diverted for them. It wasn't long before they were crossing over the palace walls. Jay noted that at least a dozen weapons were tracking *Audacia* as he slowed their flight, hovered over the landing pad, then settled the ship onto it.

"Okay, Quinn," Jay said. "Remain here. Everyone else, let's do this."

A few moments later, Jay, Char, Imaro, and Kukeb disembarked from the ship. Standing before them, at the edge of the landing pad, stood King Nobiri. He was not at all alone, as he was flanked by probably two dozen heavily armed and armored Royal Enforcers.

"Hello, Father," said Imaro, approaching the king.

"Son," King Nobiri said. Neither moved nearer the other for a handshake, salute, or embrace. Jay could feel the tension in the air like a storm about to burst.

"I have returned," stated Imaro. "As you can see, I am unharmed."

"I am glad for that," stated King Nobiri. "I presume there is a reasonable explanation for all of this?"

"There is an explanation," replied Imaro.

"Your departure was quite abrupt," remarked King Nobiri. "We were quite displeased that you chose to leave without a word, especially just before your wedding."

Before Imaro could respond, King Nobiri made a hand gesture toward the Royal Enforcers flanking him. As one, they raised their weapons to point at Jay, Char, and Kukeb.

Jay felt his stomach drop as fear clenched his heart. It couldn't end like this. He took Char's hand, and she squeezed his in return. They were just two humans making their way in the galaxy, traveling, exploring, and having adventures. To die now would suck, but at least it had been a hell of a ride.

Imaro was clearly incensed as he barked, "What is this, Father? You promised that my companions would not be harmed."

"That's true," replied King Nobiri. "They will not be harmed. However, not harming them doesn't preclude having them arrested for illegally transporting a member of the royal household, subverting a member of the royal family, and harboring a rangeen fugitive."

"What fugitive?" questioned Imaro.

The king pointed. "Kukeb Nwomga."

Maybe their end would not be immediate, but looking at all the guns pointing at them, Jay had no doubt who was in control of their situation.

"Yeah," Jay said under his breath, "this was a very bad idea."

Chapter 36 – It's a Very Plush Prison

The whole thing was distressing. Who wouldn't be distressed when they were being falsely imprisoned? Yet somehow, Char also felt oddly calm.

When she'd met Jay years ago, Char had been a workaholic. She had thrived on stress, and her anxiety tended – on a scale of one to ten, one being low and ten being high – to steadily remain at five. Her entire life had revolved around work, spending time with her parents, sister, and nephews, and occasional dates.

Earlier in her life, she'd dated seriously. She'd even been engaged once before, but that had gone poorly. When Jay had come into the picture, he initially struck Char as clever but not very ambitious, funny but not obnoxious, geeky and devoted to presenting himself without airs, without masks, and no apologies. Char hadn't wanted the attraction to be anything more than her normal flings of the time had been. That had failed to materialize almost immediately, and it hadn't been long before they were a couple, nor much longer after that they were living together.

As they had gotten to know one another, Char loved that Jay desired nothing more than to be free. Soon after they married, she had encouraged him to pursue his dream. Char had found a business she loved, coworkers she respected, and a job that tied to what she desired without either of them losing their independence or self-sovereignty. Now, they lived that life together.

Traveling across the galaxy via the *Audacia*, taking cargo and passengers veritably anywhere, had shown her and Jay things most only dreamed of seeing. Of course, there were some boring, unexciting, unadventurous trips. Yet each day they got to do something new, go somewhere different, and they met a wide variety of people across an equally wide variety of places.

All of their actions had been on the up and up. Jay had no interest in smuggling, and Char worked in a sometimes cut-throat but legitimate business.

Hence, the idea of imprisonment was unappealing, and the thought of being thrown into some dank, dingy, unpleasant cell was scary. That had been the expectation making Char somewhat anxious. The odd sense of calm was tied to the reality of the prison cell they were escorted to.

It was a very plush prison. In fact, it was cushier and more opulent than some of the finer hotels she'd stayed in or office suites she'd moved clients between.

Their prison was a well-appointed suite, featuring three bedrooms, a large, sun-lit sitting area, a small kitchenette with plenty of drink options – alcoholic and otherwise – and a restroom that put many four-star hotels to shame with its marble countertops and impressive bathtub and shower.

After making use of the restroom, Char rejoined Jay and Kukeb, who had remained with them. The males were settling themselves into chairs in the sitting room, and Char saw that Jay had gotten her a drink.

"This is not what I expected when King Nobiri arrested us," she stated. "I expected something more along the lines of a dungeon. This is a palace, after all."

Kukeb, looking utterly dejected, said, "This is because of me, most likely. King Nobiri might be a great many uncomplimentary things, but he'd never imprison a noble in a common cell, even for the most hideous crime."

"Uh, Kukeb, just what is your position?" asked Char. "Apart from being Imaro's lover, you have a job with the royalty, and are yourself a noble?"

Kukeb replied, "I've served as Imaro's personal secretary since both of us completed primary schooling. We went to the same elite, nobles-only academy and are only a few months apart in age. I am the son of a duke, and ours is a hereditary line that goes back for just as long as the royal line. Ironically, if I were female, I might well have been the chosen spouse for Imaro."

Kukeb chuckled, but there was no humor in it. "I'm a baron, but you heard King Nobiri. I'm the fugitive he accused you of harboring."

"Which is not a real charge," commented Jay.

Kukeb arose and began to pace. "It doesn't matter. Imaro ran away with me. Hence, I take the fall for his disappearance, either because I orchestrated his kidnapping or otherwise coerced him to leave his station. That's how this will be played out. King Nobiri created that narrative as soon as he made that accusation and pointed me out in front of all those Royal Enforcers. I told Imaro he knew we were not just friends, sparring partners, and work associates."

Char wasn't often a romantic, but she understood why Imaro, gay and unable to be himself, had chosen to run away with the lover he was forbidden to be with. She said, "You know, Kukeb, I sympathize. Returning here was the last thing you wanted to have to do."

Kukeb's pacing accelerated, his upset apparent. He said, "I wanted to be with him and he wanted to be with me. To hell with the expectations of his father, my family, or the rangeen nobility. We were born into lives neither of us wanted. Maybe our privilege got the better of us, I don't know. All we wanted was to be free. We did our part; we contributed to society and lived up to most of our family obligations and expectations. It was a fool's hope to think we could just leave it all behind."

Kukeb's pacing slowed, then stopped. He dropped into the couch opposite Jay and Char, then said, "I expect I shall be exiled away from rangeen space once Imaro is forced to marry."

"No," Jay said, leaning forward. "We brought you and Imaro back here to convince King Nobiri to abandon this folly. I know he must be capable of seeing reason and abandoning these devastating plans. We will succeed. We have to."

Kukeb sighed and seemed to sink even deeper into the couch. Then, he said, "I would like to believe that, Jay. I really would. But you don't know King Nobiri as I do. I have very little hope there is any reason to be found in the man."

There was silence between them for a time. Char wanted to say something to comfort Kukeb, to assure him they would succeed. However, she wanted to be careful, as she expected the room was bugged and their privacy was limited, if not outright non-existent.

Jay arose, and Char recognized the look on his face. He was thinking. "Kukeb, is there an OVERLORD consulate somewhere on Rangeenavelt?"

"Of course there is," said Kukeb, his tone flat.

"So," Jay started, beginning to pace as he said, "we should, as a registered starship crew, be able to get ourselves legal representation from OVERLORD."

Char was trying to follow Jay's logic but couldn't. "I'm not entirely sure about that. Each OVERLORD consulate has committee reps there, but legal services? Usually that sort of thing is left to the locals. But, honestly, why?"

"Well, let's look at the facts," Jay continued. "We are in Ranrop-Palast, being held not by any legal body but directly by the king. We have, as such, no resources and no obvious recourse. But we're humans, not rangeen nor subject to rangeen laws, per se. The king is obviously, per rangeen custom, tradition, law, whatever, above the law. He can do whatever he wants. But we are human beings, and sovereign individuals, as such. So, in the face of that, and if we do fail to make King Nobiri see reason, going to OVERLORD should be a viable option."

"I dunno, Jay," Char said, both because she wasn't sure why he was making the suggestion he was, and because she was equally unsure of how he was thinking it might be a viable option. "I suppose, sure, as humans, appealing to OVERLORD for assistance is viable. But I just don't know."

Jay shrugged. "A back-up plan, then," he said.

"Sure," Char said.

She arose, feeling restless. At least, she had to admit to herself, they seemed to be safe. For the time being. A nagging voice in the back of her head said you always treated the condemned like royalty before you ended them. What would that do to human/rangeen relations? That question, knowing what King Nobiri was after, silenced the nagging voice. Executing her and Jay would put the attention precisely where the king didn't want it.

Their safety, however, wouldn't matter if they failed to dissuade King Nobiri from his dangerous course, or somehow get Imaro on the throne in his place to end the danger. If they failed to stop him, it likely wouldn't matter. The interplanetary war that King Nobiri wanted to start as a distraction for profit would be devastating.

"Char," Kukeb addressed her, bringing her back to the present moment. "Truly, are you absolutely certain of the scenario you and Jay spoke of, the collapse of the economy and all-out interspecies, interplanetary war?"

"Very," she replied with no hesitation. "As bad as we have suggested that it might be, it could be even worse."

"How?" asked Kukeb.

"Depends on how many old grudges come back to the forefront," said Jay. "Races that have had lots of logical reasons to maintain peace, in the face of allies taking sides and a swiftly moving conflict, who knows what could happen? One race might decide the genocide of another is the only solution."

"Yes," Kukeb said, looking even more forlorn if that were possible. "That's worse."

"We'll find a way to stop this," said Char. Despite the challenges it would present, she believed they would make it happen.

Jay sighed. "Yes. We'll think of something. But, in this moment, this is a much better, far nicer prison than I would ever have expected. These quarters are actually quite regal."

"Yes," Char agreed. "It's a very nice, very plush prison."

Chapter 37 – How Are We Even Related?

Imaro was angry.

He was also confined in a plush prison of sorts. It was not a prison, however. It was his royal apartments.

What made it a prison were all the elements of confinement heaped upon him. For example, the royal apartments had numerous secret passages. This allowed for going places both in and out of the palace unseen. When the press and paparazzi were constantly looking at everything you did, having ways to avoid being noticed was paramount.

However, all of the secret passages out of his apartments were either blocked, sealed, or guarded. What's more, a force field of some sort was online, denying Imaro access to the MESS-work and his 'cator, though he could watch programs on the 'tangle. All access to any of the windows or his balconies was also cut off. Effectively, Imaro was a prisoner in his own home.

Whenever someone brought him food or a guard answered his summons, he insisted that Kukeb, his personal secretary, had committed no crime and was to be freed. Or, since he was his personal secretary, Imaro should be able to have him present. This was ignored.

Then, he demanded to be completely certain of how Jay and Char were being treated and to be kept with them, not separated from them. No dice, no response; all of Imaro's requests, demands, and insistences were being ignored.

For a day, all Imaro could do was make his demands and muse on how the return to the palace had gone. He was still convinced that Jay's plan would not have gone well, and rather than his human companions being imprisoned, they'd likely be dead.

He knew that because of Kukeb's station, his treatment wasn't likely to be too harsh. This was, however, the first time they'd been totally separated in longer than Imaro could remember.

Despite their arrest, Imaro felt that his father likely hadn't treated Jay and Char poorly. He just hoped that they had left the *Audacia* alone and hadn't removed Quinn from the ship or otherwise done it harm. He expected it was being left alone.

Late in the morning of the second day, King Nobiri finally made an appearance at Imaro's royal apartments.

Nobiri Iwoto was a few centimeters shorter than his son. Imaro was always struck by the similarity of the overall shape of their faces and their hair, though his father's had the streaks of black that came as part of the aging process. Like Imaro, Nobiri's default expression was a scowl, though where it was disappointment in Imaro on his part, on Imaro's part it was underlying ire for the king.

"Finally decided to pay me a visit?" Imaro said, arising from the couch in his main sitting room to stand before his father. "Have you kept your word about the crew of the *Audacia* and Kukeb?"

"What kind of question is that?" asked Nobiri. "Of course, I have. You knew full well that I would when you extracted that promise from me. Let's be honest here, Son. Do you think that you have any right, whatsoever, to question me and *my* word? Considering that it was you who abandoned his family, his commitments, and his duties on every level? There are not sufficient words to convey the depths of my disappointment in you. Were it not an incredible inconvenience, and would cause a whole host of other troubles, I would seek to name another as my heir. Do you understand the position that you are putting me in with your ungracious actions?"

Imaro snorted. "My ungracious actions? You were forcing me to be espoused to a woman that you have chosen for me, giving me no say at all in this matter. My response was in response to you."

"Idiot child," Nobiri replied, stalking past his son, the disgust evident both in his face and the hunch of his shoulders. As Imaro turned to face him, King Nobiri spun around and said, "All that you had to do was your duty as the heir to the throne and father a child or two with her. Beyond that, you could be with whomever you please, take on all the handmaidens you desire to."

Imaro squared his shoulders, making the most of the extra centimeters he had over his father. As seriously as he could, Imaro said, "I don't desire to have handmaidens, Father. In case it's unclear to you, I am a homosexual, and women do not interest me sexually in the least."

The last thing he'd expected from his father with those words was his deep, hearty, and frankly cruel, laughter. As it subsided, Nobiri said, "For the record, Son, I should remind you that there are other means, apart from intercourse, to impregnate your spouse and produce the requisite children to carry on the royal lineage. In many ways, that's preferential to natural conception via the sexual act, as the genes can be properly cleansed of impurities that way."

Imaro could not hide the disgust on his face. "Everything about that is repugnant. I won't even get into the business of 'cleansing impurities' you imply. But to carry on with a sham marriage, to make public a lie, that seems the opposite of fit to rule the rangeen people."

"You really are a fool, Imaro Iwoto," stated King Nobiri, turning away and starting to pace. As he did so, King Nobiri said, "You realize that the female I have chosen for you doesn't care if you have feelings for her or not. She gets to be the heir-consort, queen-consort in the future, and the mother of the heir-apparent. The power that comes of that is what both she and her parents desire. You are a member of the royal family and entitled as such to carry on in public howsoever you choose. Everyone knows I have handmaidens aside from my queen-consort. Need I remind you that she and I were only espoused by my father to cement an alliance and a lucrative business deal? She's not even your mother."

Imaro placed his hands on his hips and said, "And just how does that work, anyhow? I thought the whole point of you forcing me to marry was to produce a legitimate heir?"

King Nobiri snorted, then chuckled and said, "From the moment we met, the queen-consort and I were never attracted to one another. I met the requisite contract to have a spouse whom I could sire a child with, and since that was sufficient in the eyes of my father, as well as the council and advisors, it didn't matter if my heir was produced by a handmaiden rather than the queen-consort. The illusion of the crown and consort together is sufficient for the rangeen people, the council, and advisors. That would have applied to you as well, if you hadn't chosen to be a selfish child and run away with your same-sex lover. You could have remained together in private while producing the necessary heir with your spouse."

Imaro shook his head and said, "A sham marriage is a lie that I will not be a part of. The rangeen people deserve better than a lie from their royalty."

King Nobiri ceased his pacing and stalked towards his son, standing directly before him and saying, "I am Nobiri Iwato, King of the rangeen people. I don't care if you feel that the people 'deserve better than a lie from their royalty.' We are the royal family, and you are Prince Imaro Iwoto, heir to the crown and throne. You have a duty to carry on the line you will not continue to neglect. Your personal desires are nothing in the face of your duty to me, to your family, to your people. Especially when I'm on the cusp of making us even greater."

"Yes, about that…" Imaro had hoped his father would bring this up. "I think you need to give this plan of yours a lot more consideration. I'm not sure that you realize just how dangerous this course you are taking us on is."

"What are you talking about?" demanded Nobiri.

"This plan of yours to start a war between the humans, sutac, and soetub," stated Imaro.

King Nobiri burst out laughing. He turned from Imaro, walked a few paces away, then turned back and said, "You are an even bigger fool than I thought if you think my plans aren't beneficial to our family, our business interests, and ultimately to the kingdom."

"I don't think ruining the entire galactic economy is ultimately beneficial to the kingdom, Father," stated Imaro angrily.

The look on King Nobiri's face turned colder, catching Imaro slightly off-guard. "Just where would you get a notion such as that, Son? From your human companions?"

"Yes," Imaro admitted. "They also shared a tremendous amount of compelling evidence to that effect. I'm fairly convinced that they're right."

To Imaro's horror and surprise, King Nobiri laughed heartily. "Of course, they're right. I am well aware of the impact of my plan. Don't you realize who I am, child? You, and your new friends, are utterly incapable of seeing the big picture. Nothing lasts forever, Imaro, even something as seemingly stable as OVERLORD and the galactic economy. Rather than await its eventual and inevitable collapse, I'm going to take the lead and direct it. Maybe my biggest mistake was not sharing with you the totality of my plan. I think perhaps now is the time for you to know the legacy I am creating for you. How, if you do your duty and one day inherit the throne, you will be the wealthiest, most powerful being in the entire galaxy."

Imaro held back his comments; he didn't trust himself to respond.

King Nobiri withdrew a 'cator from his pocket. He activated it and said, "Have Kukeb Nwomga and those two humans, Jason Baylin and Charlotte Danella, brought to my throne room immediately."

Imaro cleared his throat.

King Nobiri rolled his eyes and added, "Respectfully request their attendance." He switched off and pocketed the 'cator. Gesturing with his head, King Nobiri said to Imaro, "Come, Son. Let me show you what you stand to gain from what you are calling the 'dangerous' course I have set."

Chapter 38 – The Mad Ravings of a Narcissistic Egomaniac

As their guards, more of the ubiquitous Royal Enforcers, marched them into the throne room, it was exactly what Jay had expected. Gaudy, over the top, ostentatious, immensely overdone. The tapestries hanging down from below the windows were finely woven and stunning, the carpets on the floor utterly plush and luxurious.

There was so much gold in the room that, in the right light, Jay expected it would be blinding. The throne was enormous, commanding the attention of the room where it sat alone atop a raised platform. It was surrounded by statuary of precious metals, gems, and a granite-like stone.

"Your mother would be so incredibly jealous of all this," commented Char.

Jay chuckled and said, "Yeah, my mom would go ga-ga for this place. She'd demand to know who the decorator is and where she can get chairs like the throne for herself."

The Royal Enforcers led them until they were standing at the bottom of the dais, three steps down in front of the throne. Kukeb remained silent, his eyes downcast. Char, like Jay, was examining their surroundings and taking in the ludicrous, extravagant throne room. Their escorts were silent, and Jay was glad they'd not barked at him or Char for their brief comments.

Nothing happened for a time that seemed to drag on and on. The more Jay took in his surroundings, the more he wondered how much was King Nobiri's versus family or even kingdom heirlooms. Still, King Nobiri chose to leave them on display, a clear sign of his wealth and power.

Finally, another pair of Royal Enforcers strode into the throne room from somewhere behind the throne on the dais. Though he'd only seen the king of the rangeen in holographic images, Jay recognized King Nobiri as he moved into the room in a way Jay wanted to describe as falling between a saunter and detached disdain. Imaro trailed behind him, then two more of the Royal Enforcers.

King Nobiri stopped in front of his throne, looking down at Jay, Char, and Kukeb, in both a literal and metaphorical way. Imaro had stopped beside the throne.

Slowly, dramatically, as if putting on a show, King Nobiri seated himself on the ornate throne. As Imaro started to move towards Jay, Char, and Kukeb, King Nobiri said, "No, Imaro. You will remain here, standing at my side."

"Yes, Father," Imaro said quietly. Jay could feel the ire coming off the rangeen prince as he resumed standing beside the throne.

"Baron Kukeb Nwomga." King Nobiri looked daggers at Jay and Char's companion. "I wonder if my son would have taken a less spineless lover had you not served as his secretary. You have proven to be an even bigger fool than my son, the prince."

Kukeb did not respond, his eyes remaining downcast. King Nobiri turned his attention to Jay and Char. "And though I have been given your names, we have not been introduced. Who are you, my human guests?"

"I'm Charlotte Danella."

"I'm Jason Baylin."

"And what world do you hail from?"

"None, currently," replied Jay. "We live on our ship and travel the galaxy. Along the way, we take passengers and cargo."

"Ah, people who don't like to be subject to anyone else," remarked King Nobiri. "Partners? Spouses?"

"We're married," Jay said.

"Isn't that sweet?" sneered King Nobiri. "So, tell me the truth. Did you know that your passenger was the prince of the rangeen people and a runaway from his duties?"

"Not at first, no," Jay stated.

"Not at first," echoed King Nobiri. "And when you did learn his identity? Why didn't you bring him home, then?"

"We had no interest in getting involved in your politics," replied Jay. "We felt no need to do anything but take our passengers where they hired us to take them."

"What changed?" asked King Nobiri. "You have returned them, and though both have made it clear they'd prefer not to be here, it was obviously not against their free will. That means you changed your mind and chose to get involved in our politics. Why?"

"Because," Char took up, causing King Nobiri to shift his gaze to her. "When we learned of your plan to start a war between the soetub, sutac, and humans, you might not have realized your plan would lead to the destruction of the galaxy."

King Nobiri laughed heartily, leaning back in his throne. "That's a bit overly dramatic, don't you think?"

"Not at all," stated Char. "Maybe you don't realize just how dangerous such an action would be because you're from a not-so-well-connected system and are, no offense, ever-so-slightly naïve."

Jay watched as King Nobiri squared his shoulders, puffing himself up to look more intimating as he leaned forward and said, "Not at all. Naïve? No, dear human female. I just know a good opportunity when I see it."

"You're referring, of course, to the sutac and soetub, and their resources?" Jay prompted.

"I see my overly-chatty son told you something about that," King Nobiri began. He arose, started to pace before the throne, and said, "This resource has been exclusive to rangeen space since its discovery. This resource has given the rangeen people a unique place as sole producers of a necessary component in all 'cators, if not the 'cators themselves. The sutac and soetub stumbled on the resource quite by accident, which I learned because they reached out to a business I have a controlling interest in to prove what they had was the resource."

He stopped pacing and turned to coldly eye Jay and Char. "If the soetub and sutac begin to mine the resource, they will disrupt rangeen control of the market. That will further open the way for more 'cator, and more importantly, 'cator component manufacturers. The exclusivity we've long enjoyed, and the benefits of that, end."

"Isn't competition in the markets a good thing?" asked Char.

King Nobiri made a dismissive gesture. "Not when compared to market control via exclusivity."

"So, you plan to somehow get the sutac and soetub to go to war?" questioned Jay.

"Yes," replied King Nobiri.

"How?" asked Jay.

King Nobiri started to pace again, and began his exposition. "Thanks to the roptera, we have been able to secretly connect via a frequency, known only to us and the roptera, to every 'cator in the galaxy. My grandsire set up the first database to store the vast amount of data we gleaned from this. Thus, I've gained information that I will use to sabotage certain sutac efforts in a way that will look like the soetub did it. At the same time, I will do similar to the soetub, while simultaneously transmitting a signal that should disrupt the soetub ability to fly – which will get blamed on the sutac."

King Nobiri dropped back into the throne. He passed his eyes haughtily over Kukeb, then Jay, then Char, before leaning back and saying, "I won't have to fire a shot or get my hands, or the hands of the rangeen, dirty. I only need to make sure that certain transmissions are interrupted while others are misdirected, while still others are broadcast, but not from their true, legitimate sources. We have implanted a code in every component we manufacture, which means it's on every 'cator in the galaxy. Hence, it will be all too easy."

"How do humans enter into this?" asked Char. "And why?"

King Nobiri chuckled. Arrogantly, he said, "You humans are so easy to manipulate. All we have to do is send a few transmissions about disrupting human commerce that seem to have come from the sutac and soetub, then make sure disruptions occur both ways to prevent understanding, so that both sides get upset. Then we interrupt human 'cator use with sutac and soetub signals and a well-placed explosive device or two in the right parts of human space. We'll make sure they're traced to the sutac and soetub, and then we have ourselves a three-way-war and further disconnect from the rangeen."

"Why humans?" asked Jay.

"Because you ask me that question, as if to imply humans are somehow more important than anyone else. Because you're the perfect combination of arrogance and foolishness, easily manipulated into impulsive reaction. Who better to draw eyes from the rangeen than humans?"

"That's monstrous," said Char.

"It's good business to know such things and take advantage of them," remarked King Nobiri.

"Your Majesty," Jay began, commanding King Nobiri's attention. "You might believe that you are starting a skirmish that will distract the sutac and soetub so you can either claim the resource yourself or prevent them from mining it. But I think you are failing to realize that it will almost instantly blossom into a broader war. The sutac, soetub, and humans all have allies that will join them in making war. You'll not just have three races fighting over a distraction, but you'll have half the galaxy at war with the other half. If you are not aware of this truth, of the alliances each of these races has, you must see and recognize that, before it's too late."

King Nobiri leaned back in his throne and smirked. "Oh, but I do. In fact, I'm counting on it."

"What?" Imaro burst out, rounding the throne to get the king's attention. "Father, if the galactic economy falls, don't we lose our fortune, too?"

King Nobiri began to laugh and once more arose from the throne. Despite being shorter than his son, it was clear to Jay he was standing to be intimidating. King Nobiri said, "Foolish child. Once again, you're missing the big picture. I told you before we entered the throne room that your new friends are utterly incapable of seeing the big picture. Even when they go to war, everyone will need 'cators. And war will lead to everyone across the galaxy needing more of them. Armies need to communicate, refugees need to communicate, and so long as there remains a supply of 'cators and 'cator components, the rangeen will be able to provide. Then, even more so, once we have the resource from the sutac and soetub."

"Your Majesty," started Char, claiming King Nobiri's attention. "If war overwhelms the galaxy, then the galactic economy will collapse. That means EVILC will have no value, so nobody will be able to pay for your 'cators and 'cator components."

"So what?" asked King Nobiri in response. "That's the loophole in EVILC. Money is issued by individual governments, planets, and corporations, and is unequal until it meets interstellar commerce. But if we no longer have the intergalactic economy of EVILC, the rangeen can still accept the monies and other resources from the various worlds, governments, and such. Or we can always arrange barter. Thus, while the galactic economy, as such, collapses, local governments maintain their sovereignty, still purchase the needed 'cators and components, and we just pile on the wealth."

"What about OVERLORD?" asked Jay. "Don't you think OVERLORD will get wise to this?"

Now King Nobiri turned to face Jay. "OVERLORD will crumble with the economy, of course. As I started to explain to my foolish son, nothing lasts forever. Even the likes of OVERLORD. Rather than await its inescapable, inevitable, eventual collapse, I'm going to direct it."

King Nobiri began to pace before the throne again. "When the war ends – because all wars end – the rangeen will have the power and the wealth to rebuild OVERLORD. But rather than the rotating representation and committees of its present form, the rangeen will be on top, directing the other races as they inevitably join, accepting and rejecting them. The new order will be dominated and ultimately controlled financially and politically by the rangeen."

"With you at the head?" asked Imaro, coldly.

King Nobiri turned on him. "Of course. And that would have been yours to inherit, foolish child. But now, this will work differently. You will espouse the bride I have chosen for you, beget a child with her, and I will raise that child to succeed me. While I do that and secure the royal line and the future you have proven to me you do not desire, you and your lover can run away. That is, of course, if you can find somewhere not at war. My legacy, however, will be assured, with or without you to succeed me. The rangeen will rule the galaxy."

"That's quite the plan," Jay said. He made his tone as nonchalant and dismissive as possible, drawing King Nobiri's attention back on him.

"Yes," Char agreed. "It would be an impressive plan, too. If it wasn't so deeply evil."

"Evil?" questioned King Nobiri with a chuckle. "No, my dear human female. Not evil. Right. OVERLORD is poorly managed and allowed this loophole to exist. Their pointless, rudderless committees are endlessly changing, never accomplishing much of anything truly worthwhile. OVERLORD could rule over the galaxy. They could set order and direction so that the strong come out on top and the weak know their place. But they don't. They never have, and that is why they are doomed to collapse. I'm right, not evil, and the galaxy needs this."

"You think the peoples of the galaxy don't want autonomy?" asked Jay. "You don't think they prefer their independence over having OVERLORD or another party ruling the galaxy?"

King Nobiri smirked as he said, "The survivors of the war will be grateful to have someone take charge, make peace, and restore order. I, and the rangeen and roptera peoples, will be beloved for that. They'll practically hand control of the galaxy to us. To me."

"You really think you're in the right here?" asked Char. "You don't think someone might work this all out and stop you before this plan of yours can begin?"

King Nobiri dropped back down into his throne. Gesturing expansively to the room, he said, "Nobody else outside my loyal circle has any idea of any of this, save you fools and my son. Imaro might be a disappointment, but he's still the prince. If he tried to tell anyone about this, nobody would believe him, because they'd believe it was just his means to usurp the throne."

Jay flinched as King Nobiri's face became colder and more menacing. "If you think you will ever leave here again, you've another thing coming to you. I won't have you killed, Jason and Charlotte, but I will keep you here to watch it all collapse while nobody ever knows the truth behind the coming war and what you have learned here, today."

"Not nobody," said Imaro, his voice strong and resolute.

"What?" asked King Nobiri, clearly caught off guard both by his son's statement and the tone of his voice.

"Jay and Char believed me when I told them what you were planning," stated Imaro with firmness and conviction in his tone. It was, Jay felt, rather commanding. Imaro continued, saying, "Also, your inner circle, your council and advisors, are no longer the only ones besides all of us in this room who know."

King Nobiri looked confused. "What are you on about?"

"Maybe," Char began, her tone oddly light and almost playful, drawing King Nobiri's attention to her. "You'd like to give the people a formal statement?"

Chapter 39 – Smile When You Tell the Galaxy Your Plan to Destroy Everything

It took all of Imaro's effort not to hoot and holler over King Nobiri's obvious confusion. Between Imaro's off-handed comment about far more people being in the know than he thought and Char's remark about making a formal statement, King Nobiri was clearly taken aback.

"What are you talking about?" King Nobiri asked once again.

"Oh, nothing," replied Imaro, keeping his tone as nonchalant as possible. "Except, of course, all of rangeen space has been witness to our entire conversation here."

"What?" demanded King Nobiri. His look was a blend of frustration, confusion, anger, and concern. He'd been holding the floor and pontificating to great effect, right up until Imaro and Char pulled the metaphorical rug out from under him.

Imaro stepped before the throne. "Let me explain, Your Majesty. You see, when I learned from Jay and Char the full extent of where your disruption of the sutac and soetub could lead, I did some checking. They are not at all wrong about how the various allies all three races have would join them if they went to war. That, in turn, would lead to even more races jumping on board, and the whole galaxy would be torn apart by that war. I couldn't believe you would knowingly do such a thing. How many innocent lives would you sacrifice to gain more power? Then I thought on it more. I realized the answer would be as many as it took. Hence, I knew that I couldn't just run away. You're right in that I must do my duty. That, however, extends beyond just the rangeen people, in this instance."

Imaro paused, seeing his words sinking into Nobiri's head. Imaro went on, saying, "You were also right that I couldn't just share this story among our people without it appearing that my intent was less to stop you from committing an atrocity as much as to usurp your throne for myself."

Imaro began to pace before the throne. "However, Jay and Char are humans, and not subjects of the rangeen, nor connected to the royal house. Since they were the ones who showed me just how depraved your plan was, and the extent of the horror you were preparing to inflict on the galaxy, Kukeb and I decided we had to act. Since we couldn't do this on our own, and not without incontrovertible evidence, we worked with our new human friends to figure out the best way to stop your plan before it came to fruition."

King Nobiri was leaning forward on his throne, anger and terror fighting for dominance of his expression. "What have you done?" he demanded in a breathy, concerned voice.

Imaro turned to face his father. "I have done nothing. Nothing, that is, but to give you the opportunity to share with me, Kukeb, Jay, and Char, the full extent of your plan. It just so happens that we arranged for you to also share your plan with a great many others."

Char placed herself on the first step of the dais, her movement drawing the attention of Nobiri. She tapped at the glasses she wore and remarked, "Despite the ease of vision correction, I always thought glasses looked great on me. Vanity aside, they also provide me with AR, VR, and the ability to glean additional data about things I see. Today, though, they've also been serving me by recording and transmitting this whole conversation."

Kukeb, no longer eyeing the floor, held up a device. "This, Your Majesty, has been using a frequency nobody in the palace would look for or take notice of to transmit the data Char has been recording via her eyeglasses to Quinn, the robot co-pilot of the *Audacia*."

"My ship," Jay said, also placing himself on the first step of the dais. "Since your Royal Enforcers don't care about the unarmed human ship in a landing bay on the palace grounds, and ignored Quinn's presence therein, he's taken the signal that Char's eyeglasses sent and has been transmitting that directly to RKNN – The Rangeen Kingdom News Network, Channel VX3410.756Q on the Interplanetary Transmission Entanglement Mediascape."

Nobiri shifted his eyes from Char, to Kukeb, to Jay, and back again several times, but he said nothing.

Imaro reclaimed his attention and said, "RKNN, of course, is a part of the Establishment Synchronized Systems network – you know, the MESS-work – in addition to ITEM, as in the *Interplanetary* Transmission Entanglement Mediascape. Interplanetary, as in your confession of your plans to start a war between the soetub, sutac, and humans - for your own gain - has been transmitted far and wide and can be viewed across the entire known galaxy."

Chapter 40 – And Now, A Word From Our Sponsor

Flashback!

Chapter 41 – The Real Idea Embedded in the Very Bad Idea (2 Days or so Ago)

"We've just received clearance to land and coordinates," said Quinn.

Jay climbed into the pilot's seat. As he did so, he asked, "Imaro, is your father narcissistic and above every aspect of the law?"

"Yes, yes he is," replied Imaro.

Jay proceeded to take control of the flight from Quinn and flew along the prescribed flight path over the sea. As he did so, he asked, "Is he the kind to believe himself the most important person in the room, and always eager to share why?"

"Yes," responded Imaro.

Jay considered his next thought, then asked, "So, do you believe, if pressed the right way, he'd share his plan? I don't just mean answer yes or no if asked about it, but full-on, complete, and total details, justifications, expectations, and the like? Think about it a moment and be completely honest both with yourself and me before you answer. If pressed, to show he's in control, has all the power, and to show off his infallibility, especially in front of strangers like Char and me that thinks he can impress and/or overwhelm, will he tell all?"

Imaro was silent for a moment, and Jay glanced back to see him thinking. Char had a curious look on her face, and Kukeb was still looking dejected.

As Jay turned back to their flight, Imaro stated, "Yes. He loves to show how big and bad he is, how very wise, how infinitely clever and always right he is. With the right goading, I'm certain I can get my father to reveal his entire scheme, down to the last sordid detail, in front of you both. What of it?"

"Quinn?" Jay questioned. "Do we still have that encrypted, special transponder? You know, the 'cator we got as an apology after that ludicrous situation we got into with Exeter's cousin?"

"Yes, we do," replied Quinn.

Jay explained, "Char remembers. My sister persuaded me to help out one of her spouse's cousins. He has like eighty of them or some other ludicrous number. Anyhow, he was moving from one system to another and needed help with that. What she failed to tell me, and what her spouse, Exeter, also failed to tell me, was that this particular cousin had a penchant for stealing. As such, while Char and I were not on the ship, he disabled Quinn and took the *Audacia*."

"Oh, that was such a clusterfuck," remarked Char.

"Anyhow," Jay went on. "This dumbass cousin went straight to Exeter with *Audacia*. Exeter, recognizing the mess his cousin had caused, got him to return the ship to us, restore and apologize to Quinn, and then pay triple to keep us from having him justifiably arrested for stealing our ship. As an added gift, and further apology for the crap we had to deal with, Exeter provided us with a special 'cator that could only communicate to the *Audacia* and reactivate Quinn if he'd been somehow shut down."

"How come you don't carry this 'cator on you at all times?" asked Kukeb.

"Because we no longer allow anyone on the ship unsupervised," replied Jay. "Also, Quinn has been modified to prevent anyone being capable of disabling him again."

"What if he got destroyed?" questioned Kukeb.

"That would be indicative of a much bigger problem," remarked Char.

"If it's not something you keep on your person regularly, what good is this special transponder, this 'cator, anyhow?" asked Kukeb.

"I'll get to that in a moment," said Jay, talking out the plan he was still formulating in his head. "Char's glasses aren't just corrective for her vision. They can record audio and video and transmit it short range. Normally, for that purpose, she keeps a tablet on her person. However, if we tweak that signal, we can probably attune it to that specific 'cator and its special transponder."

"Then what?" asked Imaro.

Jay glanced back at the rangeen prince, noting he appeared to be considering where Jay's thought was going. Turning his attention back to their flight, Jay said, "We get the king to go on his rant in front of us, revealing everything. Char's glasses will be recording the whole thing and, with the signal to the 'cator, transmitting it to Quinn on *Audacia*."

"Oh, that's good," broke in Char. "And then Quinn can transmit it out from *Audacia*."

"There's a lot of room for error here, Jay," remarked Imaro. His tone, however, was one of hope and not dismissive. He went on, saying, "One of the biggest obstacles is that signals around the palace are tightly controlled. If the Royal Enforcers or members of some other authority in the palace figure out what you're doing, they might destroy *Audacia* before anything can be transmitted."

"Not if we can establish someone for Quinn to transmit directly to, rather than transmit in the open," remarked Char.

"What?" asked Imaro.

Char said, "We send the signal to a specific recipient. Someone who will then transmit in the open to share the king's intentions with everyone. It needs to make its way onto ITEM and the MESS-work."

To Jay's surprise, Kukeb began to chuckle. "I have it," he said. "There's a permanent feed between the palace and RKNN – the Rangeen Kingdom News Network. That feed allows the crown to make statements and direct transmissions on the one channel they can control without raising the ire of OVERLORD."

"Right," said Char. "Most races have a unique channel on the 'tangle. But can you connect Quinn to that, Kukeb?"

"Yes," Kukeb replied. "Even though King Nobiri agreed to Imaro's demand that we not be harmed, he'll probably have us all arrested, to show he still has the power."

"Sorry," Imaro said. "I thought of that after I made my request. He'll be true to his word, but Kukeb is correct. He'll still do what he can to show he's in control. Because he promised no harm, chances are he'll at least not toss you into the dungeons."

"That's comforting," said Jay, half under his breath.

"Because of my role as Imaro's secretary, I have direct access to that channel," stated Kukeb. "I can veritably guarantee nobody will think to bother to remove my access to it."

"Agreed," stated Imaro.

"Then Kukeb should carry the 'cator," said Char.

"Why?" asked Imaro.

"If, as you and Kukeb surmise, your father follows through on having us arrested, it's likely everything we have on us will be confiscated. That will include 'cators, to keep us quiet."

"That's true," agreed Imaro. "Kukeb, you will probably be searched thoroughly, to make sure you're not wired as a bomb or anything of that sort. But they'll probably set up dampening fields rather than bother to take our 'cators from us, unlike our human companions."

"I agree," said Kukeb.

"There is one more question I need to ask," said Jay, observing the cityscape beginning to materialize far ahead of them. "How will the Royal Enforcers and other members of the government and nobility react? Will they come after us in support of King Nobiri, or stand against him to support you in the face of this?"

"To set any of this in motion," Imaro began, "my father would need to have most, if not all of the council and his advisors onboard. However, in the face of something that might ruin the standing of the rangeen in the eyes of the rest of the galaxy, they'll have him under arrest before he decides to out them, too. My part in this will stop any nonsense that might otherwise occur in the face of deposing the king. Then, parsing that out will be relatively easy."

Silence descended over everyone in the cockpit.

"That is a rather impressive plan, Captain," stated Quinn.

Jay glanced toward his robotic co-pilot. "Thanks."

"It requires a lot of suppositions to be correct, but I calculate you have at least a sixty to sixty-five percent chance of success," added Quinn.

"It hinges on Imaro being right about his father," added Char. "Hopefully, not only is he right, but we can do this without getting ourselves hurt or killed."

"Unless someone has a better plan?" asked Jay. Nobody replied. "Quinn, I've got our flight. Get the 'cator, please attune it to Char's glasses, and then give it to Kukeb."

"Yes, Captain," said Quinn, rising from his seat.

Looking out the forward viewport, Jay saw the city of Ranrop-Palast becoming visible, though it was still hundreds of kilometers away. He tried not to think about all the things that could go wrong. He was not a gambler by nature, but he knew this was a huge risk.

Chapter 42 – Even Nonhumans Can Be Hoisted On A Variant of Their Own Petard

King Nobiri continued to stare at Imaro. Then, he scoffed and burst out laughing. "Oh, that was too rich. For a moment there, I almost believed you had come up with something that clever. But you're bluffing."

"Oh, I don't lack the ability to bluff, Father," agreed Imaro. "After all, I did bluff both mine and Kukeb's way out of the palace and off the planet. But this is no bluff."

"Before you accuse my husband and I of bluffing," Char began. "In my business dealings, I've absolutely bluffed a time or two. Jay has done so to secure cargo and passengers. This? This is not bluff, King Nobiri."

"If you are not bluffing, why has nobody arrived to question the validity of this?" demanded Nobiri.

As if summoned, every single door in the throne room, obvious or hidden, slid into the nearby wall or ceiling or otherwise was thrown open. Two dozen more Royal Enforcers smartly marched in, as well as a dozen different rangeen nobles that Imaro recognized.

In seconds, they were surrounding the throne. More than half were on the dais beside or behind, the rest on the floor below. Imaro saw that all looked displeased in one way or another.

"Guards!" King Nobiri addressed the Royal Enforcers around them. "Arrest these humans, the prince, his secretary, and hold the Royal Enforcers already present for questioning, immediately! My son, his secretary, and the humans have been threatening me and must be withdrawn and imprisoned, now,"

Imaro watched as one of the nobles, whom he identified as the Countess Solim Iamo, a member of the council who held the position of First Treasurer, stepped forward. "With apologies, King Nobiri, but we are all aware that that is not the truth. The arrest of those you demand is not what will next transpire."

Nobiri rose from his throne, attempting but failing to be intimidating, as none of the newly arrived Royal Enforcers or nobles moved. He said, with all the malice he could put in his tone, "How dare you? Need I remind you that I am your king? Do you realize that for this betrayal, you will pay a most terrible price?"

"I think it could be readily argued that the only one who has betrayed the rangeen, Father, is you," stated Imaro. "The price our people will pay if you carry out this dangerous, thoughtless, destructive plan, especially now that it's been presented by you to the whole galaxy, is far worse than anything you can threaten any of us with. Not even your most trusted advisors, nor any in your inner circle, will stand by your side now."

King Nobiri glared at Imaro, then looked around at all the others in the throne room. Imaro could see he was seeking an ally, someone to side with him, to help him hold his place.

"I am, by birthright, king of the rangeen," Nobiri stated. "I have done nothing but advance the place of our people, made us stronger, improved our economy, and the lives of all. My actions have never been anything but pure when it comes to my kingdom and my people."

He kept shifting his gaze from person to person. He continued, his pace quickening as he said, "Do you have any idea what I can do to you for this betrayal? You alone will not feel my sting, your families will pay an equally terrible price. My rule is absolute, and you cannot take action against a seated king in good health. My heir has proven himself unworthy, and I remain in charge. Test me and see just how far I will go to show my might and right."

Once more, Nobiri paused, looking at those around him, seeking a supporter. None moved nor responded to him. His tone shifted again, becoming pleading. "I am King Nobiri Iwoto, son of Oddus, son of Ukali, son of Houli, son of Elameyahi, protector of the rangeen people. You cannot think my intentions were for anything but the betterment of the rangeen people, and to continue to make the family Iwoto strong, successful, and powerful. All I do, all I have ever done, is for the people. You must see that I am king, and this is just a misunderstanding."

The royal council secretary, Marquis Jomel Ibeme, stepped forward and said, "It must be noted, Your Majesty, that because of these non-rangeen being witnesses," – he gestured towards Jay and Char – "as well as all those present, here and now, being able to verify that they have been privy to your confession – which, as well as our presence here with you now, is still being transmitted – the authenticity of the transmission and all that has been and is still being shared is unquestionable."

"You are right about one thing, Father," Imaro said, claiming the king's attention. "Yes, I have been a foolish child. Not because I won't support this terrible plan of yours. I'm a foolish child for ignoring who you really are and what you are willing to do. You claim that it's all for the rangeen people? No, it's not. It's all about you, your ego, your power, and your wealth. What you intend, what you will do to disrupt peace and stability across the galaxy for the benefit of the rangeen – and most of all for yourself – is too high a price to pay, on any level. My own selfishness and my desire not to be forced to marry against my will or my preference, that has indeed been foolish on my part. But I was a foolish child more for being so naïve about your ultimate ambitions. Jay and Char helped me see that I could not selfishly run away, not when I could do my part to stop your mad plan."

Imaro paused and looked at everyone in the room before returning his attention to his father. "Maybe that makes me a foolish child, too. But I'd rather be foolish, in the know, and able to do some good than foolish, ignorant, and complicit in a horrible plan."

Someone across the room began to clap, slowly. Imaro saw one of the few people he truly dreaded, the head of the Royal Enforcers. Commissioner Zinibi Motua was tough, no-nonsense, and principled. She was also utterly intimidating, and Imaro had never felt comfortable around her.

She stopped applauding, and with measured, precise steps, she moved across the throne room and began to ascend the dais. As she did so, she said, "Nobiri Iwoto, I am here to place you under arrest for gross misconduct and abuse of power, conspiring to start an utterly unjustifiable planetary war, and certainly other acts beyond our jurisdiction but that I have no doubt OVERLORD will certainly be investigating."

"You think my plans were not for the good of the rangeen people?" demanded Nobiri. He had petulantly sunk back into his throne, and though his voice was clear and he spoke with conviction, the hint of desperation was unmistakable. "None of you recognize how my plans would have elevated the rangeen people. OVERLORD has no jurisdiction here, nor anywhere, because they are just an oversight committee with no real power. They're doomed, with or without any actions on my part. I'm just setting us up to lead before anyone else considers doing so.

"You say, Commissioner Zinibi, that OVERLORD will be investigating acts beyond our jurisdiction? How does that work, when OVERLORD has no jurisdiction to speak of and the rangeen are not now, nor have we ever been, subject to them?"

Nobiri arose again, on a tear, ranting and saying, "People die all the time. The paltry few who might have died from a war that would bring OVERLORD to their natural conclusion sooner rather than later are nothing in the face of the greatness that I would have achieved, the power that I would have wielded. I would be the king of kings, leader of the whole galaxy, a genuine overlord!"

The last, he practically shouted. Everyone looked stunned, and it only took Nobiri a moment to realize where he had gone. Too little, too late, he added, much more softly and calmly, "That is through me and what I do to make the rangeen great."

"I think, Nobiri Iwoto, you have made it abundantly clear your intentions," said Zinibi Motua after a too-long, uncomfortable silence. "Before you speak again, I think you should consider that all of this. Every. Last. Word. Has been recorded and transmitted across ITEM and the MESS-Work for the whole galaxy to witness. Every. Single. Word."

Nobiri looked as if he would say more, but then, Imaro saw true, full, and total realization strike him. He had outed himself and his intentions to the whole galaxy. He had done himself in with his own confession and admissions. The rangeen king appeared to sink further into the throne, remaining silent.

After another moment's pause, Zinibi Motua approached and turned her attention to Imaro. "Your Highness," she began, "with the king under arrest, as heir to the throne, you are in charge here."

"Yes," agreed Jomel Ibeme. The royal council secretary continued, saying, "Until such time as you meet with the council to decide Nobiri Iwoto's fate, and a formal ceremony can be arranged, as heir, you are Regent."

Kukeb commanded the attention of everyone in the room by loudly clearing his throat. "There are twelve nobles, all members of the council, present here and now. That's a majority. In light of his confessed crimes and the formal recognition of those present of Prince Imaro as Regent, with all these witnesses, lest anyone question Prince Imaro's authority – what about the formal declaration of disempowerment for Nobiri Iwoto?"

"Ah, yes, Baron Kukeb, you are correct," stated Jomel Ibeme. Imaro noted he sounded somewhat uncomfortable. Then, the royal council secretary turned to face the other nobles on the main floor. "I call for a formal vote, of all the members of the nobility present, as members of the royal council, to name Imaro Iwoto the Regent of the rangeen, until the fate of Nobiri Iwoto is decided."

After a pause, he went on, saying, "All those in agreement that Nobiri Iwoto is no longer fit to be king and he be formally disempowered, turn away from the dais."

Almost as one, all of the nobles turned, as did Zinibi Motua. Jomel Ibeme made it clear he was also turned away from Nobiri.

A moment later, Jomel Ibeme said, "It is witnessed, and so it is sealed. This complete, I now ask that you all recognize the heir, Prince Imaro Iwoto, as the Regent of the rangeen people, and empower him as such. All those in agreement that Imaro Iwoto be named Regent and formally empowered, turn to face him now."

Again, almost as one, all of the nobles turned, as did Zinibi Motua and Jomel Ibeme, to face Imaro.

"It is done, Regent Imaro," stated Jomel Ibeme, bowing formally.

Imaro wondered, if Char's glasses were not still recording and transmitting all that was transpiring in the throne room, unobstructed, if they would have been so quick and unanimous. Many of the council member nobles among the twelve had been Nobiri's supporters and his inner circle before his confession.

Maybe they had been fully aware of the destruction Nobiri's plan would have wrought. Maybe they had cared only for the power it would provide the rangeen people, its industry, and them, directly. Imaro knew that they were not to be trusted. But they were all smart enough to know when the end game was at hand.

"Regent Imaro," began Zinibi Motua with a formal air. Gesturing to the throne, she asked, "What should we do with Nobiri Iwoto?"

Imaro looked at his father. His eyes were cold, a mix of fury and defeat. Maybe he hoped to play some card he still had hidden, but Imaro was rather certain he had nothing left. "Commissioner Zinibi, please confine him to his apartments. And by confine him, I mean that he will receive no visitors, not even any of his handmaidens. Any requesting visitation with him will be vetted by you and I, and even palace staff who bring him food or otherwise care for his needs will be escorted by Royal Enforcers vetted by you. He will, however, be treated with the dignity of the crown."

"Yes, Regent Imaro," replied Zinibi Motua. Imaro knew she had not needed to partake in the council vote. As Royal Enforcer Commissioner, she was apart from the nobility. Yet that statement was something Imaro saw for its support of him, so he decided that Zinibi Motua, at least, he could trust.

She snapped her fingers and gestured to a quartet of Royal Enforcers. They all moved as one, taking up position around Nobiri. He only slightly resisted as they dragged him from the throne.

As he was marched away, Nobiri called out, "This will be remembered as the day you crossed your king! All of you will pay dearly for this betrayal! I will not forget who my betrayers are. Not ever."

After more of the same kind of ranting – all of which, Imaro knew, was being recorded and transmitted – Nobiri's guards, followed by Zinibi Motua, left the throne room.

Imaro looked around. There were still a lot of Royal Enforcers, a dozen nobles, Kukeb, Jay, and Char remaining. All of them looked stunned to a greater or lesser degree. More than that, all of them were looking to him to take the lead.

Imaro took a deep breath, then let it out. He had not wanted this, but he had not run away from his duty so much as his father and his personal demands of him. He would do what his people, and possibly others apart from his people, needed him to do.

"We have a lot of work ahead of us," Imaro stated.

Chapter 43 – BREAKING NEWS

"This is the RKNN, the Rangeen Kingdom News Network, Channel VX3410.756Q on the Interplanetary Transmission Entanglement Mediascape," the official-sounding, disembodied voice states.

A pair of rangeen are seated at a desk, male and female. The male has deep-set, black eyes with flecks of metallic red within them beneath his pronounced brow. His spiked hair is a bright neon green, his skin brown. The female has deep-set, black eyes with flecks of metallic gold within them, thick, long, lush neon blue hair, and a skin tone similar to the male.

Behind them is a display with the RKNN logo, and the words "Breaking News."

"I'm Dajan Ibumu," says the male.

"And I'm Laolat Njura," says the female. "Thank you for joining us on this historic day."

"If you are only now just tuning in," takes up Dajan, "let's catch you up on this breaking story from the Royal Stronghold at Ronrop-Palast."

"That's right, Dajan," Laolat says. "Two days ago, an unexpected transmission from the stronghold, on a secure connection directly from the palace to RKNN, began to transmit a conversation between King Nobiri Iwoto, his heir, Prince Imaro Iwoto, the prince's secretary, Baron Kukeb Nwomga, and a pair of humans, one of whom was doing the recording of this most disturbing and unconventional conversation."

"Indeed," takes up Dajan. "Over the course of the discussion, King Nobiri revealed that he was going to use multiple unscrupulous tactics to cause the sutac, soetub, and humans to go to war. The narrative became increasingly distressing, as he revealed that he was well aware that the overall consequence of his actions might lead to a catastrophic interplanetary destabilization, economic collapse, and even the fall of OVERLORD."

"Quite a disturbing and shocking revelation, Dajan," says Laolat. "This behind-the-scenes look into the mind of the rangeen king was truly disturbing. Even when he realized that the discussion was being recorded and shared, he worked to convince the heir, his secretary, and the humans that his plans and subsequent actions were all quite justifiable."

Dajan says, "We wanted to test those claims, so we had our own Unbussu Wifali speak with respected historians, economists, and military officials."

Dajan turns as the camera pans to show Unbussu Wifali beside him. "Unbussu, what can you tell us?"

The screen now shows Unbussu and several numbers appearing on the screen at his side. "Thank you, Dajan. All of the experts I spoke to agree that the death toll resulting from a war between humans, soetub, and sutac would be in the tens of thousands. However, as the humans speaking with King Nobiri pointed out, all three races have allies who would join the battle in support, raising that death toll dramatically to the hundreds of thousands. As more races get drawn into such a combat, all of our experts agree that such a war would have resulted in tens, if not hundreds, of millions of deaths across the galaxy. A truly horrifying notion."

"Unbussu?" queries Laolat, and the camera cuts to her. "What about the threat of the collapse of the Enigmatic Valuation Institute of Leverage Currency?"

"Truly distressing, Laolat," replies Unbussu, as the camera cuts back to him. As he speaks, new numbers appear. "All of the experts we spoke with agree that an interplanetary war involving a majority of the races across the galaxy would disrupt commerce and collapse EVILC in a matter of months. While some worlds would be able to make do with their own currency, certain moons, space stations, platforms, and unaffiliated worlds dependent on EVILC would be swiftly impoverished. Without EVILC, trade would become almost impossible, and that would lead to unprecedented medical emergencies, famines, and possible lawlessness impacting billions. It's an awful, frightening picture that would be presented to us all."

"Those are some startling numbers," says Dajan. "Thank you, Unbussa." A graphic of the OVERLORD badge appears on the screen behind Dajan. "No representatives from OVERLORD have yet issued any formal statement about this situation. However, it is expected that investigators will be dispatched to verify certain legalities. Additionally, OVERLORD will also be sending a special committee, at the request of the Regent, to oversee the transition of power and to coordinate with the investigators on whether Nobiri Iwoto will be charged with any crimes that will require his extradition into OVERLORD custody."

"Meanwhile," says Laolat as the camera pans to her, "most officials, pundits, and general citizens continue to be impressed by the clear-headedness and definitive actions on the part of the Regent, Prince Imaro Iwoto." An image of Imaro appears behind her. "While previously dismissed as naught but a puppet of King Nobiri, Prince Imaro's clear and direct speech, honesty, and defiance of tradition have impressed not only the rangeen people, but others across the galaxy."

"That's right, Laolat," says Dajan as the camera pans back to him. "In fact, multiple polls have placed Prince Imaro's approval rating at record highs, sometimes greater than eighty percent, far above any others in the Iwoto line of rulers. Though many had awaited Prince Imaro's future reign with deep trepidation, most now view it with hope and excitement."

"Yes indeed, Dajan," says Laolat as the camera cuts back to her. "One of the most unique traits of Prince Imaro is his extreme humility. While it was accepted that King Nobiri would take and accept any and all credit, real or otherwise, Prince Imaro is unexpectedly, unabashedly humble. When various leaders across the galaxy reached out to the Regent to express their gratitude for him saving the galaxy from war and collapse, he repeatedly stated that he could take little, if any, credit for this."

"It has indeed been quite unexpected and amazing, Laolat," says Dajan as the camera returns to him. An image of Jay and Char appears behind him. "In fact, Prince Imaro has stated repeatedly that the credit goes to the humans who he and Baron Kukeb Nwomga took ship with, one Jason 'Jay' Mortimer Baylin and his spouse, Charlotte 'Char' Angela Danella. During his most recent press conference, the Regent had this to say."

The screen cuts to Imaro, standing in an opulent room in the Royal Stronghold, where announcements to the press are regularly made. The question asked, Imaro says, "Once again, I must state that while I did my part, I did not save the galaxy from my father's machinations. Jay and Char saved the galaxy."

Chapter 44 – The Surreal Aftermath of Unplanned Heroism

The past three days had been surreal and utterly crazy. Char was not a fan of the spotlight. One of the things she loved most about her job was that, though she had direct interaction with clients at times, overall, her work was not in the public eye.

They had done their best to avoid speaking to the press. Yet their best had not resulted in zero contact. The press wanted their story.

Imaro had decided that Jay and Char had saved the galaxy. Char could hardly believe he'd stated it so plainly. She felt that it was a gross overstatement of the role she and Jay had played. Imaro disagreed.

With the crisis averted, Char had wanted to leave as soon as they could. Yet Kukeb and Imaro had persuaded her and Jay to remain in Ranrop-Palast. Both rangeen had provided an extremely reasonable argument: concerns for Jay and Char's safety.

While nearly all the nobles and advisors to the crown either already had, or would, switch sides, disavow Nobiri, and support Imaro, trusting their word would remain questionable for some time. Nobiri had ruled for forty years as king, and Imaro had no doubt that, even discredited as he was and as awful as his plans would have been for the galaxy, Nobiri still had followers who'd go anywhere he led them.

Some, as such, might see Jay and Char as targets of opportunity. If they left the protection of the Royal Stronghold and Ranrop-Palast, a Nobiri loyalist might think to capture or kill them to somehow force Imaro's hand. Because Imaro didn't want Jay and Char to be used as bargaining chips in that way, he and Kukeb felt that they should stay.

Char disliked it but couldn't argue with the reasoning. There was, Jay pointed out, another practical reason not to leave. The authorities that were en route to Rangeenavelt specifically desired to speak with Jay and Char. What's more, while the process of the formal removal of Nobiri and Imaro's elevation were worked out, the press, representing various ITEM channels and MESS-work sites, wouldn't be harassing them and getting in the way of going back to work.

Thus, Char and Jay were lounging in the suites that Imaro had provided for them in the palace. If their prison had been plush, this was downright sumptuous. They had a beautiful courtyard, open to the outside, with a lush garden, as well as a balcony off their sunroom. There was a large kitchenette, which was unnecessary when livery could be summoned instantly to get them anything they desired. They had a magnificent bathroom with a massive tub and shower, a cushiony sitting room, and an opulent bedroom.

Char and Jay had visited some incredible places across the galaxy. They'd stayed in deluxe vacation accommodations many times. All of them paled in comparison to the royal treatment on Rangeenavelt.

During their stay, Jay and Char had full access to both ITEM and the MESS-work. Char was reading and watching multiple reports about the news of the former rangeen king's plot as it spread around the galaxy. Planets more or less on the other side of the Milky Way were aware of all that had transpired. Again and again, Char came across clips of the recording of Jay, Imaro, and Kukeb confronting Nobiri and getting him to reveal his plan. Char could be heard multiple times and wasn't only on the recording because it had been made via her eyeglasses.

One of the most bizarre and distressing elements of the whole thing, Char felt and Jay agreed, was the number of pundits, commentators, and leaders across the galaxy calling them heroes. It didn't help that Imaro had publicly stated that Jay and Char had saved the galaxy. That just seemed utterly far-fetched.

Char conceded that the war Nobiri had intended to start would have been atrocious. The devastation, as well as the economic and other repercussions, would have been catastrophic. Char had seen more than one estimate of the potential death toll and ruin that would have followed, and it was just unimaginable. She recognized all of that but couldn't wrap her head around the idea that preventing that meant they'd saved the galaxy. That was totally crazy, right?

At all of the many press conferences Imaro was holding, he kept insisting that the credit was Jay and Char's. Had they not shared their perspective and told him how devastating King Nobiri's actions could be, Imaro would not have accepted his responsibility and taken action to stop his father.

Jay had attempted more than once to get Quinn recognized for his part. Had the robot not tied the feed into the palace hardline to RKNN, they'd have been unable to make the rangeen king's confession visible to the galaxy in real time. Jay kept crediting Quinn for his part, and while some of the reporters and interviewers accepted it, most glossed over the robot because he was a robot.

Char appreciated that Jay made the effort. She was also quite sure that Quinn, artificial intelligence though he was, also appreciated receiving his due credit.

Quinn had left the *Audacia* and visited them in the Royal Stronghold. Although the robot was welcomed and invited to join them in their suites, he preferred to remain aboard *Audacia*. He'd only come to visit them, he claimed, because Thalia and Cosima were being unusually needy and had communicated to him that they wanted to be with their humans. So, he'd brought the spacecats to Jay and Char.

The herpestelines, Quinn had stated haughtily, had been bothering him and had even deigned to communicate directly with him, something they normally didn't do. For the most part, the spacecats stayed on the ship, content to keep it vermin-free and roam all about. It wasn't usual for them to demand to be with their humans, even when Char and Jay departed for more than just a few days.

It was, of course, pleasant to be with their companions. Like Char and Jay, the spacecats also received the literal royal treatment. All four of them, as such, were being pampered, catered to in every way, and were enjoying the luxuries and being spoiled.

They'd not been left wholly to their own devices. Imaro reached out to them every day, and Kukeb visited frequently. Both, however, apologized for not having more time, but there was a ludicrous amount of work for them to do.

Now Char was lounging on a couch, reading on a tablet, with Cosima sprawled on her lap. Jay was similarly lounging on another couch, watching something on his tablet with Thalia on his lap. There was a gentle and pleasant breeze blowing into their suite from the open balcony.

A tone sounded, and Imaro strode into the room. He appeared to Char to be carrying himself larger, with more dignity and a sense of purpose. The runaway rangeen male had transformed into the rangeen Regent, taking his responsibilities seriously.

"Your Highness," Char addressed him. "Forgive me, I'd stand and bow, but you know I dislike shaking Cosima off."

Imaro grinned and waved a hand dismissively. "Of course. Besides, it's nice to get a chance to just be with friends and not bowed to or otherwise given formalities."

"How are you doing?" asked Jay, also not rising, though Thalia stretched and removed herself from his lap.

Imaro sat in the nearest cushy chair with a sigh. "I have been so incredibly busy. I knew accepting this would make my life a lot more difficult but never appreciated the scale of that."

"Want to talk about what's got you constantly on the go?" asked Char.

"Of course," Imaro said. "First, figuring out who I can genuinely trust has been a challenge. Save one or two, all the nobles, council, and various advisors have offered their loyalty to me. They know which way the wind is blowing, so of course they're siding with me. But I'm not foolish enough to trust them without testing them. So far, I only mostly trust Commissioner Zinibi and Countess Solim. The only people I completely trust are Kukeb and you two."

Char grinned at the compliment. Cosima removed herself from Char's lap and made her way to Imaro's. The rangeen regent let her settle herself and began to rub her ears.

"What's more," Imaro continued, "I've had to do a lot of politicking with OVERLORD, the sutac, and the soetub. Because you humans are so scattered and were not targeted in the same way, that's not been an issue. The threat alone has caused the sutac and soetub to seek possible retribution. Fortunately, OVERLORD has been extremely helpful in managing that."

Despite Cosima's protest, Imaro arose. He was clearly restless, as he began to pace, and said, "I've also been working with a huge number of very distraught business owners who find themselves working with me now rather than my father. Of course, the share in all the businesses didn't belong to Nobiri specifically, but the crown. Ergo, they're my problem now. I have no doubt that several of them were in cahoots with my father but flushing them out is going to take time."

Still pacing, but slowing, Imaro sighed. "Then, on top of all this, there's the formal removal of Nobiri as king and my coronation to replace him. It's been more than a lifetime for many of my people since a new king was coronated, not to mention it's been centuries since a king was removed against his will. Even so, there's a ton of pomp and circumstance that's unavoidable, and the whole ceremony is, I think, a bit much. Fortunately, Kukeb is back in his element and doing an incredible job managing everything with me. I'll work on having him accept my proposal to become my spouse after this is done."

Imaro stopped pacing and sat back in the chair. "Of course, you both will be invited as guests of honor at my coronation. The first non-rangeen ever in attendance at a coronation, I'll have you know."

"Wow," was all Jay said.

Char felt momentary anxiety. A coronation? The number of people that would be there was an uncomfortable thought. Also, the whole idea of being at an alien race's coronation was uncomfortable.

Still, after all they'd been through together, she couldn't say no. "Of course. We wouldn't miss it," she said.

"It'll be somewhat awkward," said Jay, "But one of those once-in-a-lifetime events we're honored to be invited to."

Imaro chuckled. "You really do not recognize just how big a debt of honor you're owed, do you? You also don't realize how large a debt I personally owe you. I know it wasn't your intent to get involved in rangeen politics, nor to save the galaxy. But you did intend to set me and Kukeb on the right path. You are how I found my way, in more ways than one."

Char saw Jay starting to blush. She felt the same, but said, "I'm glad we could help."

"Help," Imaro scoffed. "So much more than help," he went on, standing. "I wish I could stay and chat longer, but there are things I need to do and places I need to be. However, may Kukeb and I join you here for supper tonight? Even if it's a little late?"

"We'd really enjoy that," Jay said, knowing Char would agree.

"Excellent," Imaro said. He turned to leave but then turned back. "Oh, one more matter. There's not going to be time to have anyone travel here, but do either of you have anyone you'd like to invite to be here, holographically, both to serve as witnesses and be your guests of honor at my coronation?"

"Oh, I can't tell you how much my mother would love that," said Jay. Char coughed to cover her grin. She agreed. Though, like Jay, she suspected his mother would mostly want to compare what the rangeen royals had to what she didn't, and vice versa.

"Certainly. Char?" asked Imaro.

She considered that a moment. "I think my sister would love to get a chance to attend this. She's always had a thing for human royalty of the past, so this coronation she'd enjoy witnessing."

"Great," said Imaro. "I'll make that happen. If you'll excuse me? See you later."

Imaro departed, and Char saw the Royal Enforcers fall into step with the regent before the door slid closed.

Char already knew the answer but decided to voice the question, nonetheless. "Jay, do you really think it's a good idea to invite your mother to something as ostentatious and officious as this coronation?"

"Absolutely," replied Jay. "Why not? Let's give her a chance to attend this utterly special event, which she can only do because of us. At any rate, if she gets obnoxious, we can always cut the holographic feed."

Char laughed at that.

"Besides," Jay continued, "maybe by getting her invited to a royal coronation, and her seeing how we're treated as guests of honor, maybe she'll see that what I do is far more than play a glorified space-trucker."

"Jay, my love, don't hold your breath," Char said with a chuckle.

Jay started to laugh. "I won't. I like breathing."

Chapter 45 – And Again, A Word From Our Sponsor

Hi there. This is your friendly neighborhood author once again. We're not quite to the end but getting close. There are some bits and pieces that you might care to know about that are behind-the-scenes, so to speak, and not part of the main story. However, since they tie side and background bits together, I thought I'd share them now.

When they watched the transmission sent by Char from the rangeen Royal Stronghold, the leaders of the soetub and sutac did something they never did. They communicated with one another. Discussions ensued about setting aside their nearly racial dislike of one another and allying together, sans their other allies, to attack the rangeen. They reasoned that it might be time to deprive them of their formerly exclusive resource altogether.

Imaro, it turns out, is a far more skilled diplomat than he would have credited himself as. Frankly, nobody thought he had it in him. Maybe he didn't bluff his and Kukeb's way off Rangeenavelt as much as he negotiated it. At any rate, Imaro managed to persuade them that he had things under control, his father's plans were utterly foiled, and he had zero interest in carrying them out in the slightest.

Imaro also started to negotiate with both the sutac and soetub to help them extract the resource and get it to market on their terms. Unlike Nobiri, Imaro feels that competition will be good for the economy in ways beyond exclusivity. The sutac and soetub leaders are intrigued by Imaro and look forward to further working with him.

Speaking of Nobiri Iwoto, we can drop his title. He ceased to be king as soon as Imaro was installed as Regent. Because you might be curious what happens next, and this story isn't going to cover that, Nobiri is exiled to Sovereign Boundary along with certain loyalists that Imaro and Kukeb identify. Nobiri and his loyalists will remain on Sovereign Boundary under a combined guard of Royal Enforcers – hand-picked by Commissioner Zinibi – and OVERLORD Special Constables.

The legal case against Nobiri will drag on for years, but for the most part, he will suffer enough in his exile. He and his fellow exiles are isolated, under constant guard, and have limited communication and freedoms. They're under a form of house arrest that, for people as powerful as they were, is quite awful.

Jay and Char might not fully accept it, but they really did save the galaxy. Had they not learned who Imaro was and persuaded him to go back to Rangeenavelt, Nobiri would have set his plan in motion and destroyed the galaxy. It would have been a grim, unfortunate place for all if he'd gotten away with his scheme.

Jay and Char will have to contend with being celebrities for a while. They won't get to work as much as they'd prefer at either of their jobs. People will make a huge fuss over them for a time. However, like all celebrity, it'll fade. In time, they'll go back to their normal, chosen, contented existence.

Unless, somehow, they wind up having to save the galaxy again. Just what are the odds that two people, two humans among tens of billions of other humans, trillions of other nonhumans across the whole galaxy, and thousands of worlds, would save the galaxy even once? I am not very good at math and calculating those odds ("never tell me the odds") is a miserable proposition. Yet I'm fairly certain that they're utterly ridiculous and improbable.

Ergo, the same two people, and all those other factors, saving the galaxy again? I'm betting it's statistically impossible.

That means, however, that it's far too probable.

You never know.

Chapter 46 – But We're Just Normal People With Normal Lives

Jay had never felt as out of place as he was feeling now. He wasn't as introverted or adverse when it came to crowds as Char was. This, however, was a bit much.

The nobility of the rangeen were there en masse. All were present, either in person or holographically, save a few who had made themselves scarce with Nobiri's downfall. Jay marveled at the many neon colors of hair in elaborate styles and ornate, often gaudy outfits both male and female were wearing.

Jay and Char stood with Kukeb at the front of the throne room, atop the dais. Kukeb, looking especially resplendent in his formal outfit, had done his best to let them know who many of the important dignitaries and leaders of the rangeen people were. This included several of Nobiri's handmaidens and Imaro's mother.

The room was packed with observers, all under the watchful eye of the Royal Enforcers. Jay glanced towards one of the VIP galleries and saw his mother, present as a hologram, chatting amiably with a couple of other humans, a rumel, and several rangeen. He knew she was having the time of her life and noted she was wearing something new and especially colorful for the occasion. His stepfather was at her side, sometimes joining the conversation but largely observing.

Char looked amazing. Imaro had sent tailors and seamstresses to visit the pair, and they had had new elaborate outfits made for them. Char's dress was a gorgeous purple, accenting her curves in a way that reminded Jay how attracted to his wife he was.

Jay, for his part, was in what amounted to a tuxedo, although it was far more comfortable, the material soft and black with purple accents to match his spouse. Char had commented that both their outfits were way fancier than anything either of them owned and were more costly than her dress and his tux had been for their wedding. Jay remarked that their coronation outfits were probably more expensive than their whole wedding had been.

"What are we doing here?" Char whispered to Jay.

"Standing out like humans," Jay replied.

"Humans who saved the galaxy," Kukeb added.

Char rolled her eyes and Jay grinned.

Imaro's coronation would be broadcast across ITEM and the MESS-work. The final act after a near-catastrophe of unimaginable proportions.

A fanfare began to play. The conversations faded out, and all eyes turned to the far side of the throne room, away from the dais.

Regent Imaro Iwoto, prince of the rangeen, stood looking especially regal. He appeared quite different from the young rangeen man who had hired Jay and his ship. He held his head high, his shoulders squared, and he wore elaborate ceremonial garb.

Jay had expected a herald to make a boast as Imaro moved through the throne room towards the dais. Instead, the fanfare took on a more formal march, Imaro walking with two heavily armed Royal Enforcers before him in full armor. Two more were behind them in more ceremonial gear. Behind Imaro was Commissioner Zinibi Motua and Marquis Jomel Ibeme, recently named acting prime minister. Behind them, two more ceremonial guards and two more fully armed and armored Royal Enforcers.

As Imaro passed, people saluted, bowed, or simply gawked. It felt to Jay like a very sedate, practical affair, but still a heavily embellished occasion.

Jay watched his mother observe the passing rangeen leader. He knew that look. She was measuring the being, his wealth, how he carried himself, and cataloging any and all ways she could equal or better him.

"Try to look less obvious about your jealousy, Ma," Char whispered to Jay. He stifled a chuckle at her similar thoughts.

At last, Imaro and his entourage arrived at the dais. The guards ascended the three steps, as did Imaro, Zinibi, and Jomel. Imaro paused as Zinibi and Jomel stepped past him, placing themselves between Imaro and the throne.

The march turned back to fanfare, reached a crescendo that made Jay feel moved, and concluded. Silence echoed through the throne room, interrupted by a squeak when someone hiccupped from the gallery.

Marquis Jomel cleared his throat. "People of rangeen, witnesses near and far, welcome. This day, we are gathered to elevate a new king to lead the rangeen people. As acting prime minister, it is my place to stand for the rangeen people to formally commence this action. Who stands before the empty throne?"

"I am Imaro Iwoto, Regent, son of Nobiri Iwoto, and heir to the throne."

"Imaro Iwoto, will you accept, as is your birthright and rightful place, the role of king of the rangeen people?"

"I will do my duty and accept the crown," stated Imaro.

"I am Marquis Jomel Imbeme, acting prime minister, and I accept your claim." With that, he took a sideways step, opening the space between Imaro and the throne.

"I am Royal Enforcer Commissioner Zinibi Motua, council member, and I accept your claim." With that, she took a sideways step, opening the space between Imaro and the throne.

Imaro stepped to the throne. He nodded to Jomel, then Zinibi. After that, he turned to face the attending crowd and the cameras.

"I am Imaro Iwoto, king of the rangeen," he declared. With that, Imaro sat on the throne.

The fanfare blared and almost startled Jay. He saw Char put her hand to her chest, reacting the same. Jay had expected a cheer, but not the fanfare. When it ended, the echo remained atop silence from all those attending the coronation.

Just like that, Imaro, the passenger with his boyfriend paying for passage away from rangeen space, was no longer prince nor regent, but king.

For a fleeting moment, Jay wondered if he could offer the stateroom aboard *Audacia* at a new, premium rate. "King Imaro Slept Here!" or the "King Imaro Stateroom." But he wasn't that kind of person, for one, and the kind of attention it would get them was likely not worth it.

Imaro spoke, and Jay wondered what sort of amplification system was in the throne room, as his voice seemed to come from somewhere above. "Thank you, one and all, for attending this day. I appreciate you being witness to this historic moment."

He paused, changed his tone, and then said, "I should like to begin my time as king by continuing the work I began as regent. Thus, I welcome any ambassadors to meet with me, both so I may learn from you how your past relations with the rangeen have been, as well as to learn how we might improve upon them moving forward. My special secretary, Baron Kukeb Nwomga, will be arranging appointments over the coming days. It is my greatest desire that the rangeen have open and honest relations all around."

There were murmurs and then applause following his statement.

As it faded, Imaro continued, saying, "To all the roptera present or watching on the 'tangle, I would like to get to know more of you personally. Unfortunately, my father kept me away from relations with roptera leaders of government and industry, and that is not something I shall continue. You are as much a part of rangeen space as the rangeen, and it is my hope to be certain that we continue to live as symbiotically as before, if not more closely in the future."

Jay had not previously paid much mind to the roptera. Now, he noticed there were quite a few in the crowd. He saw that they had the same general build as humans and rangeen, with bat-like ears and beady brown eyes that, upon closer examination, contained shiny red flecks. What stood out were their vestigial bat-like wings. Jay remembered, at some point, Kukeb remarking that the roptera hadn't flown in millennia.

There was a high-pitched, almost imperceptible reaction from the collective roptera. It was almost uncomfortable, but only just on the edge of his hearing.

As that subsided, Imaro stated, "There is a matter of a personal nature that I should like to resolve, and I shall do so now, in this forum, at this time. Baron Kukeb?"

Kukeb, who had been standing beside Char, came forward.

"For many years, Kukeb Nwomga has served as my personal special secretary. Yet he has been more than that to me. While I expect him to continue to serve in that role, I should like it to be known that I am choosing Kukeb as my consort. The tradition forcing crown heirs to marry for the sake of producing new heirs is both a nonconsensual nightmare and an antiquated custom I will be breaking."

Jay could see that Kukeb blushed as Imaro arose and embraced him. There was applause, but Jay also saw confused looks among many of the rangeen nobles and council members.

Releasing Kukeb, but not resuming his seat, Imaro continued, saying, "This is the first of many changes to tradition, custom, and law coming soon. Further, there will be more positions shifting among the council, advisors, and even the nobility in the coming days. While I honor my heritage and my birthright, there are changes that need to be made to keep the rangeen whole, not just today, but into the future."

Again, there was a combination of applause and confused looks among the rangeen. Jay wondered how much Imaro was going to change now that he was the king.

"Before this ceremony ends, there is one more important piece of business I must attend to," Imaro intoned. "I would ask Jay Baylon and Char Danella to attend me."

Jay had not expected that. He could tell that neither had Char. Taking her hand, they moved to stand before Imaro and Kukeb, in front of the throne. Jay was nervous. He also worried that Char would be deeply uncomfortable. Not for the first time since their transmission of Nobiri's confession, they were being seen by potentially billions across the galaxy.

He stole a glance towards the hologram of his mother and stepfather in the VIP section. It wasn't lost on him that she looked proud of him. That had never been their issue.

"When Kukeb and I left Rangeenavelt, intent on leaving rangeen space behind forever, it was this couple who had the starship we would book passage on," Imaro began. "They knew only that they had a pair of rangeen hiring them for passage to a planet far away from rangeen space. They had no clue just what they were getting themselves into by bringing us aboard."

"No, we most certainly did not," remarked Char. It had been meant to be soto voce, but it carried through the speakers. Imaro, Kukeb, Jay, and Char began to laugh at that.

"I know you don't see this as I do, but were it not for you, we'd be on the verge of paying a terrible price," Imaro said in a softer tone. Then, for the assembly, he continued and said, "The rangeen, the sutac, the soetub, the human race, and, frankly, the whole galaxy owes you a debt. You convinced me to change my course, confront my father, and stop the terrible plan he was about to carry out. Your actions saved a lot of lives and prevented unspeakable misery."

"Imaro… Your Majesty," Jay started. "While I, we, appreciate the sentiment, all we did was bring you here to do what had to be done."

"You're the one who saved everyone," added Char.

Imaro shook his head. "No, yours was the idea to get my father to confess and transmit that as irrefutable, undeniable evidence to stop his plans. You emboldened me to stop running away and face my responsibility to my people and the greater good. For that reason, I am presenting both of you, Jason Mortimer Baylin and Charlotte Angela Danella, the highest honor the rangeen people can bestow, the King's Esteem of Merit."

Kukeb had a pair of ornate, gaudy medals on what looked like gold fabric ribbon. Imaro took them and, one at a time, hung them on first Char and then Jay's shoulders.

"Thank you, Char and Jay," stated Imaro. The crowd erupted into thank yous and applause. Imaro directed them to turn and face the crowd.

Jay had done theatre in his youth. He didn't mind performing. Char had done behind-the-scenes theatre and preferred not to be in the spotlight. Still, they both accepted the accolades.

Finally, Kukeb guided them back to their place on the dais beside the throne.

"Thank you all for joining us today," Imaro stated again. Once more, the fanfare sounded. As its last note echoed away, the people began to move about, mingling.

"Sorry," Kukeb said, turning to Jay and Char. "Imaro insisted."

"That's okay," said Char. "It's only majorly awkward."

"He got you, too," commented Jay.

"That he did," agreed Kukeb. Jay saw him throw a knowing grin at his lover.

Jay and Char were both inundated by numerous ambassadors, nobles, councilors, and other representatives of various races. Jay knew it would be hard on Char, given how it was nearly overwhelming for him.

As the crowd pressed them less, they began to make their way towards the hologram of his mother and stepfather. They were able to move about because there were holoprojectors in place all over the throne room.

"I think, my love, the next few months are going to be very interesting for us," Char commented for his ears alone.

"In so many ways," Jay said. "We're either going to attract tons of new clients and have jobs too plentiful to easily choose from, or the celebrity will cause people to avoid us and we'll have no work. Either way, I suspect getting currency won't be a challenge."

"How did we get here again?" Char asked.

"You suggested I buy a starship," Jay said. They kissed and then made their way to his mom and stepdad.

Jay's mom was holding an animated conversation with a small crowd of rangeen and rumel. They parted, however, as Jay and Char approached.

"Hi, Mom," Jay said. "Hi, Bob."

"I'm sorry I can't hug you two," his mom said. "I suppose holographic VIP presence is better than having to watch on the 'tangle like your father."

Jay didn't bother to take the bait. He had invited his dad and stepmom, but they had declined, which Jay had expected and understood. "I appreciated the king inviting you."

"He is impressive," Jay's mom said. "And this place is amazing."

"Excuse me, Ma, Dad," Char said. She kissed Jay on the cheek and stated, "I need to go talk to Mirella."

"I'll join you shortly," said Jay.

"Tell your sister we'll try to come say hello as well," Jay's mom called. Char moved off and Jay's mom went on, saying, "I hope you know how proud I am of you. Of both of you."

"Me, too," added Bob.

"Thank you," Jay said, appreciating her sentiment. "I think Imaro is going to want to speak with you, before you end your transmission."

"I look forward to that," Jay's mom said.

After some more small talk, which Jay was impressed remained light and judgment-free, Jay promised he and Char would pay them a visit as soon as they could. He saw Imaro starting to make his way over. He and Char would be supping with the king and his intended consort later.

Jay found Char talking to Mirella, her sons and her spouse. They exchanged pleasantries – Jay had always liked his in-laws – then Mirella and the family ended the transmission.

Jay and Char were alone for the moment. They were both looking at the people still moving around the throne room conversing, probably striking deals and the like. A quartet of official-looking people, two humans, a kijivu, and an ajerari – whose look screamed bureaucrat – approached them.

"Jason Mortimer Baylin and Charlotte Angela Danella?" addressed the ajerari. The four each flashed a digital identity card. "We're here from the Organization for Verification of Extraplanetary Rules and Logistics for Overall Referential Definitions. We are transmitting to your personal 'cator codes a summons to be interviewed tomorrow morning."

"Thank you," Char replied. "We'll be there."

"Congratulations on your achievement," stated one of the human OVERLORD bureaucrats as the foursome moved along like an odd wave.

"I wondered when they'd get to us," Jay commented.

"Of course, they're here in time for the coronation," said Char.

"Oh, you missed it," Jay began. "My mother said she's proud of us. And she meant it, with no caveats."

"Wonders never cease," replied Char. "Maybe she'll stop trying to convince you to 'get a real job.'"

"Maybe," Jay said noncommittally. "But I expect that things will be back to normal with her all too soon."

Char took Jay's hand. "You think saving the galaxy can be topped?"

"No, but you know how it is," said Jay. "The novelty of this achievement will fade, and it'll be like this never happened and we're still not doing it right. Just wait."

Chapter 47 – What Does A Hero's Mother Think About It All?

As overwhelming as it was, there was something oddly right about it.

Imaro had been so caught up in his own drama and his need to be with Kukeb, bucking tradition and the duties and expectations he'd come to loathe, that he hadn't seen the danger. He'd known Nobiri was a blowhard intent on expanding his power and influence. That it would go so far and be so destructive, however, he'd never imagined.

For all their disconnect, Imaro didn't hate or wish ill on his father. Yet for the greater good, he had no choice but to take his place and stand as the new king of the rangeen people.

Now that the formalities were out of the way, Imaro was doing his expected duty. He was greeting an endless parade of dignitaries and guests. He was shaking hands, bowing, respecting various racially and culturally unique greetings, and speaking formally and informally with many.

He had not at all planned for things to end here. In fact, his plan had been quite the opposite. Give it all up, run away from his duty to the crown, kingdom, and people, and live a life in solitude, hiding away with the male he loved.

Kukeb, he noted, was also busy making notes, taking appointments, and settling into the business of being personal secretary to the rangeen king. From time to time, Imaro shared a look with his newly chosen consort.

Despite matters taking a decidedly different and unexpected path, Imaro was happy. He knew that as the new king of the rangeen, he could do some good. He knew, however, that it rocked numerous boats and upset many.

Several of the nobles and councilors didn't know it yet, but they were going to be answering for some things. That would be a necessary starting point for the ongoing changes he'd be making.

Imaro had been making his way to a specific person he just had to meet. After all that Char and Jay had done, even though they disbelieved that they'd saved the galaxy from devastation with their actions, Imaro had to meet Jay's mother.

What kind of person must she be, Imaro thought, to have raised a man such as Jay? Clearly, he was something more than just the captain, pilot, and co-owner of a starship. Was he a descendant of some sort of secret noble line? What was one of the people who had raised him like?

Further, given that his own parents were mostly indifferent to him and his existence, what did a genuine hero's mother think about him being honored as he'd been? What impression did her son's unintended heroism leave on her?

Imaro was finally able to approach her holographic form. She and the man Jay had identified as his stepfather – a term Imaro had been unfamiliar with, but Char had explained meant the man Jay's mother was now married to that was not his biological father – were chatting with a group of rangeen, rumel, and humans.

"Your Majesty," one of the rangeen addressed him as Imaro reached them. "It's an honor to be here to witness this today."

The others expressed their appreciation and gratitude as well. The rumel thanked Imaro for his part in stopping Nobiri's plot.

Finally, Imaro was facing Jay's mother and stepfather. "I am Imaro Iwoto, and it is a great honor to meet you both."

Jay's mother bowed awkwardly, saying, "Thank you. I'm Sindi Reznik, and this is my husband, Bob." Jay's stepfather bowed slightly more gracefully. Jay's mom continued, saying, "It's truly an honor to be present for this auspicious occasion. If I may say so, you have a lovely home."

Imaro didn't think of the throne room as home, but was still appreciative of the statement. "Thank you, ma'am. Truth be told, though, I must admit, I am honored that you are here. Were it not for your son, none of this would have been possible. But more than that, we'd all be facing quite the troubles."

"Oh, yes," Jay's mom remarked. "He did make quite the impression, didn't he?"

"More than that," Imaro said, feeling somewhat confused. "You must be proud of him and what he's done here."

"Oh, yes, of course," Jay's mom said.

Imaro chuckled. "I don't think he or Char fully grasp the magnitude of it." Imaro leaned in closer. "They don't realize that their actions really did save the galaxy. More than anything I did, they're the ones who spurred me to action. Char and Jay have done us all an amazing service. Don't you think?"

Jay's mom sighed, which confused Imaro. Then, she said, "Yes, it's impressive, of course. My son, the savior of the galaxy. But he could have been a doctor, a lawyer, or business mogul, if he'd just settled down and put his mind to it."

Chapter 48 – One Last Word From Our Sponsor

I want to thank you for reading this story. It's been a real departure from my usual style. I hope the absurdism of this book has been as much fun for you to read as it has been for me to share.

I'm going to break this wall again in asking you to support me and other indie authors. When you don't have the backing of a major publisher, you wear a lot of hats and do a lot of work to put a quality book out into the world. While buying our books supports us, reviewing them on whatever site you bought them from, Goodreads, and the like, helps generate buzz and gets us more readers. Also, if you have friends – and I hope that you do – please let them know that they should buy this book, too.

Unless you really disliked it. But if you did, have you gotten to this final chapter because you wanted ammo for a truly abysmal review, or are you some sort of masochist who likes to torture yourself with reading? Whatever, I don't kink-shame (though I might kink-judge).

Me and the other indie authors of the world appreciate all the support we can get. Thank you!

Finally, if you did enjoy this, you're probably wondering – will Jay and Char have more adventures? Of course, they will. They have a starship and a wide galaxy of people, places, and things to explore. Even if Jay's mom thinks he'd be better off flying a desk on some planet somewhere.

Might they do something grandiose and save the galaxy again, causing your humble sponsor here to share another story of their unintended, unexpected heroism with you? Anything is possible.

The End.

.

.

.

.

Maybe.

Acknowledgments

There are several people I need to thank for all their continued assistance and encouragement. In no particular order:

Rose Butcher, my cover artist. She gets me. She understands my vision, and she does an amazing job of making manifest the image in my head. Thank you for being so incredible!

Vicky Skinner, my editor. Thank you.

My wife Chrissie. Without her support, I couldn't do this. She is incredible, my best friend, biggest cheerleader, and unabashedly the inspiration for Char.

My dad, for always supporting me by paying attention to all I do and buying everything I write.

My mom and stepdad, for letting me create this caricature of you.

My sister, niece, sister and brother in-law, and nephews.

My friends and their continued support. Thanks for following along on social media as I keep oversharing.

Heather Texle for taking my attempt at creating an interesting blurb for this book and making it sing!

Everyone on the Sci-Fi Unity Discord. You've offered me so much help and insight along the way, and I appreciated the community of writers!

Last, and certainly not least, YOU. I love and appreciate my readers. I hope you've enjoyed reading this first entry in this series as much as I enjoyed writing it.

Before you go – again, I'd like to ask you to please leave a review on whatever platform you purchased this from, and/or Goodreads. Also, please tell a friend or two!

About the Author

MJ BLEHART has been writing sci-fi/space opera and fantasy all his life, finishing his first book when he was nine years old. *Star Wars* and *Star Trek* were some of the biggest influences in his childhood.

He is a history aficionado. MJ has been a member of the Society for Creative Anachronism (SCA - a medieval re-enactment society) for over thirty years. As part of the SCA, he studies and teaches 16th-century rapier combat (fencing), court heraldry, and spends time with friends.

When not writing sci-fi and fantasy, MJ blogs regularly, exploring mindfulness and creating an amazing life. He strives to live a kickass life and consciously create his reality (and share that process to help others do the same).

MJ lives in New Jersey, just outside of Philadelphia, with his wife and their three feline overlords.

Links

Author website (where you can join my newsletter and learn more about me and my ongoing process):
mjblehart.com

YA Fantasy series *The Source Chronicles*: sourcechronicles.com

Facebook **@blehartmj**
Instagram **@mjblehart**
Bluesky **@mjblehart.bsky.social**

Other books by MJ Blehart

The Savagespace Trilogy

Alliances and Consequences
Revelations and Reconciliations
Challengers and Survivors

Forgotten Fodder

Unexpected Witness
The Clone Conundrum
Unraveling Conspiracy
Bold Moves
Turncoat's Gambit (Autumn 2025)
Shell Game (Autumn 2025
Conspiracy Theory (Winter 2026)
Shifting Sands (Winter 2026)

The Void Incursion

Opening Gambit
Critical Position
Strategic Crush
Antipositional Moves
Check and Mate

Standalone

Jay And Char Save The Galaxy
Infamy Ascending

Short Stories in Anthologies

Crooked V.3 (Edited by Jessie Kwak)
Spells and Swashbucklers (Edited by Val Griswold-Ford)
Rum and Runestones (Edited by Val Griswold-Ford)

www.ingramcontent.com/pod-product-compliance
Lightning Source LLC
Chambersburg PA
CBHW071522110726